THE LOTUS FLOWER EMERGES

By Patty Ronchetto

The lotus flower emerges from the dirty and muddy bottom of a pond. Its unique quality is said to symbolize the human who rises from the darkness of the world into a new way of thinking and living.

MW01538462

This book was printed in the United States of America.
Copyright © 2017 Patty Ronchetto
ISBN-13:
978-1975805456
ISBN-10:
1975805453

Part One

(1936 – early 1940's)

Secrets and Consequences

Chapter One

Anna

1936

"How beautiful to realize life is growing inside of me," Anna thought. "Although I cannot yet feel the stirrings of this tiny person, it is miraculous to know it does exist. Unfortunate timing has condemned this miracle. Knowing what I must now do, how do I live with myself? God, please see a way to make this right. I know it is against your laws but Karl and I love each other and if my father finds out about this baby, he will kill him. I am giving a life for a life. I wonder if this tiny new life would be a boy with Karl's thick, black, curly hair and the firmness of his stocky, solid body; or, if a girl, would she have my slight build, pale skin, and chestnut hair. My eyes are brown yet Karl's are blue...but I will never know."

"Dear God, sometimes you have us on earth play such cruel roles. If only my family didn't care how poor Karl's family is, maybe this could all be different. God, I don't know if I can live with myself after I do what must be done, but Karl does not deserve this even though I know I may be condemned to Hell for what transpires today." Anna closed her eyes in prayer while she cringed at the thought of killing their baby.

It was 1936 and the country was in turmoil with rumors of war. Karl was 19 and Anna was 17. They were neighbors living out in the country farmland of southeastern Minnesota. Anna's family immigrated from the Ukraine and were proud of their nationality and Ukrainian-Orthodox beliefs. Her family did very well in farming and although not wealthy, they were better off financially than Karl's. Karl's family had entered the United States almost twelve years ago from Czechoslovakia. While Karl's father did extra odd jobs in order to supplement their small farming income, Karl, being the oldest of five children, had to drop out of school in the fifth grade in order to help with the family's finances. Following in his father's footsteps, Karl went about town seeking odd jobs as well as working for other neighbors to secure extra income. Karl worked hard all the time, but he would never have enough money or be educated enough to please Anna's father. Religion was also an issue with Karl's family being Catholic. Anna's father preached how when Anna became old enough to marry, she must marry within the Ukrainian-Orthodox faith. The only way they continued to see each other was because Anna's father and brothers spent so much time out in their fields. In between Karl's jobs, Anna and Karl would meet in their secret place down by the Mississippi River. Anna loved this place that was so open with the water flowing and where daisies grow wild. It was so peaceful, a place where they could shut out all the problems and unfairness that life seemed to dictate to them. This was where Anna gave herself in love to Karl. This place would always be special to them.

2

Anna remembered the first time they made love. She was so scared but she wanted to give herself completely to Karl. On that day, Anna and Karl lay side by side in the wooded area by the river, staring at the trees and sky, planning their future as if no one would interfere. Anna loved Karl's tingling touch whenever he caressed her. This time, as he gently cupped her breast, Anna was so sure with the talk of their future that she begged Karl to go further. As Karl slowly and silently removed Anna's clothing, all she could dream of was that someday she would be his wife. It was with this thought when she felt the heaviness of his body on hers and the firm yet slow entrance into her. There was hurt and Anna winced in pain, but only momentarily as for now, if not in name, at least emotionally and spiritually, Anna was his wife.

Now, something that was so beautiful must end so tragically.

Earlier that day, in desperation, Anna confided to Peter, her older brother, of her pregnancy and her plan to contact a midwife to perform the abortion. Anna had heard about a woman called "Midwife Katrina", who lived not far from her Midwestern town. The cost would be $25, and Anna was short $5. Peter reluctantly gave Anna the $5 but begged her not to go through with this. It was a crime and so dangerous. Maybe something else could be worked out but Peter knew their father would never forgive his sister. He would have Karl put away; or at the very least, make life difficult for Karl and his family. Peter also thought Karl should be told. Once Anna took the money and left, Peter immediately regretted giving Anna the money. He decided to go into town to find Karl. He knew some of the places where Karl worked on small jobs. He promised Anna he would not tell Karl, but Peter was so concerned for Anna's safety that he decided now he must try to stop her.

It was in Midwife Katrina's shack that Anna now sat praying and contemplating the child that she felt she was murdering. Would Karl ever forgive her for not telling him and letting him be part of the decision? She was doing this because of her father and to protect Karl. They could have children later, once they worked on Anna's father to accept Karl for the good, kind hearted person he was.

Katrina appeared from behind a ragged curtain in the next room. The curtain was made of an old tattered blanket thrown about a stretched out clothesline. She looked so sloppy and fat that Anna wanted to run but Katrina calmed her with a smooth motherly voice as she guided Anna to the makeshift cot where gray, dingy sheets and towels were spread. Rusty looking instruments were simply placed on a cardboard box that was covered with a towel.

"Now Anna, please remove your garments at least waist down," Katrina said as she helped Anna. Anna noticed how dirty Katrina's fingernails were and she cringed as she cried out, "God, forgive me!"

Karl was baling hay for a nearby farmer. He was depressed over Anna's sad state the last few weeks. Karl loved his family and knew that they needed every cent of what he earned to survive but if only he had a little extra money. Then he could go to Anna's father to show him what a hard worker he was and how, no matter what, he would support Anna as he loved her more than anything in the world.

Suddenly Peter came running toward Karl. As Peter relayed the story of Anna's pregnancy and intended abortion, Karl could not believe it. "Oh my God, why didn't Anna tell me? We will find a way; we must find a way! Do you know where she went, Peter? You must help me find her and stop this before it is too late."

"Anna told me her name. Midwife Katrina. I asked around and know it is not far from here. We have to hurry."

"Oh, no," Karl yelled as they ran faster. "I have heard talk of her in town. The police are trying to find Katrina as she is also known as 'Katrina the Butcher'! We must hurry!"

Peter had borrowed one of his father's work trucks telling his father he needed to go into town for supplies. Karl and Peter arrived at a decrepit building which was about five miles from the farm where Karl had been working. They ran into the shack only to find that it was too late. The deed was done.

Anna lay on the blood soaked cot, listless and pale. Karl rushed to her side while Peter took off after Katrina who had stormed out the door as the boys stood by Anna's bedside.

"Anna, why didn't you tell me?" Karl was sobbing now as Anna barely lifted her head to slightly smile at Karl. With a cold, limp hand, she stroked his head as she whispered, "What is done now, Karl, is done. We have too many other problems. Now we can start fresh. Please do not hate me for murdering our child."

"Oh, Anna, how could I hate you?" Karl cried, "It is you I worry about, you I love no matter what!"

Anna sobbed but even her sobbing was weak.

"Hush, darling", Karl pleaded, "we must get you help now."

"My father must never know, Karl," Anna cried.

"It no longer matters. Now what matters is that you get better. We must get you to the city hospital."

Karl went outside to find Peter. Peter was gone, in pursuit of Katrina, however, the truck was still there with the keys inside. Karl feared Anna was dying. He wrapped her up in towels and blankets that were in the shack. He then carried her in his arms and placed her in the truck to rush to the hospital.

Anna was bleeding so much. Karl could not understand how with so much blood she was still somewhat lucid. Soon Karl saw Peter running toward the truck. Peter jumped in the truck. While speeding through the roads, Peter gave a vague explanation of what had happened. He had caught up with Katrina, tackled her, and tied her wrists together. He had taken her to a neighboring farmer begging the family to call the police and hold her as he had to get Anna to the hospital.

Karl stayed with Anna at the hospital while Peter had the unfortunate task of breaking the news to his parents.

Chapter Three

Anna and Karl

Karl held Anna's hand while the doctor and nurses kept close watch over her, continually monitoring her blood pressure and heart. Only for a moment did Karl leave Anna's side to seek out the doctor in charge to find out Anna's condition as she lay there, still bleeding. The doctor looked grave as he explained to Karl that he must wait for Anna's parents to inform them as she was only 17, and they were her next of kin. He said that Anna's condition was critical. Karl, with tears streaming down his face, went back to Anna's side, accompanied by the doctor.

"Is there anything we can get you, Anna, before your parents arrive?" the doctor inquired. "Anything to make you more comfortable?"

Anna looked up into the doctor's face and said, "No, nothing." As her tired eyes passed from the doctor's face to Karl's, a sudden flicker of light jumped into her eyes as she smiled and said, "Yes, doctor, you can do something for me. You know and I know that I am going to die. Please get a chaplain or priest and let me die as Karl's wife. Please, please, I beg of you to grant me this last request before my father arrives."

The doctor could not refuse this small, loving creature as he knew with each minute her life was slipping away.

"Very well, Anna," the doctor solemnly replied.

The hospital cleric was by Anna's bedside within minutes. He first asked them if they were sorry for all their sins, and then gave them reconciliation. An edited version of "Holy Matrimony" was recited, and Anna and Karl exchanged wedding vows while an orderly and nurse stood by as witnesses. It was all Karl could do to keep from breaking while holding this precious girl's hand, the one whom he owed so very much, while he knew the end was near.

As the chaplain pronounced them husband and wife, Anna smiled up at Karl and said, "Now I am happy."

Then she died.

No crying out, no screams of pain, no sorrow. She just closed her eyes and died. Karl stood there no longer crying, just staring at the one person who had made his life meaningful and knowing he would never be the same.

Anna's father came into the room, ranting and raving at everyone to see his daughter. Once Peter had told his parents, Anna's father screamed in rage and swore he would kill Karl, but Anna's mother only sobbed quietly as she told her husband that for now, the main concern was to have their daughter rest in peace.

Now, Karl looked Anna's father in the eye and said, "It is over," and walked out.

The few days that followed were ones of grief, guilt and loneliness. Katrina had been taken into custody and would surely be sent to prison. There had been other women who had died under Katrina's knife.

Anna's family forbid Karl to attend the funeral. They also threatened serious charges would be made once their daughter was laid to rest.

Karl's family was, of course, understanding toward their son's ill fate; however, they knew Karl would never survive in this town with the wrath of Anna's family. The only thing this heartbroken family could do, with the threat of war not far away, was to convince their first born to join the U.S. Army - to leave what had become his American home during these past dozen years. Karl would have to send pay from his army allotment home to help the family. Karl, not really caring what was to become of him, left his home the day of Anna's funeral, after he had stood hiding behind a tree at the cemetery, waiting until all her family members had left. Karl then laid a bouquet of daisies on Anna's gravesite - the daisies from their "secret place." The place where the daisies grow wild. The place where they found love until their love had turned to death.

Karl said goodbye to his family and walked by himself into town to the Federal Building. At 5:00 pm in the autumn of 1936, Karl officially enlisted in the United States Army. Karl knew he would never again know such love as he had with Anna.

Chapter Four
Elizabeth
1940

"I'm so excited, Mother. After all the planning, my wedding is almost here, and it will be the event of the year in Seattle!" Elizabeth was giddy with the plans of her upcoming marriage to Captain Ronald Mathe, a handsome naval officer.

Elizabeth Phillips met Ron Mathe last summer while vacationing on Gull Lake, Minnesota. Every year, Elizabeth and her mother, Olive, would spend a few weeks there as Olive's family had a vacation home right on the lake.

Elizabeth's father, Dwight, had always been too busy to go on a family vacation. He was gone so much because of his military career. After school Dwight began his military service with the 116th Field Signal Battalion for the Washington National Guard in the Mexican border conflict of 1916. During the First World War, he was gassed during Army duty at Soissons, France. After his recuperation, he began flying and worked for and operated commercial lines in the state of Washington. In 1929 he received national fame when he flew the New York to Los Angeles air races in the Chief Seattle, a plane that was purchased through public donations. Now, during the Second World War, he was flying transports for the Royal Canadian Air Force from Canada to Europe. To most people he was almost a hero, but to

Elizabeth and her mother, his drinking created much tension and arguments over the last few years. He promised Elizabeth he would be home for the wedding. Her parents had been separated for a year, and not yet known to Elizabeth or anyone in the family, they agreed to divorce sometime after the wedding.

Ron lived with his parents in Minneapolis until his enlistment in the Navy. They often spent a few weeks vacationing on Gull Lake.

Olive and Elizabeth were now renting an apartment in South Minneapolis so that Elizabeth and Ron could see each other. It was in the same building where Olive's aunt lived and only across town from Ron's parents. It was helpful that family was close by to help with wedding plans and be of support during the Dwight and Olive separation. It also gave time for Olive and Elizabeth to get to know the Mathe family. Previously Ron had flown out to Seattle several times to meet Elizabeth's relatives and help finalize plans for the wedding.

It had been such a whirlwind romance last year. Elizabeth and Ron met on the fourth of July, 1939. Elizabeth lay sunbathing on the dock. Ron came swimming over to meet her. He noticed her earlier and wanted to invite her to see the fireworks. Elizabeth, not looking up at him and acting cool and standoffish, said she had plans with her family. Without a beat, Ron invited all of them to come along. Shocked by the 'family' invite, Elizabeth took off her sunglasses to stare at Ron. Her heart leapt as his steel blue eyes flickered in the sun.

That was only one year ago. Elizabeth was eighteen and had just graduated from Lillian Stern's School for Women in Seattle. Ron was twenty-four and had just been accepted into the Naval Officer's program, following in his father's footsteps.

Olive was concerned that Elizabeth and Ron were moving too quickly. Her fear was that Elizabeth was trying to fill the void that her father left in her heart. The war did not help either as it was certain the newlyweds would soon be parted. She begged her daughter to wait for a year or so but Elizabeth's mind was made up.

Olive had married when she was younger than Elizabeth. She had not known Dwight very long before they wed. Olive tried to talk with Elizabeth about how difficult it was to get to know each other once you are living together and that things do not always turn out as you expect, especially coming from a privileged family. Things change and people change, but Elizabeth was determined. There was no doubt about it that Elizabeth, an only child, was a very spoiled child. Olive tried to protect her from the turmoil of her own failed marriage but most of all the problem stemmed from the family's wealth. Olive's father, Arthur McAlister, had made a fortune the last several decades selling and shipping timber on the West Coast. Arthur was a powerful business man, extremely rich, and feared by many.

The Phillips were well taken care of by Olive's family. Their spacious four-bedroom home was given to them as a wedding gift. Elizabeth attended only the best private schools and hobnobbed with

13

Seattle's high society. All this was thanks to her maternal grandparents, the McAlister's. They never expected their grandchild to want for anything. Elizabeth's father, Dwight Phillips, came from a comfortable home life but it was no comparison to the McAlister wealth. They were all so proud of Dwight and his war record. They recently heard he would soon start reporting as a commander under Colonel Theodore Roosevelt's Post No. 24. The McAlister's did not yet know their daughter and Dwight had agreed to divorce. They would not have approved.

Elizabeth and her mother had been busy the past six months traveling back and forth to Seattle. There were engagement parties, bridal showers, shopping for just the right pattern of china and silver, and, of course, the Waterford Crystal must be the perfect cut for impressing all the important people the newly married Captain and Mrs. Ronald Mathe would be entertaining. The exchange of wedding vows would take place at a prominent Presbyterian Church where the Phillips attended for years and was well supported by the McAlister's. The wedding reception would be held at Elizabeth's Grandfather's Seattle country club. It was large enough to hold the venue where over 300 guests would be attending.

The only disagreement Elizabeth and Olive seemed to have with the wedding plans was in choosing the right wedding gown. Elizabeth would be walked down the aisle by her father under an arch of swords held by some of the highest ranking officers in the Navy. Olive thought it would be appropriate for the gown to be a fitted satin with exquisite pearls and no ruffles. Elizabeth wanted to look like a princess with ruffles and flounces and the longest train she could have. Elizabeth usually got her way, especially if her father got involved. After consulting with a well renowned dressmaker in the Seattle area, a compromise was made and the perfect dress was ordered. It would be a fitted satin but with a lace overlay. A matching fingertip length veil was chosen. It would fall softly on Elizabeth's short, auburn curls and round face. Tiny crystals would reflect her emerald green eyes, a trademark of her Irish descent. A stunning train, seven feet long, would complete the gown. Elizabeth's mother thought the train was too elaborate as her daughter was a mere four-foot eleven inches, but the dressmaker assured her it would be more elegant than gaudy.

Elizabeth knew everything had moved fast once Ron proposed; but she wanted this life and knew it would be perfect. How smooth he was, this six-foot, sandy brown haired man, who seemed to know exactly what he wanted out of life and was so sure of himself. Such soft features, except for his stern jaw, didn't make you want to take a person like Ron seriously; however, Elizabeth soon learned that when he made up his mind about something he went after it with all this broad-shouldered naval officer's strength could muster. It always made Elizabeth laugh when they kissed as Ron would lift her small frame up like nothing to meet his lips and steel blue eyes. It had been difficult to refrain from going all the way before their wedding. There had been heavy petting for almost six months now, and each time they were together it was more difficult. Elizabeth often wondered how Ron could be so patient with her. Sometimes when he drank more than usual, he seemed to get angry. It did concern Elizabeth but his mood soon passed. She had read about how men usually got what they wanted, and she only hoped and prayed that during these last months before the wedding Ron had not been finding his satisfaction with other women. He would soon need to be stationed in different places around the world and that worried her. She wanted desperately to give in, but she wanted everything to be just perfect. That perfection included giving herself completely to him on their wedding night. They had nothing to worry about for they would be very happy, and their wedding would be on the grandest scale.

Chapter Five
Elizabeth and Ron

It seemed strange that so many life changing things could happen in just one year.

Elizabeth and Ron's wedding was perfect. Her parents were now divorced. Her father was still flying, and he remained using Seattle as his home base. Olive decided to stay with her aunt in Minneapolis as Elizabeth and Ron made their home not far from that apartment. Ron would be gone more now in wartime, and Olive wanted to be close to her daughter. Olive suspected that her daughter struggled with Ron being gone so often, but she was too proud to let her mother know. More than a few times while having lunch with Elizabeth, Olive had seen stress on her daughter's face. She noticed her troubled eyes and thought she smelled liquor on her breath. Ron insisted on calling her Liz instead of Elizabeth and wanted her to dress less conservatively. Olive recognized the signs of marital problems beginning and did not want her daughter to be subjected to the life she had had with Elizabeth's father. Maybe it was wrong to keep things from her child, to try to protect her from the ugliness that developed over the years with Dwight, but this was the life Liz had chosen. Maybe Ron would not develop the issues that Dwight had with drinking, arguing, and hitting his wife. Elizabeth did not know all the abusive times that Olive had kept from her. She still idolized her father.

The Mathes celebrated their honeymoon in Niagara Falls. The first three months of their marriage had them attending many parties. Elizabeth was introduced to officers and their wives. Most of them seemed quite worldly and liberal, but Elizabeth had been raised to be proud of her heritage and wealth so she was quite confident in herself and stature. Or so she thought.

Elizabeth was getting ready for their latest dinner party when Ron came into the bedroom with his second martini in hand. Elizabeth had spent all afternoon getting her hair done and her nails perfectly manicured. She had her slip on and her favorite moss green cashmere suit lay on the bed.

"Liz, you're really not going to wear that suit, are you?" Ron's tone was sarcastic with a half smile across his face.

"What's wrong with this outfit, Ron? I thought you always liked me in green to match my eyes." Liz was hurt as she had prepared all day for this evening and thought she would look stunning.

"Liz, that outfit is fine for all your mother's little social gatherings but you are now an officer's wife. Let loose a little bit for God's sake. Don't you own any dresses with plunging necklines or slits up the side?"

Elizabeth was taken back. How could her own husband want her to dress so cheaply? Exposing her body was a pleasure she shared solely with her husband in the confines of their bedroom.

18

"Ron, why do you want me to flaunt my body to other men?" Elizabeth seemed timid asking.

"Liz, Liz, Liz, you are such a damn prude sometimes," Ron emptied his second martini with one gulp and went swiftly to their closet. He threw out a tight red sheath dress that he had purchased for Liz on their honeymoon. Liz had worn it one night to dinner after Ron pleaded with her. She felt uncomfortable that entire night as she could see other men's eyes roaming hungrily over her body. That night when they returned home, Ron had made love to her differently than he ever had. On their wedding night, Ron was so tender and gentle, knowing it was Elizabeth's first time. He lovingly guided her through each phase of their love making so that Liz never regretted any bit of it, and in fact, the crying she did that night in her wedding bed were not tears of pain but tears of complete love.

It was not so on the night she wore the sexy red dress. When they returned after dinner, Liz headed for the bathroom to change and get ready for bed.

"Liz, where are you going?" Ron demanded, in a drunken stupor after the four martinis he devoured during dinner. "I want you here! I want you to undress in front of your husband!"

Elizabeth knew by now when Ron had a few drinks it was useless to argue with him. She had a couple glasses of wine with dinner, but she could not get used to the awful taste of martinis. Ron often lost his patience with her because she wouldn't drink with him at night.

She was trying to get used to the taste of alcohol by drinking a little each day before Ron came home. She worried her mother may have sensed the scent of alcohol on her breath when they would meet for their late lunches.

"I mean it Liz, take off your clothes!"

She began to unzip the red sheath dress.

"Oh, no," Ron demanded, "first remove those tight underthings."

Liz was getting frightened with Ron's tone. She lifted her dress up far enough to remove the nylon stockings from her garters. She then pulled off the garter belt which held them. Liz was so small there was no reason for her to wear the girdles most women needed to wear. Liz next removed her panties.

"Now get over here by the bed," Ron said while he laid out on their double bed.

"I'm not finished undressing, Ron," Elizabeth said.

"Get over here now!" Liz jumped at Ron's orders and walked silently to the bed.

"Now stand there and lift your dress up to your waist." Liz obediently did so but felt embarrassed by her husband's drunken antics. While Liz stood there, Ron explored her with his fingers. Being unnecessarily rough, Liz let out a small sob of pain. Ron immediately became angry and demanded she now remove every piece of her clothing. After doing so, he also removed his clothing.

Elizabeth now remembered how rough he was with her that night. He had done things to her she never even heard of.

She had sobbed, begging him to stop as he was hurting her. He had then sprung up and slapped Elizabeth across the face, "You fucking little innocent girl! You are my wife, you do as you are told!"

After what seemed to be an agony of time, Ron asked if his little bitch was satisfied. Liz choked out a yes, and Ron said he knew how to make his little bitch feel good. Now it was his turn. He turned her over and plunged deep inside her with no gentleness whatsoever and emptied himself into her. He then fell into a deep sleep while Liz soaked her battered and bleeding body in the bathtub.

So now Ron wanted her to wear the dress again. Afraid of refusing him once he was drinking, Liz reluctantly slid into the dress, and they went out to the party.

Six months to the day that Elizabeth and Ron were wed, Elizabeth found out she was pregnant. She was ecstatic. This would make everything all right. It would be perfect, just like she always wanted. The last six months had been difficult. Ron was absolutely convinced he had married a frigid girl. Now the baby would change everything. Liz was sure once the baby was born, Ron would start coming home earlier in the evenings and limit his drinking. Maybe even Liz's mother would ease up on her. Recently Ron had brought up to Olive that he and Liz had little spats. Liz complained he drank too much and worked too late. Liz felt betrayed when Olive sided with Ron.

Olive even shamed her daughter in front of Ron saying that she did not believe Liz had the audacity to question such a wonderful, important man as Captain Mathe. She should count her blessings for marrying a man of such high esteem.

Liz needed to talk with her father. She had left so many messages for him but none were yet returned. Talking with her grandparents wouldn't help as they were so old fashioned and righteous. They believed that you should not discuss marital problems with anyone.

On Ron and Liz's six-month anniversary, Liz waited up for Ron. At midnight he came home with the smell of martinis on his breath. Tonight Liz didn't mind because tonight would be as special as their wedding night. Liz had gone out earlier in the day, after she received the news and bought a lovely, purple organdy nightgown. She now waited in their bed with a bottle of chilled champagne and glasses. She even had candles burning to add a special touch of romance.

As Ron entered the bedroom, he shouted, "What happened, did the electricity go out?"

"No darling," Liz said softly. "This is in celebration! I have wonderful news. We are going to have a baby!"

Ron stared at his wife in disbelief. "Well, what do you know," he sneered, "it's almost like the 'Immaculate Conception' for as much sex as we've had."

"Please, Ron," Liz pleaded, "I promise to try and loosen up from now on. I promise."

"You damn well better and don't go getting fat either just because you got knocked up."

"I'll take good care of myself as always, Ron, now let's have a toast to our baby." Liz opened and poured the champagne. As they touched glasses, Liz said, "To the 'three' of us...happiness always."

Ron smirked and said, "You better give me a son, and he will not be raised as a wimp." Ron gulped down his champagne and undressed. He lay on the bed and slipped into a deep, steady snore. He did not say good night to Liz, and she sat in bed for hours trying to remember the last time he had told her he loved her. After a while, Liz once again cried herself to sleep.

Chapter Six
Kimberly Margery Mathe

Kimberly Margery Mathe arrived on January 28, 1941. She weighed in at a healthy eight pounds, one ounce. What a beautiful baby girl she was. Ron did not get his boy, but he seemed pleased with the whole situation anyway, declaring that his daughter was a chip off the old block and she was of good stock...his good stock. Of course it did help that his mother-in-law, Olive, was there as this indeed contributed to his act of good nature.

The next months seemed to go by more smoothly than before. Liz was busy every minute of the day learning to be a mother, as being an only child there were so many things she never learned. In her privileged upbringing, there was always a live-in nanny for her as well as hired help to do the house cleaning and cooking. Ron still had his martinis every night and now there were some occasional all nighters.

On December 7, 1941, when the Japanese bombed Pearl Harbor, Ron was told he had to report for active duty within the week. Liz was heartbroken that she and Kimberly would be alone. She was now happy and thankful that her mother lived nearby to help her. On the night before Ron was to leave, instead of spending the evening with his family, he stopped at his favorite spot for liquid refreshment. A new waitress was working. A new young, very young, waitress. Ron's eyes poured over every inch of her small but well endowed frame. What he could teach that little thing, he thought. He roughly called out to her to bring him another martini. She cowered at the sound of his voice but quickly went to fill his order. When she returned with his drink, he asked if she was busy after she got off work that night.

"Sorry, but I don't date customers," she replied.

"What's the matter, aren't I good enough for you?", he grabbed and twisted her arm as he informed her that he was a Captain in the United States Navy - a Captain leaving in the morning to fight overseas for this country, for her.

"Please mister, I don't want any trouble. I'm only eighteen, and I need this job. Sorry."

With that, Ron released her arm in disgust. He emptied his glass and left.

It was 1:15 am and the young waitress walked toward the car that her father let her use to get back and forth to her new job. As she opened the door, a voice behind her whispered, "I'll give you just one more chance to help serve your country."

She whirled around and there was the drunken Captain. She started to scream but he was too quick for her. He muffled her mouth with his hand and dragged her into the nearby alley where his car was hidden. She started to cry out again, but he warned her if she did, he would kill her. The young girl was so terrified she sobbed but remained quiet. Ron pulled rope out of his uniform pocket and tied

25

the young girl to the handle of the car door. He then proceeded in a drunken stupor to rip her clothes off and rape her.

The bar owner was leaving his establishment and noticed his employee's car was still in the parking lot. He heard muffled sobs. He peeked down the alley and saw by the streetlight the young frightened girl and the creep who was molesting her. He quickly ran to her rescue. Ron was so thoroughly absorbed in this act of violence that he didn't even hear the approach of the bar owner. He dealt blow after blow to Ron's face and Ron was left unconscious only to awaken in a jail cell.

Ron and his parents tried to use his military record as justification that he was a good person and this was his only offense. They argued that his time would be of better use remaining in the military and serving his country. The legal system, however, did not take likely to his molestation of the young, innocent girl. Later that year Ron was sentenced to ten years in prison, and during his first year incarcerated, Liz divorced him. Liz's grandparents did not want the marriage broken. They told Liz to stand by Ron. They did not want another divorce in the family. Liz knew they were only thinking of their name and their many friends. Didn't they understand how she had been hurt and betrayed? She no longer felt any love for Ron. He had finally broken her. Unfortunately, whenever she looked at her daughter, Kimberly, instead of seeing a sweet little girl that constantly asked where Daddy was, she saw a reflection of Ron.

Chapter Seven
Kimberly and "Betty Lou"
Wartime

The last year had been traumatic for Liz. Her grandparents were not happy with her decision to divorce Ron. With her grandfather's influence, he arranged to have all records of any association with the Mathe name expunged. Liz would go back to the last name of Phillips, and the process was started to legally change Kimberly's name. Liz decided that she would no longer go by the name of Liz as that was what Ron called her. She wanted every memory of him erased from her life, so she now would go by Betty Lou Phillips. She wanted a whole new life without any reminder of the past few years, including her daughter.

Kimberly spent most of her days with her grandmother, Olive. Kimberly was too little to understand what had happened. She only knew that her daddy would be gone for a long time.

Betty Lou knew it was not her little daughter's fault. She tried to be a good mother to Kimberly but was relieved to have Olive take over the burden of parenting whenever possible. She needed to find a way to start over, to get a new life. She started looking for a job. In wartime jobs were difficult to find.

27

After months of searching for a job with no luck, Olive started noticing that Kimberly was getting increasingly withdrawn when she was around her mother. Kimberly would cry when she left Olive's apartment to go home with her mother. After much soul searching, Olive decided to pay for Betty Lou to attend a business school to learn shorthand and other secretarial skills. She would take care of Kimberly while Betty Lou attended school. This would give Betty Lou a better opportunity to find a good job and maybe, for now, it would be best if Olive spent more time with Kimberly. Olive knew Betty Lou married Ron too fast without really getting to know him. Maybe having more time to herself and with people her own age would help her want to be the mother she needed to be.

Business school was exciting for Betty Lou. She could attend classes all day and forget about her former life. She could finally look forward to a future again. Betty Lou was quiet and secretive during classes as she did not want anyone to know of the scandal in her former life. Her last name was officially Phillips again, so she felt safe with her secrets. Her mother took care of Kimberly as much as Betty Lou wanted, so there was no need to let anyone know she was ever married or that she had a child. She made a few friends at school. Her best friendship was with Margie. She clicked with Margie immediately as her own daughter's middle name was Margery. Margie was single and had been raised on a Minnesota farming community. Her parents immigrated from Czechoslovakia. Her father spoke some English, but her mother had never learned the English language. Margie's mother had only completed the second grade. Once the family immigrated to America, it was understood that the children would need to be interpreters for their parents. Margie's mother, Victoria, wanted her to have the education she never had. She saved money from the household fund to pay for Margie's business schooling. Margie felt obligated to her parents and had never yet dated. She was a tall, good looking young woman but extremely shy. In business school Betty Lou seemed as quiet as Margie, so becoming best friends seemed right. She thought they had a lot in common. They confided in each other and once they swore to be best friends forever, no matter what, Betty Lou finally told Margie about her daughter but she avoided the whole truth. Maybe it was her previous high society life but Betty Lou told Margie that Kimberly's father was killed in the war.

Business school lasted for nine months. Both girls graduated with exceptional grades and were very proficient with their newly acquired skills. The only problem was good jobs were still hard to get. The war would surely end soon and better times were ahead. Until then, both girls applied to and were accepted in a stenographer pool. They worked with a large group of women typing letters and purchase orders for the Hennepin County Government. The jobs were boring but helped to increase their typing speed. They both were able to save money, and every payday Betty Lou would stop at F.W. Woolworth to buy Kimberly a small toy or candy. It helped ease her guilt.

One of Margie's siblings, an older brother, was in the army and had been wounded in the attack by the Japanese on Pearl Harbor. He had been moved to a military hospital in Texas. Margie so wanted to visit her brother but was afraid of traveling by herself. Betty Lou asked her mother if she would be willing to keep Kimberly for a few weeks while she went with Margie to Texas. Neither one of the girls owned a vehicle. The American automobile factories had converted to wartime production which caused tires and gasoline to be rationed making bus travel the most popular and affordable way to commute at this time. It would take approximately 34 hours to get from Minneapolis to Dallas without any overnight stops. They were told there would be plenty of rest stops but the girls didn't think they would mind the long trip as the Minneapolis Greyhound Bus Terminal had opened less than five years ago and all the busses were new and modern. It would be a comfortable but long form of transportation.

Olive was concerned with the distance Betty Lou had already created with Kimberly, but she knew if she told her no, Betty Lou would hold it against the young girl.

The girls were tired when they arrived in Dallas. They couldn't wait to get cleaned up once they checked into a tacky motor lodge that was close to the military base and hospital. The next morning, they headed out to visit Margie's brother. Margie's brother had been moved from a wounded stage area to a ward where other wounded army privates were recuperating. Karl was now out of danger and would be released in a few weeks. The extent of his injuries were no longer debilitating but would keep him out of further military assignments. His injuries consisted of a bullet in his shoulder and shrapnel in his neck. The bullet had been removed; however, some of the shrapnel would need to stay in his neck as it was too close to the spinal nerves to remove without causing permanent damage. He had also developed malaria while stationed on Oahu but was on the mend, no longer contagious, and in good condition. In a way, he was one of the lucky ones as he would be heading home, his tour of duty finished, and although wounded it was not serious.

Margie introduced Betty Lou to her brother, Karl. Betty Lou was immediately attracted to him with his kind blue eyes. She could tell his army buzzed black hair was starting to grow back into the cutest black curls. Margie told Betty Lou about Karl and Anna but asked her not to mention it. It had been almost seven years ago, but Karl still felt the loss deeply. He had spent some time with a few women in Hawaii when the soldiers went out together, but he could never get past the deep love he had for Anna, the baby that could have been, and the death of both.

The girls stayed in Texas for almost two weeks. Most of the time was spent at the hospital. After the first week, a friend of Karl's came to visit him. Leonard met Karl while both were stationed in Honolulu. They were both privates in the Army. Leonard was from Texas and was tall, dark haired and extremely handsome. Margie was infatuated with his sexy, southern drawl. One night he took both Margie and Betty Lou out on the town to show them a little bit of Texas. Leonard and Margie hit it off right away. They seemed to click together, and it was difficult for them knowing that Margie had to go back to Minnesota. The last few days of the girls' vacation, Betty Lou insisted that Margie and Leonard go out alone to spend time with each other. During this time, Betty Lou visited Karl at the hospital. They had some good talks. Karl was talking more and could now look Betty Lou in the eye without the haunting of ghosts. He wanted to be cordial to her as she was his little sister's best friend. He was surprised when he felt a little bit of sadness on the day before their trip ended. He of course would miss Margie but he had to admit that he had grown to like Betty Lou. She helped him get out of his shell a little with their talks. She had helped him feel comfortable again in the company of a woman.

The saddest part of the girls' departure was the intensity of the farewell between Leonard and Margie. Leonard took the girls to the bus station and carried their bags.

A perfect southern gentleman he was! As the girls said their goodbyes, Margie could no longer hold back the tears. She already knew she was in love with Leonard and wondered if she would ever see him again. He had often commented that his home had always been in Texas, and he could not imagine living in the snow and subzero temperatures of Minnesota. Margie was sad and doubtful that a long distance romance could survive, although many did in war time. They never went "all the way", but their relationship had gotten into some heavy petting. Leonard was a respectable Texan and had total respect for Little Margie from Minnesota. He liked to call her "My Little Margie" after the television program. He promised to write to her, and it was evident there were tears in his eyes when he kissed her goodbye.

Chapter Eight

New Beginnings

The war was over! Karl's parents were getting on in age. Karl's father, Charles, had suffered a minor heart attack after his son was wounded at Pearl Harbor. Farming was too much for them now. Their children were adults and did not want to continue with the family farming. Charles had been selling his home grown produce on the roadside for several years and had some money set aside. He decided to take some of his nest egg and invest in a small grocery store that was in a predominately Polish neighborhood in the northeast section of Minneapolis. He was familiar with a small Italian grocery store in town. It was in an area where many Italian and European people had immigrated. The neighborhood was very ethnic, so Charles thought, "Why not cater to the European and Polish community like the Italians did?" Many people were starting up new businesses. The mood of the country was one of new beginnings and renewed hope.

One day while Charles and his wife were taking a stroll around the neighborhood dreaming of this possible new endeavor, they came across a property for sale. It was across Central Avenue, a few miles from the Italian grocery store. It definitely needed some work but was a good sized building. There were empty living quarters attached alongside the small vacant clothing shop. Above the shop were additional occupied living quarters. They climbed the stairs to inquire about the 'For Sale' sign posted in the front yard. The people living above the shop had been renting for several years. They explained that the clothing shop had closed during the war. The entire property was for sale. The owners previously lived next to their shop and always rented out the living area above. Their only child, a son, had been killed in the war, and they no longer wanted the responsibility of renting out or running a business. After their son died, they moved to a small flat as it was too sad for them to continue living where their child had grown up. They would sell for a reasonable amount to the right buyer. This was the perfect opportunity for Charles and his family. Within six months, they had sold their farm for a good profit, moved to the new house, and started their own grocery store, 'Charles' Self Service'. They knew it would take months, maybe a few years, until a good customer base was established, so the rent they would receive monthly from the existing upstairs renters would help them through the time needed.

Karl had been home now for a few months. He helped his father with the move and setting up the store. There was remodeling that needed to be done and bookkeeping to be learned. Charles wanted a walk-in cooler where he could butcher, wrap, and store meat. New wood and glass food cases had to be installed as well as open bins to store fruits and vegetables so customers could inspect produce to place in their hand carried baskets that the store would supply, just like a European open market. Karl persuaded his father to add a candy counter and a gum ball and trinket machine he had seen at a store in Texas. The machine was a glass ball filled with gum balls and small trinkets. The glass ball attached to an iron stand. The ball was filled by unscrewing the large nut and bolt on top of the glass. The customer would insert a penny into a slot at the bottom of the ball, and then turn the handle. You never knew what you would get, but you could be sure at least one trinket and one gum ball would roll out. The gum balls were brightly colored red, blue, yellow, and green. The trinkets were cheap little plastic and metal figurines with a hole that children laced through a string to make a necklace or bracelet.

Karl and Charles were busy making contacts with vendors and suppliers to estimate their first few orders. Karl seemed like a new person. His mind was occupied by all the work that needed to be done helping his dad set up the store. He poured himself into his work. That was his life now. His mother and father did not think it was healthy for him to work so hard and so many hours, but they were grateful. They did not believe they could have managed without Karl's help.

Margie and Betty Lou continued working in the steno pool. Margie knew that soon the store would open and her weekends would be needed to wait on customers and run the cash register. She did not have a problem with that as she had not heard from Leonard in about a month. She was depressed, and everyone close to her could sense the loneliness she carried.

Betty Lou, Olive, and Kimberly decided to visit Betty Lou's grandparents in Seattle for their summer vacation. Betty Lou did not want to go back to Gull Lake as it would bring back too many memories of her previous life with Ron. Ron had made no attempt to contact his daughter. Kimberly's name change was not yet final, and Ron did not seem to care one way or another. He was very careful not to show any anger or resentment to the guards or warden during his stay in Stillwater State Prison. His hope was to cut his sentence in half and get out in five years for good behavior. He would start a new life when he was out and not settle for mediocrity. He would be sure to make up for lost time.

"Charles' Self Service" would be officially ready to open in a month. It would be mid-summer and would be a good time for selling fresh fruits and vegetables. Charles had negotiated with a reputable vendor to deliver the best Polish and Kielbasa sausage he had tasted in this country. He advertised this as well. The price would be costlier than most meats, but Charles would take only a small markup so that he could reel in the ethnic community in hopes they would feel and taste 'a little bit of home'.

Everything was going well, and Karl had a wonderful surprise for his sister. He had been in contact with Leonard. It was obvious that Leonard was head over heels for Margie, but he was depressed over not being able to find a good job and with Margie so far away. He had been a good cook in the army and there were a few jobs in Dallas he could get, but the pay was poor. He was starting to feel like a failure. Karl suggested that Leonard take a break. He could get on a Greyhound bus and visit Minnesota for the grand opening of the store. Maybe Leonard could find a decent job in Minnesota. Leonard still did not want to live in a cold climate like Minnesota, but as it was summer now, he agreed to visit and surprise Margie. He couldn't write to her now because he was afraid he would let his news of his upcoming trip slip and ruin the surprise. Karl made a pact with his parents to keep it a secret from Margie. Leonard would arrive in time for the grand opening of the store.

In the early morning of the store opening, the family was busy blowing up balloons and making sure everything was in place. The stores hours would be Monday through Saturday from 7am until 10pm. Sundays the store would be closed as this was a strong Catholic and Ukrainian Orthodox community. The grand opening would not begin until 8 am. Karl had taken a break from stocking shelves the night before to pick up Leonard at the bus station. Leonard stayed out of sight until Margie was in bed that night. Afterward, Karl sneakily led him into the house. He hid out in Karl's bedroom while Margie was there.

People started lining up outside the store at 7:30 am. They were happy to find a store catering to their heritage with reasonable prices. It was also heart warming that the owners spoke a form of Slovakian. The store was situated in the middle of their own neighborhood and as most immigrants did not drive, the store offered delivery of groceries. Karl would happily do that as long as there was someone to help his dad manage the store during his absence. Charles' entire supply of sausages were sold out by noon that day. The gum ball machine as well as the penny candy were big hits with the neighborhood children. "Charles' Self Service" was open and the outlook was truly 'The Great American Dream'.

During a lull in the day, Karl asked Margie if she would see if the man at the counter needed some help. The tall man had his head hung down and was looking in the candy case. Margie went behind the counter and asked, "May I help you, sir?"

"Only if you are as sweet as the chocolate in this candy case," Leonard replied in his sexy southern drawl.

Margie couldn't believe her eyes! At first, she wasn't sure it was Leonard because she had never seen him out of uniform. His hair had grown out with the cutest dark brown curl in the middle of his forehead. Then he looked up, and she knew it was Leonard! Margie burst into tears and held her hands up to her face. Leonard came around the counter and took her in his arms. He looked into her eyes, and he knew then that he would do anything for her. He had missed her so. He tenderly kissed her lips, and because there were a few customers still in the store, he pulled away but told her he would stick around for a few days. He would like to take her out to dinner that night.

It was a successful night all around, except for Karl. He was excited about the store's success and happy for his sister; however, he could not help but feel the pangs of loneliness and emptiness as he watched Leonard and Margie hold each other.

Chapter Nine
Karl and Betty Lou

"Charles Self Service" had now been open a month. Business was better than the family ever expected. To no one's surprise, Leonard remained in Minneapolis to be close to Margie. He started looking for a full-time job and helped out part time at Karl's family's store. He was unsure of his long-term plans but for now wanted to be close to Margie. He shared a bedroom with Karl until he could find full time employment or until he returned to Texas.

It was almost 10:00 pm on Friday and Karl was getting ready to close up for the night when he heard the bell on the top of the door jingle, signaling a customer.

"We are just getting ready to close, but I will be right with you," he yelled out.

The customer's back was toward Karl and as Karl approached her, he felt his heart beat up to his throat. She had the short, cropped, auburn hair he remembered Betty Lou having.

"I'm looking for a friend." she said with a smile in her voice as she quickly turned to face Karl.

He recognized Betty Lou's cute, impish nose, and his heart raced but all he could do was stare at her. Just then his sister, Margie, came into the store with Leonard.

"Hey, you two. Glad we caught both of you together. Betty Lou is home from her summer vacation and we thought the four of us could go to the Bijou tomorrow night to see a motion picture."

"No, thanks," Karl quickly came to his own rescue, "I've got a lot work to do."

"Come on, now," Betty Lou pleaded. "Can't you take time off from stocking shelves to accompanying us to a harmless picture show?"

Margie interjected, "I've already mentioned it to Papa, and he will be fine alone tomorrow night."

This Betty Lou was a tease with some kind of unknown agenda, Karl thought.

Karl was too tired to argue with his sister. Besides, he could not remember the last time he went to see a motion picture. He agreed to go. All four planned to meet in front of the store and go together.

The Bijou Theater was located on Washington Avenue in downtown Minneapolis. Whenever the girls would go to the movies together, they would go to the neighborhood theater, The Ritz, as it was within walking distance. It would be exciting to go to the downtown Bijou which had been remodeled a few years earlier.

They met and walked up a block to Central Avenue to catch the streetcar. It took them to Hennepin Avenue, then they walked a few blocks to Washington.

The four of them sat in plush, red cushioned seats in the balcony. Red velvet drapes adorned the walls of the theater and the golden scrolled woodwork was unlike anything at their neighborhood Ritz Theater. The movie playing was a brand new release. 'Leave Her to Heaven', starring Gene Tierney, Cornel Wilde, Jeanne Crain, and Vincent Price was a drama about obsessive love. The picture was over dramatic but good. Everyone enjoyed it.

Afterward, Betty Lou talked them into going to a small bar off Hennepin Avenue where there was music, dancing, and beer. Margie was still too young to legally drink alcohol, but surprisingly got in without a problem. She ordered a Coca-Cola, and Betty Lou turned her nose up and told her to live a little.

Karl was concerned. This young woman, Betty Lou, was attractive and usually very kind to Margie yet, at times, she seemed too old and too experienced for his little sister. Betty Lou acted as if she were out to prove something. Karl could not quite figure her out. She was an interesting person, and he really liked her yet, he couldn't help but sense some sort of danger with her.

The music was loud and jubilant. Karl could not remember the last time he had danced. When both Margie and Betty Lou pulled him out on the dance floor to do the jitterbug, he was not even sure he knew how. He felt foolish, yet it was fun to laugh again. Suddenly the music changed to a rendition of Glenn Miller's slow, romantic tune, "Moonlight Serenade." Karl found himself pushed into Betty Lou's arms as he watched his little sister parading back to the chair next to Leonard. He sneered at the victorious smile on Margie's face.

As they danced, Betty Lou filled in the awkward gaps with chitchat about her job and how wonderful it was to have Margie as her best friend. When Karl asked her more about herself, she seemed to clam up but did tell him she was an only child and her real name was Elizabeth but she preferred Betty Lou as it seemed more modern. By the end of that slow dance, Karl was beginning to feel throbbing sensations in his upper thighs and groin. It had been so long since he had those feelings. His heart began to beat faster and there were small beads of sweat across his forehead. After the dance, he apologized and said he was not feeling well. The all decided to go home.

The next day was Sunday, and the store was closed. Karl spent most of the day alone in his room. The memory of Anna haunted him intensely. He could not concentrate on anything. He slept that afternoon and all through the night. It was a restless, tired sleep, but the next morning he had to admit he felt much better and was ready to work.

Later the following week, Margie and Betty Lou announced that as the store was closed on Sunday, it would be the perfect time to go on a picnic at Moore Lake. It was several miles from the house so they would need to use Karl's delivery car. They wanted friends and family to join in. The girls would make sandwiches and potato salad if the guys would bring pop and potato chips. Margie's mother would make strawberry shortcake. Everyone thought it was a good idea. Even Karl said after working so hard to set up the store, it would be fun to enjoy some summer sunshine.

Early Sunday morning, family and friends gathered at Moore Lake. Charles voiced his concern about missing Sunday mass and made sure that before anyone ate, a prayer was said. There was more than enough food. The best part was two huge watermelons Karl had picked out as the best ones in the store. Everyone sat around the picnic tables indulging in the succulent slices of deep red melon. The guys had a watermelon seed spitting contest, which Betty Lou found disgusting, but laughed along with the others.

After gorging on food, Margie, Leonard, Betty Lou, and Karl decided to walk around the lake to make room for strawberry shortcake. The others, including Karl's other siblings, stayed back to play a card game of 500 Rummy. Halfway around the lake, the foursome reached an alcove. They all had swimsuits on underneath their clothes. Margie and Leonard were ready for a dip in the lake. Once they persuaded Karl and Betty Lou to join in, all four were frolicking in the water. Karl's eyes kept returning to Betty Lou's chest. Her breasts were quite large for such a petite girl. They were full, yet proportioned well. He could feel the hardness in his swimming trunks swell as his gaze settled on the wet swim suit outlining Betty Lou's hard nipples. He decided to swim out alone for a while before retreating to the beach. He must get back to the others at the picnic table, to the unthreatened safeness, to his imprisoned mind holding Anna.

That evening everyone was tired from all the fresh air, sunshine, and exercise. Margie had fallen asleep on the living room couch so Leonard went to bed. Betty Lou asked Karl to take her home but not awaken Margie as they both had to be at work in the morning. Karl felt uncomfortable driving Betty Lou home. The entire ride was in silence until they reached Betty Lou's apartment. It was already arranged with Olive to keep little Kimberly until morning as Betty Lou did not know what time she would be home.

"Would you mind helping me carry in these dishes and blankets from the picnic?" Betty Lou asked Karl.

Karl shrugged his shoulders but immediately got out of the car to help. When they reached the door, Betty Lou insisted Karl come inside. He cautiously entered and carried the picnic dishes into the kitchen. Betty Lou went straight for the refrigerator and opened a beer for both of them.

"Just have a quick beer with me before you leave," Betty Lou said as she sat on her couch.

Karl reluctantly took the bottle of beer and sat down next to her. His heart was beating fast and he wondered if Betty Lou could hear the pounding of his loud, rapid heartbeat.

As Betty Lou sipped on her beer, she knew that she had every intention of showing him she was not a shy, frigid, girl. Not like Ron had thought! She would never make that mistake again.

"I had a wonderful time today, Karl," she said in a soft, seductive voice.

Karl felt something stir inside him as he replied, "It was fun. I haven't relaxed like that since I was in Pearl Harbor before the war started."

"You need to relax more, Karl. Let me show you." Betty Lou set down her beer and turned toward Karl. She placed her hands on the nape of his neck. Karl was startled and started to resist but then Betty Lou began massaging the muscles in his neck. They both laughed and Karl let the enjoyment fill him as the tightness seemed to be lifting away. Once the stress seemed gone, Karl felt tingly all over. He could no longer resist the sensations surging through his body. It had been too long. He had been so lonely for too long. He reached around his neck and took Betty Lou's small fingers in his hands. Their eyes met and before Karl could consider what was happening, his lips were on Betty Lou's soft, tender mouth. They kissed and embraced without either one speaking. As Betty Lou's fingers played with Karl's curly black hair, the passion that arose in Karl was too strong for him to deny it any longer. His hands caressed those perfect breasts he had earlier admired in the wetness on the beach. As he removed her clothing, his bereft mouth and tongue explored every sensuous inch of

47

her body. She moaned in pleasure, guiding his head along in places she never before wanted known to Ron. Ron had never been this tender, this caring. She did not want to spoil this so as Karl parted her legs she whispered his name in pleasure and kissed him full on the mouth as she felt his fullness enter her.

Afterward, as Karl drove home, he had mixed feelings. He knew this girl had not been a virgin. His sister had told him about baby Kimberly some time ago. Karl had asked Betty Lou why she had not told him. She explained she was afraid what he would think of her. She also came clean with the true story of Kimberly's father. He felt sorry for both Betty Lou and Kimberly. Maybe this was part of Betty Lou's secretive evasiveness.

When Karl left, Betty Lou asked him to call her. He said he would but now as he drove home, he did not know. He still felt guilty somehow. Once Karl was home in his own bed, memories of Anna jumped before him as tears rolled down his face. He finally drifted into a much needed sleep.

Chapter Ten

Home is Where Your Heart Is

Leonard and Margie's relationship continued to develop into a deep friendship that was getting more intimate each time they were alone together. Leonard worked hard impressing both Karl and Charles. He had a real knack with bookkeeping, so he was an asset when help was needed paying bills and balancing the books.

Charles' health seemed to be deteriorating, and before Thanksgiving, the family asked Leonard if he would accept a full-time job, working alongside Karl in their family business. They could not afford to pay the salary they knew Leonard was looking for, but they would continue to offer him room and board in their home without any expectations of him paying rent. Leonard had been trying to save up enough money to go home to Texas for Christmas and as he was not having much luck finding another job, he agreed to the family's offer.

Christmas was a month away. Leonard knew in his heart that he wanted to ask for Margie's hand in marriage. He did not have enough money saved to buy her an engagement ring. He knew she would accept that. Margie was well grounded and very much aware of the tight finances. She was still working with Betty Lou at the steno pool and was also helping out at the store.

In the beginning of December, the renters living up above the grocery store, announced they would be moving at the end of the month. They would be going back to Wisconsin to live with family and help out on their family farm. Charles was concerned he would not find another renter soon enough as the family depended upon the rent to help with the monthly house payment.

Leonard thought he had the perfect solution. He knew that he and Margie deeply loved each other. They could marry and with both of their salaries, could afford to move in above the store.

Accepting he would not return to Texas, Leonard asked Charles for Margie's hand in marriage and if they could live in the apartment above the store. Charles agreed with the condition they would marry before living together.

On New Year's Eve, Margie and Leonard were united in matrimony. A small, simple wedding was held in the sacristy of St. Anthony's Catholic Church with Karl and Betty Lou standing up for them. Margie bought a white two-piece suit and matching pumps. Betty Lou helped with the bouquet arrangement of white lilies and pink and red carnations. The greenery added to the bouquet was festive for the time of year. Leonard wore a brown suit he had picked up at the Veteran's thrift shop. He had been correct that Margie did not care about diamonds or a fancy wedding. She was ecstatic simply for finding such happiness. They decided in the spring to take a honeymoon drive down to Texas to meet Leonard's family.

New Year's Day was spent with the entire family helping the newlyweds move in above the store. Karl had taken a wooden crate from a grocery delivery and painted it with flowers and hearts to have in the newlywed's entry way of their new home. The sign read "Home is where you hang your heart."

Chapter Eleven

Acceptance

Once Karl knew about Kimberly, he spent a few weeks going through everything in his mind. He wanted to meet Betty Lou's mother and Kimberly before he felt committed to this relationship. Betty Lou agreed but warned him her mother, Olive, came from wealth and sometimes came off as a snob, even though she felt Olive's heart was in the right place. Karl remembered he felt that same way about Betty Lou when he first met her.

They met for lunch at Olive's apartment. Kimberly was a cute little girl who seemed to cling to Olive like she was her mother instead of her grandmother. Olive was pleasant at first but throughout lunch, Karl felt as though he was being grilled about his intentions with her daughter. Once Olive realized Karl had not even graduated from high school, she looked appalled and made no secret that her daughter should be with someone who was more than a grocery clerk in a store. It meant no difference to Olive that Karl, having been in the army, had served his country or that he was injured in service. Karl and Betty Lou both tried explaining to Olive that they were only dating and it wasn't serious enough to be concerned about his financial status.

Olive looked her daughter straight in her eyes and responded, "You should always be concerned about financial status."

The rest of the afternoon was uncomfortable and Karl could not wait to leave. The only bright spot of the day was Kimberly seemed to really warm up to Karl and he thought she was sweet.

A week passed and Karl did not contact Betty Lou. He felt so belittled in Olive's presence. Then Saturday afternoon, both Betty Lou and Kimberly came into the store. Kimberly ran right up to Karl and hugged him at his knees. Karl felt a tug at his heart. He picked her up and brought her over to the gumball machine with the trinkets. He gave her a few pennies. Kimberly was thrilled with the little colorful plastic and metal pieces that came out of the machine. Karl took a piece of twine from the store counter and showed her how to make a necklace out of the pieces. It was obvious that Karl and Kimberly adored each other.

Against Olive's objections, Karl and Betty Lou continued to date. The store was doing well and Karl was finally feeling some peace with his life. He knew he would never get over Anna. She would always be the love of his life, but he had to move on if he was going to have any kind of life. The last few months had been enjoyable with Betty Lou, and he felt he was getting more attached to Kimberly. Maybe it was guilt from the child he could have had, or maybe he felt sorry for Kimberly as she did not seem to warm up to her mother. Karl felt he truly loved this little girl and wanted to take care of her. He often invited her along with Betty Lou on outings. Betty Lou wasn't crazy about it, but accepted it.

Three months after Karl had met Olive and Kimberly, Betty Lou realized she was pregnant. First, she told Olive. It did not go over well.

"What do you intend to do now?" Olive asked with a look of disgust on her face.

"I intend to tell Karl tonight, and he will do the right thing," Betty Lou replied with an air of guile.

"Oh my God," Olive screamed at her. "Did you purposely get pregnant to trap that boy? What were you thinking? Why would you want that nobody in your life? We should have never stayed here. I should have moved you back to Seattle and found someone for you with prestige, someone that comes from money. Karl is not up to our status and if you go through with this, you will be damned. Please don't do this. It will be an embarrassment to our family."

"Mother", Betty Lou replied without any fear in her voice. "I never listened to you when you said I should stay with Ron, even when he was in prison. Wasn't that an embarrassment to the family? I didn't listen to you then, and I won't listen to you now."

Olive could not believe how her daughter, her only child, could react like this. After all, she had stayed in Minneapolis only for Betty Lou and Kimberly. She had given up her friends in the social circles of Seattle to help her daughter and granddaughter. She must now play the trump card with her daughter.

"I will take Kimberly away from you if you marry this man. I would rather see her without her mother than be subjected to a life of poverty, which you will be. Can't you see what a mistake you are making? You need to take care of this right away. Find a doctor who can terminate your condition, or I will find one in Seattle to do it. You don't even need to tell Karl. In the morning, I will take Kimberly to Seattle with me for a few weeks. Call me when you've reached your senses."

The next morning, after Olive and Kimberly left, Betty Lou stayed in bed going over and over in her mind her situation. She had been so hurt by Ron, so embarrassed. Ron had presented himself as a moral and upstanding naval office and came from a family of money. Look where that had gotten her. Karl did not have any family money but he was determined and a hard worker. She loved him for that. He also adored Kimberly. Her mother would come around eventually and accept the situation once they were married. She had to. What else could she do?

That night, Betty Lou decided she needed to tell Karl. Walking around the park by her apartment, Betty Lou asked him to sit down on a bench.

"What's wrong?", Karl asked. "Too tired to walk?"

"No", Betty sheepishly replied. "I need to talk to you about something. My mother took Kimberly to Seattle for a few weeks. She wanted me to straighten out my life."

"What do you mean? You have a good job and a wonderful little girl. Straighten out your life how?"

"Karl, I haven't been feeling well lately. I went to the doctor, and he confirmed that I am pregnant."

Karl could not believe what she was saying! He sat there in dead silence for several minutes. Betty Lou started crying. Could she have been wrong about Karl's conscience?

After what seemed to be a lifetime, Karl took Betty Lou's hand and asked her to marry him, to become a family with Kimberly and the new baby.

Betty Lou was ecstatic. Her tears of worry now turned to tears of joy.

Karl's thoughts went to Anna. He felt trapped, but he knew he must move on and do what was right. He would not see another baby die. In his own way, he did love Betty Lou. He would make this work.

They married in the small chapel at St. Anthony's Catholic Church where Leonard and Margie had exchanged vows. It was a small wedding with Leonard and Margie standing up for them and only Karl's family present. In order for the priest to marry them, Betty Lou was required to sign a paper for the Catholic Church agreeing to raise all their children in the Catholic faith. Betty Lou did this but she had a deep gnawing in the pit of her stomach that she had given up so much and everything was changing. This was not the way she was brought up and not how she always dreamt her life would be.

Chapter Twelve
Life's Journey

The first year of marriage is always tough. Getting to know every intimate detail about each other is one thing but add this with the stress of living with your in-laws and being pregnant, Betty Lou felt like she was losing her mind.

A few weeks after Betty Lou and Karl's marriage, they flew to Seattle, at Karl's insistence, to get Kimberly back. Karl begged Olive to let him raise Kimberly. If not, he would have to get the authorities involved and charge Olive with kidnapping. Since Olive had taken Kimberly to Seattle she knew there would be trouble. Karl also confronted Betty Lou's grandparents. They all knew Kimberly adored Karl and missed him as she had been asking about him since her arrival in Seattle.

After much pleading and arguing, an agreement was finally reached. Olive would release Kimberly with the understanding that Betty Lou be written out of the family will. Any affiliation with the family would be severed. Karl said that was fine with him but Betty Lou was devastated. This was not in her plan. She thought she would always have some financial security based upon her grandparents' money but her grandfather had enough and was through with her. He had pulled too many strings to wipe the slate clean when Betty Lou divorced Ron. He felt if his granddaughter wanted to marry into poverty, she could live in poverty. In the end, Betty Lou's family was disowning her for her marriage to Karl. They were not only disowning Betty Lou, but Kimberly and any future children conceived through this union with Karl.

Karl could not believe how cold Betty Lou's family was. He was determined to raise his family with as much love as possible and someday show Betty Lou's family that love and family meant more than money. He would work as hard as he could. As the three of them headed back to Minneapolis, Karl told Betty Lou they didn't need her family or their money. They would be fine. Betty Lou wasn't so sure.

Betty Lou's grandfather never finalized the name change for Kimberly. Karl said Kimberly was now his daughter and would take his last name. From this point on Kimberly went by Karl's last name, including when she entered the school system. No legal name change was made and as Kimberly was so young she did not realize her real last name was different from her family's.

The store was running well and with Karl's parents, Charles and Victoria, getting on in years, they decided to retire to a small house not far from the store. They turned the store over to Karl and Betty giving them some relief and comfort. The living area attached to the store now provided more than enough room for Karl, Betty, Kimberly, and their expanding family. It was the perfect solution for everyone and Karl and Betty were in charge of the family store.

Eventually, having a family of seven children was not easy for a woman who was an only child with no domestic skills. For Karl, his first true love could never be replaced however hard he tried. The perfect solution that was created for Karl and Betty's dreams became a series of shattered and hopeless nightmares.

Part Two

(1950's to present)

Patty's Story

My Journey to Peace Through

Hell

I asked God for strength,
that I might achieve...

I was made weak,
that I might learn humbly to obey.

I asked for health,
that I might do greater things...

I was given infirmity,
that I might do better things.

I asked for riches,
that I might be happy...

I was given poverty,
that I might be wise.

I asked for power,
that I might have the praise of men...

I was given weakness,
that I might feel the need of God.

I asked for all things,
that I might enjoy life...

I was given life,
that I might enjoy all things.

I got nothing that I asked for,
but everything I had hoped for.

Almost despite myself,
my unspoken prayers were answered.

I am among all men, most richly blessed!

--Anonymous

Prologue

My mother used to tell me I had an overactive imagination. I never had an invisible friend like other kids, but my dreams would often wake me and seemed so real.

To this day, some 60 years later, I remember in detail the scary dreams. I was sure there were witches and demons in the closet or under my bed. It took much consoling and my parents doing closet checks and under the bed searches in the middle of the night to get me back to sleep. Once my parents thought I was convinced that all creatures were gone, they would tell me to go to sleep and they would see me in the morning. I lay in bed saying my prayers. There were many times that I would say my prayers all night, still not convinced the monsters were gone. It was those times that I would unfortunately wet the bed, afraid to get up in the dark in the middle of the night. Quite often however, while saying my prayers, I would see an older man standing at the foot of my bed. He was short in stature, wore casual work clothes, and had a brown derby hat on his head. The hat was always tilted to his left side, and each time he visited me, there was a smile on his face that seemed to spread from ear to ear. I was never afraid of this man. He made me feel at peace and not afraid.

Those nights I would drift off to sleep without any worry. When I would awaken in the morning, he would never be there, but I knew he would come back to visit me. He never spoke to me, he just smiled and seemed to beam with light. I didn't mention this man to my parents because previously I insisted the tooth fairy was real.

Yes, I was convinced that whenever I lost a tooth and put it under my pillow, I would see a tiny colorful fairy flying about my pillow holding a magic wand that would produce the shiny change under the pillow for my penny candy desire to be fulfilled.

That enchantment came to an abrupt end one night when my mother gave me a good night kiss. I felt her hand slip under the pillow case and open up. I jumped up and found the reward for the lost tooth. I screamed at her saying she was too big to be the tooth fairy. That night I cried myself to sleep knowing the little colorful fairy would never return.

The old man did return however, not every night but several times until I couldn't remember seeing him anymore.

It was a few years later in the late 1950's when I was in elementary school, our class was doing a project on family history. It was a simple project, just to identify our parents, grandparents, and siblings. The teacher insisted we should know the given names of our grandparents not just "grandma" and "grandpa".

I did not know my grandparents very well. The only surviving grandparent was my dad's mother. She came over from Czechoslovakia and did not speak any English. My sister and I would sometimes spend a night at her house, and she would bake the best rolls and raised donuts. She would speak in her native Czech tongue, but we had no idea what she said. We were somewhat afraid of her because she would speak loudly, and we could not understand her. But the language of food won out, and we spent the night devouring her perfectly sugared raised donuts and prune filled kolaches. It was on one of these nights that I studied framed pictures on an old wooden table by her couch. I never paid much attention to them until that night because we had discussed knowing our grandparents in school. There were pictures of all my siblings, my aunts and uncles, and their children. Then I noticed a picture behind these others. It was a picture of my grandmother a few years younger but what I saw next to her sent shivers up my back and I felt as if the hair on my arms stood up and froze. The man standing next to her was the same man who had visited me many times at night when everyone else was asleep! He had the same derby hat on, worn at an angle and that wonderful smile radiated across his face. I couldn't believe it! I could not speak to my grandma as she wouldn't understand what I was asking. I asked my sister, Veronica, who is two years older than me, who that man was. She told me that it was Grandma's husband, our grandpa. She explained that he died several years back of a heart attack, and I was too young to remember him as I had been a baby when he passed. I told my sister about him visiting me, but she only laughed and said that I must have seen the picture an earlier time when I was at the house and simply forgot. When we got back home I told my parents, but they laughed and said that because he had the same clothes on as in the picture, it was again my overactive imagination. I was so sure it was really him. It felt so real, and I knew I had never seen that picture before. I just knew my grandpa, Charlie, had visited me from heaven to comfort me.

I never saw Grandpa after that. Many claimed experts of the supernatural and mind phenomena have stated that children do see spirits until they reach the age of reasoning and simply don't believe anymore. The spirits may still be there, but as children we do not recognize them or see them any longer because we have accepted that it was a figment of our imagination. I am not so sure of that.

Chapter One

My family consisted of seven children. I had three brothers and three sisters. I was the youngest for ten years and then my little sister came along. Before my little sister was born, we lived in northeast Minneapolis. It was in the mid 1950's, and our house was a large four-plex that belonged to my paternal grandparents. We lived in both the upper and lower left side of the house. The upper right side of the house was rented out, and the lower level was my favorite, our neighborhood grocery store owned and operated by my father's family.

One of my fondest memories of the store was when I was in kindergarten. Kindergarten was only a half day, and I went in the morning. School was only a few blocks from our house. I walked everyday with my sister who was two years older than me. Coming home I had to walk by myself, but back then people didn't worry about that. Each day I came home from kindergarten was like a holiday. With my other siblings at school all day and my mother working part-time, Dad would close up the store for lunch. He would prop the 'Closed for Lunch' sign against the bright blue Masterbread metal sign on the door. I had my choice of anything in the store to eat. Dad loved food as you could tell from his 300-pound frame. Everyone in the neighborhood loved my dad. They called him "Big Carl", and the store was named 'Carl's Self Service'. We had the large wooden cases with glass windows that held the best candy. At Easter time, we sold chocolate eggs and crosses, all decorated and in individual packages. At Christmas time, my dad put out the brightly colored Coca Cola Santa Claus sign that was taller than him. We also had a variety of penny candy from red licorice whips and black licorice pipes to pastel colored dots that you ate right off the paper. I liked the little wax bottles filled with fruity liquid. Once you drank the liquid, it was cool to chew the wax bottle and spit it out. My favorite fun thing in the store was the bubble gum machine. This tall red machine had a glass dome on it. Inside was assorted colors of bubble gum balls and little trinkets. These trinkets were probably made of lead, who knows. There were trinkets of little animals, flowers, and toys. Each trinket had a molded loop on top. It was fun watching children put their pennies into the machine, turn the knob and squeal with delight and anticipation at what prizes they received with their gumball. The popular thing with little girls was to collect and put their trinkets on string to make a necklace or bracelet. During my lunches with Dad, he would take out of his pocket the secret key that he used to fill the machine. He would unlock the top of the glass dome, and I could take one handful just for myself. I had the best trinket necklace in the neighborhood. Once we had our lunch picked out, we would go into our living room to watch TV. Our living area was actually attached to the store. We could enter our kitchen through the store without going outside. My dad and I would sit down and watch the same show each week day. I can't remember the name of the show, but there was always a pretty woman with a mink stole wrapped around her, and she seemed to float down a long stairway. We also watched "Queen for a Day". Dad always asked me, "What would you do if you won a lot of money?" He was always trying to win contests.

Dad had a habit of giving the larger families in the neighborhood credit during tough times. Mom used to take money out of the store's cash register to go to the VFW and play bingo a few times each week. The cash register was also her bank for beer money. My mother was attractive. A petite but busty, reddish dark-haired woman, she was an only child and often told us that she hadn't planned on having so many children so she sometimes needed to get away by herself. Her getting away time was playing bingo. I remember telling her that she got away when she worked part-time. She didn't think that was funny, and I often felt she didn't like her own children.

Dad didn't drink much. Occasionally a beer, so there was constant arguing, and these issues eventually led to the store going defunct.

Dad then went to work as a truck driver delivering furniture. Once the store closed, it remained vacant and became a huge play area for us. At Christmas time, we would get the biggest tree we could find. We all decorated it, but Mom would be the only one to put the tinsel on as she insisted on hanging the silvery strands one by one. My oldest sister, Kimberly and I danced the polka around the tree to the tune of "Beer Barrel Polka". These were good times.

One slick winter night while my dad was driving home in his semi-truck, he crashed and rolled over. He had no idea that he had acquired

7

diabetes and had gone into diabetic shock. Luckily, he survived the crash, but unfortunately his truck driving career was over.

My mother now had to work full-time to support the family. She did have secretarial skills from before she was married. It was in the 1950's, and women were not paid even close to what a man would make. Our family was now poor. So many mouths to feed and so little money. My dad became the "house husband" and mom was the so-called "bread winner".

In the 1950's, the Welfare program was called "Relief". To say your family was "on Relief" was like saying you were a displaced person in a soup line. I don't know how we would have survived without the government's help because not only did they give us orders for food, but they found us a place to live in the north Minneapolis projects. My parents were given "relief orders" for clothing. These orders allowed each child to have a certain number of clothing items. For example, we were each only given seven pair of underwear and socks. It was worse for the outside clothing because welfare only allowed us two to three complete outfits, so we would wear some clothes to school twice a week. Kids can be so mean as they would tease us and say we were poor and didn't have many clothes.

For me one of the most embarrassing times was when I got my first bra. I developed at a young age, as did all my sisters. I was only nine years old and in the fourth grade when I got my period. Along with that, I developed noticeable breasts. I was teased in gym class because of my bouncing breasts. The Relief Department could not believe that a nine year old girl needed not a training bra but a full-fledged cup sized bra. The school nurse contacted my mother that we needed to meet with her after school. The nurse took us down to the school basement and there were racks and tables stacked with used clothing. This was clothing that had been donated for needy people. That is how I got my first bra at age nine. My first bra had been worn by some other person, and it had noticeable yellow stains from the armpits. Looking back on this now, I wonder why my mother didn't take me to a clothing store to get my first bra. It should have been a special "grown up" occasion. I would think my parents could have afforded to get me a new bra. They certainly had money to keep playing bingo. Dad had now joined Mom to play bingo with that endless hope that he could double the grocery money with a huge win. Mom always had her beer, but I guess I accepted what I had.

Another benefit of being on Relief was that you received monthly "surplus commodities". We received bags of rice, cornmeal, powdered milk, sugar, and flour plus cans of dried beef, which we would serve on bread for dinner. My dad, remembered it from his army days, calling it "shit on shingles". We received canned, powdered eggs and clear bags of oleo. The oleo was white in color with a yellow-orange center dot. You would have to knead the bagged oleo with your hands so that the yellow dot would work into the white oleo and turn it yellow. That way it looked more like butter. The worst food was the cornmeal and the powdered milk. Each morning before we went to school, my dad would cook up cornmeal and serve it with the powdered milk. This was not the skim milk we have today. This was a powder that you mix with water. It would be blue in color and taste nasty. My sister and I referred to this as "cornmeal mush with blue milk." We hated it so much that when my dad left the kitchen, we would run it down the sink. There weren't garbage disposals so one day the sink got plugged, and my dad got wise to us, so he started to stay in the kitchen until we finished our breakfast. My sister handled it OK, but I often ended up throwing up on my way to school. So I went to school hungry. To this day, I avoid skim milk, thinking of that blue milk I just about gag.

The projects were comparable to a double bungalow where you lived side by side with another family. A cement patio separated our unit with our neighbors. Our neighbors had twelve children, and their house and children were always dirty. Most people that lived there were in the same boat. It often happened that we would need to share utilities with our neighbors. Our electricity would get shut off due to non-payment. My dad concocted an agreement with our neighbors when our electricity was shut off, we would run a cable from our neighbor's house to ours at night so we could have some light, watch TV, and eat. We would reciprocate with our neighbors when they couldn't pay their bill.

Chapter Two

Living in the projects brought so many changes to all our lives. My oldest sister, Kimberly, had already graduated from high school and did not move with us. She worked and lived downtown. After Kimberly graduated from high school, Mom and Dad told her she had a different father than the rest of us. Kimberly, at eighteen years of age, was devastated. Why didn't she know sooner, and who was her father? None of us knew mother had been married once before. Kimberly wanted to know who her father was. My parents explained to her he was not a good person and she would never have to see him. He had served time in prison and was now out. He was re- married and had another family. Kimberly insisted on knowing more about him. My mother finally gave in and told her when Kimberly was just a baby, her father, who was a naval officer, went out one night and got drunk. He tied a young girl to the back of his car with rope and raped her. Mother no longer had any contact with him, as were the terms of the divorce. Kimberly was appalled that she was never told any of this before now. Apparently, Dad had never legally adopted Kimberly, but she had always used our last name, the only name she knew. She planned on looking up her birth father to hear his side of the story. Kimberly felt this revelation was a betrayal. It was the determining factor for her moving out of the house.

My brothers, Bill, Richard, and Curt, seemed to always hang out with the wrong crowds and get into trouble. Fighting, drinking, stealing cars and money now seemed to be the norm for them and their friends.

A few months after moving into the projects, we found out that my mother was pregnant. I was ten years old when she gave birth to a little princess named LeeAnne. My little sister seemed to be an answer to my prayers. I had felt so alone with my family changing and falling apart. I no longer was the baby of the family, and I had a little one to take care of and play with. Maybe my siblings would stop calling me a tattle-tale and Daddy's favorite child.

LeeAnne was cute and perfect in every way. She had the curliest brown hair and blue eyes. Everyone who met her could not believe how her hair had such long, natural curly ringlets. I was born with a streak of silver-gray hair next to my dark brown hair. My older sister, Veronica, was born with Albinism. Her skin and hair were shockingly white. She could not stay outside in sunlight or in neighborhood pools very long without blistering from the sun. Her eyesight was poor. Her eyes were light blue but when she looked at the sun or any light they would take on a pinkish tinge. She wore glasses before she started school. Everyone in our old northeast neighborhood accepted her. Her best friend then was a blind girl. I believe moving into the North Minneapolis Projects was the downfall of my sister. It was difficult for her to make new friends.

The schools where we now lived were nothing like we had been used to. Children our age knew much more than we did. They used terrible language we had not yet been exposed to. We were growing up way too fast. There were many blacks in the new neighborhood, and those boys seemed to stare at Veronica all the time. When Veronica was in sixth grade, one afternoon before lunch, several black girls in her class locked her in the skating room and were going to beat her up because they didn't want their black boyfriends looking at her. It was fortunate a teacher heard the commotion and put a stop to it before any violence started. The girls were talked to and apologized, but Veronica still had to go back to school. It was scary, and she now realized how different she was. That began her downward spiral.

Veronica's attitude toward me changed after that incident. Whenever my parents would go out, Veronica and I would babysit LeeAnne. I dreaded those times because as soon as we heard the car leave our driveway, Veronica was in the kitchen getting a butcher knife. She would threaten me with it saying I was "miss goody two shoes" and maybe she should cut my face to turn me into a freak so I would know how she felt. I would cry and ask her why she hated me so much. She just laughed. Worst of all, we shared a bedroom and the same bed. At night, she would dare me to fall asleep saying she might strangle me in my sleep. She had changed so much so quickly. Whenever I threatened to tell my parents, she said if I did, she would hurt me worse and maybe even LeeAnne. I felt fearful, and I started wearing panties under my nightgown with a note tucked inside that simply said "Veronica killed me". Sometimes I wrote it on my skin in ink. Every night I fell asleep praying, not knowing if I would be alive the next morning.

I don't know what I did to set her off one night. She had a black belt with a big metal buckle on it. We were in bed after the lights were out. All of a sudden, she whipped this belt right across my face. I didn't realize what was happening and screamed. My father yelled up to us wanting to know what was going on. While I cried and held my face, Veronica told him I just had a bad dream.

The next morning, my face was red and swollen with welts. Dad took one look at me and said, "What the hell happened to you?" I told him I was just tired and didn't sleep well.

Later that night, I cornered Dad. I couldn't take it any longer. I told him everything. I sobbed as I recalled how Veronica used to be my friend but now she hated me and I didn't know why. I was afraid if Dad confronted Veronica she would go after me and LeeAnne.

Dad just sat there for a long time and said nothing. He hugged me and said, "It'll be alright. Don't say anything to anyone else. Dry your eyes and go upstairs."

Nothing happened right away but within a few weeks, the association that managed the projects, allowed us to move to a larger unit that had an additional bedroom. Mom and Dad said it was because of the birth of LeeAnne that our family increased in size. Dad insisted that LeeAnne would continue sleeping in Mom's room, the boys would all sleep in the same room, but Veronica and I would each

14

have our own room. Also, we would not be returning to the same school.

My mother checked out the school at the Catholic church we attended. She had heard they sometimes took charity cases with tuition being paid by the convent. Veronica and I were accepted. I enjoyed the Catholic school, but Veronica did not. She was embarrassed by always needing charity. Every other week the nuns would have the neediest families come to the convent after school. We would be given large brown bags filled with free bread and donuts based on how many children were in our family. My sister would ditch me so I had to carry the bags home by myself, usually smashing the bread. Even kids in the Catholic school were mean. Veronica couldn't handle the ridicule of others who would call us paupers and try to steal our free bread. We spent two years at North Minneapolis St. Joseph Catholic School before its doors closed for lack of funds.

The following year I started seventh grade and Veronica started ninth. We were both anxious going back to public school, especially Lincoln Junior High as it had a bad reputation. Strangely, Veronica started fitting in better than I did. Often avoiding me now walking home from school, she started hanging out with questionable people. I wasn't included in her circle of friends. They would bully me. At least it was better than getting hit in the face with a belt buckle.

That summer, when Veronica was fourteen years old, she attended the night time Aquatennial Torchlight parade in downtown Minneapolis with her new friends. Little did she know these friends, still amazed by her whiteness and different eyes, were setting her up. Asking her to save a place for them near some tall bushes, they were off to buy snacks to bring back and watch the parade. Once they left, their black boyfriends appeared. Veronica was dragged into the bushes, raped by these four boys, and deserted by all her friends.

My parents wanted it all hush, hush. No charges were to be filed as it would be more difficult for my sister. It was summertime, so Veronica did not have to face the embarrassment of returning to school. She would get over it and start at North High in the fall, even though those same "friends" would also be attending the same school.

I know now that if my sister had been given the counseling and support she so desperately needed, her life could have turned out differently. I could never hate her even after what she had done to me. I felt sorry for her, and that was the last thing she wanted. After she found out that her so-called friends were the farthest thing from "friends", she started getting along better with me, sometimes.

One Saturday late afternoon on December 23rd, Veronica and I went to F.W. Woolworth on Olson Memorial Highway. It was Christmastime, and we wanted to see if we could afford any last-minute gifts to get our parents with the babysitting money we had earned. We ended up just having a cherry coke and French fries at the deli counter.

It was nice spending time with Veronica again without those friends, but I would always be careful what I said. Woolworth's was only a few blocks from our house. It was starting to get dark, so we headed home. Veronica sensed that someone was following us. We turned around and saw a tall thin man hovering several feet behind. We weren't sure if he was following us, but I remembered seeing him at the deli counter staring at Veronica. We decided to speed up our pace. We got home, laughed at ourselves, chalking it up to being paranoid.

The house seemed too quiet. Mom and LeeAnne were home and who knows where my brothers were. Mom said Dad stormed out of the house after another fight. We could tell Mom had been drinking. She went upstairs with LeeAnne to lay down. Veronica and I watched TV. We loved the multi-colored Christmas lights that my dad hung in the living room windows, but we couldn't pull the shades down while the lights were up. We did not realize we were being spied on through those windows.

I took a bath, set my hair in pink sponge rollers for Sunday church, and went to bed. Veronica eventually went to bed but didn't lock the door as she worried my dad didn't have his house key.

Suddenly, I awakened to someone standing over me whispering, "Veronica, Veronica, come with me." It was dark in my bedroom, and I remember jumping up on the bed screaming that I wasn't Veronica. Suddenly Veronica flew out of her bedroom and turned on the hall light to see what was wrong. I screamed, "Veronica, look out. He's after you."

I realized from the light this was that same tall man who had been following us. All of a sudden, he pulled a gun out of the pocket of his black leather jacket. Veronica screamed, "Who are you? What do you want?" He said that he wanted her. She was a beautiful white goddess, and he wanted to marry her. I was crying and screaming. He grabbed Veronica by the arm and said he would not harm her. Once he grabbed her, I somehow got away and ran into the bedroom where my mother and LeeAnne slept. I knew my mother was probably passed out, but miraculously I was able to awaken her. She came out of the room after I screamed what was happening, and she seemed to sober up. This man was holding Veronica in front of him. He had the gun pointed at her head saying he didn't want to hurt her, but he wouldn't let anyone stop him from having her.

Mom tried to hush me. Veronica looked like she was in shock. Mom said, "OK, let's talk about this. You need to put your gun away. Let's go downstairs and discuss this." Surprisingly, he agreed.

The three of them headed downstairs, and I stayed upstairs to try to keep LeeAnne safe in her crib. If only we had a phone! Yes, my parents couldn't afford a phone after it had been turned off for many months of non-payment. After awhile I heard yelling. It was my brother Richard's voice. Then there was loud arguing and fist fighting. I ran downstairs. My brother had come home, wanted to know who this man was, and what was going on. The stranger was wearing boots and pulled a knife out of the side of his boot. He threw my brother against the wall and cut his arm. There was blood splattered on the wall. My mother screamed telling him to stop.

Somehow, once again, she had gotten this strange terrorizing man to calm down.

He said he wanted to talk about Veronica and would calm down if we wouldn't call the police. My mother promised not to call the police, explaining we did not have a phone. He put down his knife and said he had seen Veronica at Woolworth's. He was immediately attracted to her because of her purity and beauty. God had spoken to him saying she would be his. He had to marry her.

Veronica was crying and telling him he was crazy. My heart was racing. Mom and Richard told both of us to calm down and this would be settled. My mother made him a proposition. She wanted to know his name and what he did. If he told her this, she would allow Veronica to go out on a date with him. Of course, Veronica was adamant that this would never happen, but Richard mouthed to her to say it would be OK.

His name was Steve Hughes, and he worked on motorcycles and cars. A plan was made that he would come to the house in a few weeks after the holidays to meet my dad and take Veronica to a movie. Veronica just stood there staring at the floor with tears rolling down her face. Steve insisted on shaking everyone's hand as they would now be his family. Veronica and I refused as we were still so frightened, but Mom and Richard demanded we do so. He then left. We stood around the living room feeling numb. Then we saw how he had unwrapped all our Christmas presents under the tree. Mom bandaged Richard's arm. Thankfully it wasn't as bad as it looked.

Richard said he was leaving to go the gas station and call the police. Mom said, "I told him we wouldn't call the police." My brother said, "Well, I didn't make that promise." Mother insisted that Veronica and I rewrap all the gifts the best we could while she washed the blood off the wall. We were instructed not to mention a word to Dad as he would get mad and blame Mom for drinking and falling asleep when it happened.

Deep in my heart, I feared more for Veronica and myself than my mother. As we rewrapped all the gifts knowing what they would be on Christmas, Mom told us to be sure and act surprised. Veronica didn't say a word, but just sat on the floor rewrapping the gifts.

It was amazing that the crazy man had given us his real name. The police came to our house right away after Richard called. Mom was nervous that Dad would come home before the police left. The police ran his name, and found that he had recently escaped from Stillwater State Prison. He was dangerous and mentally unstable. They agreed to patrol the area each night and contact us when they caught him.

Later that night, Dad came home and went to bed unaware of anything that had transpired earlier. We didn't know that Dad had hidden some money in the dining room buffet. The next morning, he noticed it was missing. Dad was angry and blamed the boys for stealing it. Then he blamed Mom. Everyone was yelling, and it was Christmas Eve. When I was alone with Dad, I finally broke down and told him what happened. He hugged me and said he was so sorry.

20

Then he confronted my mother. She just glared at me. I didn't want my dad strapping the boys again and blaming them for stealing as it was most likely the escaped convict.

That was the worst Christmas of my life.

A week passed, and it was New Year's Eve. I couldn't believe my mom and dad wanted to go out and play bingo that night. We were still so afraid Steve would come back as the police had not yet caught him. Mom said she felt safe leaving us as the police would be patrolling the area. Our brother Richard was mad at our parents for leaving. He decided to stay home with us.

It was just about midnight when we heard a loud crash. The windows in our kitchen as well as the living room were shattered. Shortly after that, sirens were heard and rotating red lights were glaring through our windows. The police came to our house telling us Steve was in the area. They had been tracking him and would let us know when he was apprehended. The shattered windows were caused by gun shots. I remember one of the police officers asking where my parents were and saying, "If they have money to play bingo, tell them to get a phone." If my older brother had not been with us, the police would have called Child Protection Services.

The escaped convict was finally captured about two months later after he stalked my sister at school. That was the last we ever heard from him. The police did follow-up that he had been convicted and institutionalized.

Veronica was never the same after that. She ran away from home after stealing all the babysitting money I had saved. She spray-painted her hair black. The police soon found her as it was easy to identify the fake hair color with her albino skin.

When school let out for the summer, we finally moved out of the projects. The incidents that happened were never discussed any further.

Veronica became an atheist and remains one to this day.

My brothers took turns in and out of reform schools. There was not much laughter in our house anymore, and my brothers became strangers to me. One night two of my brothers observed me kneeling at my bedside praying the rosary. My older brother, Bill, said he was sorry and didn't mean to disturb me. My younger brother, Curt, laughed at me and said, "What has God ever done for you or this family?" He continued to ridicule me. I don't know what it was, but I was more determined than ever to seek God's help. I always had faith in God. I found peace in knowing God was watching over me. After all, I could have been shot or stabbed by the crazy man. I decided not to miss any more church on Sundays and pray to God that things would turn around. Each night I said my prayers. Each night I heard my mother's tears.

Chapter Three

It is hard to believe we only lived in the projects about five years and yet everything went so wrong during that time.

My mother continued to drink but managed to hold down her job and started earning good money. The Welfare Agency could no longer justify allowing us to live in subsidized housing with my mother's income and because my brothers were older and had all quit high school. If not in reform school, the boys lived elsewhere, except for Richard. Richard always tried to fit in. He never got into serious trouble but tried to show the other brothers he was "cool". Richard spent six months in a reform school only because he had taken the wrap for Curt. Curt had been on probation and had robbed a gas station. Richard was there as the lookout, his first time. If Curt had been charged, he would be sent to prison instead of reform school and for a much longer time. Richard, thinking he could be part of the "in crowd" and win Curt's respect, confessed to the robbery. Curt let him do this even though Richard served six months' time.

My parents thought they could save the rest of us if we moved back to the old neighborhood where we had all been so happy. After months of searching, they found a rental home a block away from where we used to live.

I didn't mind moving, and Veronica seemed just OK about it. She never seemed happy anymore. After a few months, we realized that old saying "you can't go home again" really rings true. We had been away five years, and most of our old friends had new "best friends". My mother was now only sober when she left for work in the morning. We never knew when she would be home. She would leave at seven in the morning to catch the city bus and wouldn't come home until late at night without care or concern about us. Dad always made dinner and waited for her to come home. His temper was getting shorter, and he seemed so mean.

One day when I was in tenth grade, I was called into the school office, and my father was there to pick me up. He had told the office clerk that there was a family emergency at home. I couldn't imagine what it would be, but I gathered my books and left with him. I was worried something had happened to my little sister. Dad told me he would explain it to me later. When we got to the car, Veronica was there and told me LeeAnne was still in school. We needed to do something for Dad, and he did not want LeeAnne to know about it. I could not figure out what was going on. Veronica explained. My dad was taking us out of school to help him "investigate" my mother. Apparently, he had been trailing her for days but was always back home in time to make us dinner. Mom had been leaving work around four in the afternoon each day in a car with her boss. Dad had followed them to a not-so-good part of town by Loring Park where they entered a rundown apartment building.

A few nights before, while my mother was passed out at home, Dad had gone into her purse and found an apartment key. The key had the apartment number imprinted on it. He had taken the key, made a copy, and slipped it back into her purse. She had no idea.

Now the three of us were on a mission. I didn't know exactly how I felt about it as I had no say. I was a kid, and Dad was mean so I didn't dare question him. I only knew it did not feel right, and I didn't want to know what we would find.

My dad had given Veronica a Polaroid camera to take pictures. I was simply to be a witness, and my dad told me I would see what my mother was really like. We entered the apartment, it was just a large room and a small dingy bathroom. It was old decor with dark woodwork. Yellowing pink flowered wallpaper was torn and hanging in several places. There was a double bed, small kitchen area, tiny closet, and a bureau. The furniture was scratched and wobbly. The kitchen sink had a plastic container filled with dishes in dirty water. The room itself had a sour smell to it. My sister and I noticed there were doilies and knick-knacks we had missed at our house. Here they were with some dishes, knives and forks, and towels that had once been in our kitchen. I watched as my dad opened the bottom drawer of the bureau. It was rickety and creaked when he opened it. It was filled with bank statements in the name of Mom's boss. Dad told me to gather up several of these thick envelopes to take with me as it was proof and for security. He had Veronica take pictures of what was in the drawer as well as many pictures of the apartment. As we drove home, Dad instructed us not to say a word to our mother and to act "normal", whatever that was. For my earlier dismissal from school to assist him in this mission, he wrote a note to my school telling them my little sister had fallen, and he needed help to take her to the hospital. I thought about how I would need to lie if any of my friends or teachers asked about her. That night I stared at the framed picture hanging in our dining room that read "The family that prays together, stays together." I was so confused. Where did that picture come from? It had been on our wall a long time but I couldn't remember where it came from. Our family never prayed together. That night I fell asleep with my rosary in hand asking God to keep us safe even if I was the only one praying.

Chapter Four

Dad's plan was to confront my mother while she was sober so she could comprehend what he was telling her. This had to be in the morning or on the weekend before she started drinking. He also wanted my sister and I to call the wife of my mother's boss and beg her to have her husband leave our mother alone. We did that at the drug store pay phone. The woman on the other end of the phone calmly thanked us and said she would definitely do that.

I don't know what any of us expected. We were being pulled into situations that children should never have to deal with. Dad still had not confronted Mom but the day after we placed that dreaded phone call, Mom surprised us by coming home right after work. She was not drunk. It seemed almost like a holiday the few times Mom was home and sober. We were happy until she called us all together and yelled at us, telling us we had no idea what we had done. Dad showed her the Polaroid pictures. She laughed! She said she could not understand why he would do such a thing as she was the breadwinner, and he wasn't. My mother had enough clout at work that she did not lose her job. Besides, she was sleeping with the boss. She did however, tell us she had given up the apartment.

She started coming home from work at a reasonable time. This lasted about a month until we noticed by the end of the night she was always drunk. Dad searched her closet and found half empty bottles of rye whiskey in her shoes and the pockets of her robes. It was easy for her to hide it as I honestly cannot remember my mom and dad ever sharing a bedroom. We were often awakened with my mother's screaming. She had what my father referred to as the "DT's". She would think snakes were coming out of the walls.

Life went on with mother being disassociated from us but still living in the same household. I was in high school, and outside of going to school each day, my main concern was taking care of my little sister. LeeAnne and I were the only children now at home.

My oldest sister, who had moved out long ago when we had first moved into the projects, had gotten pregnant and was now married. Veronica quit high school in the 12th grade. She had gotten pregnant and was now married to the first guy she ever dated. They met at a nursing home they both worked at after school. He did not have a high school diploma either. My brother Richard joined the army, but the other two boys seemed to always be in trouble. Curt did end up spending time at Stillwater State Prison for armed robbery and being an accomplice to a deadly shooting. He was guilty. He just never pulled the trigger — his best friend did.

Dad wouldn't let me date. He often told me I had to wait until I graduated from high school. His reasoning was he did not want me to get pregnant like Kimberly and Veronica. Other than meeting boys in my classes, I didn't have an opportunity to meet anyone. I wanted to be sure that LeeAnne and I would always remain close, but the time would come when we became separated and did not speak or see each other for ten long years.

Chapter Five

It was in my senior year of high school when things went from bad to worse. In the winter, my dad was changing a flat tire. His car was parked in our back yard by the alley as we did not have a garage. Somehow the jack slipped, the car shifted, and my dad's foot was injured as the jack fell on his foot. That was in 1969. The sore on his foot looked awful. I told him to go to the doctor, but he was stubborn. The only doctors we ever went to were at Hennepin County General Hospital where there would be hordes of people waiting long times to see a doctor. After several weeks, the sore was not healing and looked worse. I took a day off school to go and wait at the hospital with Dad.

The news was horrible! Apparently with Dad's diabetes, gangrene had started to set in. If they could not get the infection under control, his foot would need to be amputated.

Mom could not handle cleaning his wound, so Dad would clean it himself and on occasion would allow me to clean it with hydrogen peroxide, put on the antiseptic, and bandage it. Often when he was depressed, he would not clean it. When I would ask him about it, his response was, "To hell with it." Sometime later I noticed a horrible odor whenever I was around my father. It was coming from his wound, and I could tell he wasn't feeling well. I told him we should go to the doctor again and was surprised when he agreed.

The doctor took one look at the oozing wound and gave him the worst news. The foot would have to be amputated. The infection was spreading up his leg. You could tell by the discoloration of the skin. The amputation would need to be made just below his knee. That may have been the first time I saw my dad cry. He was only 53 years old, but he looked and sounded like an old man. I held his hand while we both cried. The surgery was done right away the next morning.

Dad stayed in the hospital for several days. We had to make our house easily accessible for him. The hospital would send him home with a used wheelchair, but we had to be sure he could get around the house without too many issues. The house had narrow doorways and a few steps up to both the front and back doors. The only doorway that was large enough for a wheel chair was into the living room so we set up a cot for him there where he could watch TV. He had to use a bedpan and as Mom hadn't changed her ways, I was the care giver. Sometimes he was so embarrassed for me to empty his bed pan, he used an old milk carton or bottle, closed it up, and waited until Mom was home to have her get rid of it. Being a large man, we did not have the physical strength to help him much, and Mom didn't really make the effort. Instead, she somehow convinced the American Red Cross to get my brother Richard home from the army on a hardship case. Richard was stationed in Korea at the time, and his tour of duty was almost done.

In the meantime, my brother Curt was out of jail and on probation. He married his girlfriend from the projects. They were renting an upper duplex not far from us. They had one son and were expecting again. Curt had taken a job at a foundry. It was dirty, hard labor but he made good money. It seemed like he was trying to turn his life around. He worked evenings for the better wages, and during the days, he would come over to see if I needed help with Dad. At first, he was helpful, but after a few months it was obvious he had started drinking or whatever. He came over one day, and as Dad was resting in bed, he approached me in the kitchen. He said I was really filling out well and maybe he should show me how to take care of a man. I couldn't believe it as he unzipped his pants and pulled out his penis asking me if I had ever seen one! I was scared and started crying. He laughed and said, "That's right, you're the good one. Daddy's little girl." He zipped up his pants and said, "You've got it so good. You have no idea the beatings your father gave us boys."

I said, "He's your father too."

Curt laughed and told me I was pathetic and stumbled out of the house. Watching my brother weave as he got into his car, I feared for him driving in this condition.

I remembered years ago, my three brothers getting strapped with the belt. Back then it wasn't labeled "child abuse", and I knew several families who punished their children with spankings or the belt. One time my dad had a large five-gallon plastic jug that held any loose change he had accumulated. Sometimes he would throw in a dollar bill. The cap on the jug was sealed with duct tape and a slot was cut into the top of the bottle where the money was slipped in. Dad asked if any of us had spare change to throw it in there. When it was full, he would count the money and see if we had enough to go to a lake for a weekend or do something else fun. The bottle was filling up. It was clear plastic, and you could see the money stacking up. Not a good idea for the weak and tempted. Once the jug was over half full, it seemed to start going down. Dad looked at the tape around the cap, and it was still intact, but when he moved the jug, coins started coming out of the bottom. Someone had cut a hole in the bottom and was stealing money. He called all of us together, including my mother, and wanted to know who took the money. We all stood there while Dad asked us one by one, "Did you steal the money?" Everyone said no. Dad made us all go down to the basement where his bed was. He said, "Now I'm going to ask you again." No one's response changed. He then said he did not think Veronica or I would have done it. He believed one or more of the boys had. By not coming clean, the boys were told to lower their pants and lay down on the bed on their stomachs. Veronica and I were told to stay and watch to see what happens when you disobey your parents. Dad took off his belt and one by one yelled at the boys, "Did you take the money?" As each of the boys said "no", a sharp, taut, slap from the leather belt landed across their buttocks, immediately turning the flesh red. Each of my brothers cried in pain but one by one they still denied taking the money. After Dad was finished, he handed the belt to Mom. She didn't seem to have a problem with it. The only thing she said as she strapped each one was "This is going to hurt me more than you."

Veronica and I just held onto each other and cried. Shortly after that, Curt ran away with a friend, stole a car, and robbed a store.

After Curt stumbled out of the house that day he was so vulgar and cruel to me, I wondered what I personally had ever done to him to be treated like this. A few days later, Dad was up in his wheelchair when Curt came back drunk. He came into the house and started slugging my father in the face and chest! Curt yelled, "You fucking old man! You were never a good father to me. I hate you."

I started screaming for him to stop. Dad didn't fight back, he just sat there and took it. I yelled at Curt that I was going to call the cops. He said, "Why bother, I'm out of here forever," and he left.

That night we called an ambulance as Dad was having a heart attack. His stay in the hospital was about a week. During that week, Curt was arrested and thrown in detox. After his release, he was remorseful and wanted to be given another chance. He did not get fired from his job as it was a tough position to fill, but his boss put him on probation. I never mentioned the episode of me in the kitchen with him. I didn't want to put any additional stress on Dad, and who else would care?

Kimberly's husband, David, was a rough looking truck driver that none of us really cared for. He was in a motorcycle group and seemed rowdy. He was not personable, but he came through for my dad. After visiting one day with Kimberly and seeing the limited and poor conditions my father suffered through, he took out his check book and asked how much it would cost to get an artificial leg. We had

33

given up hopes for Dad to get a leg as we knew we couldn't afford it. Surprisingly, David wrote out the check for the amount needed. He made Dad promise the money would go for the artificial leg only. No money to Mom.

Getting that artificial leg made such a difference in Dad's attitude. After getting used to it, he could once again drive a car and get around the house with little trouble. He even started cooking again.

Other than Kimberly, I was the only child at that time to graduate high school. LeeAnne would graduate ten years later. Dad was proud of me but did not attend my graduation. It was too difficult for him to get into the bleachers. Mom eventually made it in time to see me get my diploma. My sisters Kimberly, Veronica, and LeeAnne were there along with my brother Richard.

I often thought of going to college, but money seemed the determining factor. My grades weren't bad. I had been on the B honor roll until the eleventh grade. I was unable to participate in after school activities as I had to be home for Dad and LeeAnne. I graduated with a little better than an average GPA. Not good enough for a scholarship. My mom never talked to me about college, and whenever I mentioned it to Dad his response was, "What for? You will just meet someone and get married." That thinking may have been what temporarily changed me when I was a senior. For over a year I went down a path I can't believe today I would ever do.

Chapter Six

During my senior year of high school, I turned eighteen. I hadn't yet gone out on a date. I didn't drive either as we couldn't afford behind the wheel training, and I didn't have anyone who could teach me. Dad was the only one in our house who drove. Mom had given up her license years ago. Dad told me she never renewed it as she didn't want to stop drinking and knew she couldn't drink and drive. Getting groceries was sometimes a problem if Dad wasn't up to driving. We didn't have the big grocery stores in our neighborhood. There was a small corner store LeeAnne and I would walk to several times during the week. Maybe my dad liked us to do that because of the small store he once had. He was supporting the "mom and pop" stores. We became friendly with the store clerk and would spend much time visiting. His name was Ed, and he only worked nights. His day job was as a buyer at a large paper firm. He needed to earn extra money to support his three children. He was divorced and wanted to go back to college part-time. He was ten years older than me and was very kind to me. One night he asked me out on a date. I told him I would think about it and let him know.

I mentioned it to my father when I got home, and he was furious! "You don't know anything about him. He could be a murderer! You may be eighteen, but I won't allow you to go out until you have a diploma in hand. Do I have to stop you from even going to the store?"

I usually listened to and obeyed my father, but at eighteen, especially after being cooped up most of my life, I could feel my hormones pulsating. I was sick and tired of not being like the other kids in my class who were always going out and having fun.

I had become friendly with a few girls in my classes who had cars. One day at lunch, I confided to my friend, Luba, about my situation. She suggested I tell my dad that we were working on a project together for our Modern Problems class. As a team project, we needed to do research together at the library. As the library was close to school, she would pick me up. Then I would let Ed know to meet me outside the school, and we would go on our date. The lying began. Dad believed me, or so I thought.

My first date with Ed had me head over heels. He was wearing a suit and had brought me a bouquet of flowers. Now how was I to explain flowers to my dad? I couldn't bring them home, but the thought was all an innocent eighteen-year-old needed. It didn't take much for me to be swooped in by his charm and attentiveness. Once we kissed, and he started touching me, I felt all tingly, like I was dizzy and on fire. My heart was racing, and I loved every minute of it. Our first date was spent just talking and getting to know each other, followed by passionate kissing and his tender touching. I honestly didn't know what to do. When he drove me home, I told him to drop me off a few houses before mine as I was sure Dad would be looking out the window waiting for me. When I got home, all was good. Dad asked me where my books were. Of course, I forgot my books and fake research papers in Ed's car! Quickly I responded that Luba was compiling our papers to present to class. Dad seemed to accept that.

I continued dating Ed on the sly until one night he told me he wasn't good for me, and we should stop seeing each other. We had not yet had sex, and I thought maybe this was why he was going to break up with me. After much prodding and crying on my part, he told me why but made me promise not to say anything to my family, especially my dad. Seems like my dad had been following us a few times. I should have known after he followed my mom, but that was different. She was his wife. I was his eighteen-year-old daughter who was graduating from high school. Ed said it wasn't so much my dad following us, it was that two of my brothers paid him a visit one night while he was working at the store. My brother Richard was the nicer one, Ed told me, but Curt threatened him. Curt told him he would pound the shit out of him if he continued seeing me. Ed told me he had fallen in love with me and wanted to keep seeing me. Those words were all I needed to give in to him. We weren't concerned we were being watched as Ed had told my brothers to let him have some time to tell me, and it would be over.

I couldn't stand it! As obedient as I had been all those years and as I had taken on the role of the mother in that house, this made me furious. When would it ever be my time? Why did I have to sneak out to see this person who made me feel so special, so beautiful, and so loved? That night we made love. Losing my virginity in Ed's car wasn't very romantic. It wasn't how I always dreamt it would be. Regardless, I felt loved and now devoted to him.

We continued seeing each other but were more creative with our rendezvous times and places. Meeting during the daylight had less chance of being followed. For the first time in my life, I skipped school while Ed left work early. I felt more grown up now that I was no longer a virgin, but that wasn't always good. I started questioning why we never went to Ed's apartment. Why would we always be in a car or a motel that Ed had rented? We had gone out for lunch a few times and a movie once, but lately it was just sex. Ed told me he shared an apartment with a guy who worked as a mechanic, and the apartment always smelled like grease and oil. He didn't want to bring me into such a dirty place. Another thing that bothered me was Ed would always call me. I didn't know how to contact him. Since my family moved back to northeast Minneapolis, we did have a phone and there was an extension phone next to Dad's bed in our living room. I usually knew when Ed would call me so I tried to be by the phone in the kitchen. I started hearing clicks while I was talking to Ed and knew that once again I was being spied on. I told Ed I needed his phone number so I could call him. He gave me his number at his daytime work and of course the store where he worked at night. He said there was no phone at his apartment. I accepted that for a while. One day I called him at his daytime work. A co-worker answered his phone. He said, "Ed just stepped out for a second. Is this his wife, Carol?" I hung up. When I got home from school that day, Ed called me immediately wanting to know if I had called him earlier. I told him yes. He asked if I could walk up to the store that night as he had to talk to me. As LeeAnne and I walked to the store, I had mixed feeling about seeing him. Ed asked if he could talk to me alone in the back of the store. My worst nightmare had come true! Ed explained that he wasn't yet "legally divorced". He was still living with his family. He said he and his wife did not have sex anymore, but they still lived together. He said he would have told me but was afraid I wouldn't see him anymore. I was devastated. I couldn't do this. He had small children. How could I break up a family? How could he have lied to me, and how gullible was I to believe everything he told me?

I left the store with my sister and begged her not to tell Dad I had been crying. It was hard for me to stop the tears, but I had no choice. I could just hear Dad telling me, "What did you expect?" or "I told you so."

That night I lay awake crying, berating myself for how stupid and gullible I was. I had given myself to this man. Now I thought that no man would ever want me as I was no longer a virgin. I wanted to talk to someone; I wanted a mother I could confide in. That morning while Mom got ready for work and before I left for school, I told her. She had this half smile on her face and said, "Well, I guess the apple doesn't fall far from the tree." She told me, "We sometimes get ourselves into situations that we may not like, but we need to make the best of it."

What the hell did that mean? Here I was sobbing and pouring my heart out to this woman who was an "occasional" mother to me. I wanted her to tell me what I did was OK and that I would still be desirable to someone else — someone single and my age. I wanted her to encourage me never to see Ed again. She told me that she loved her boss, but he couldn't leave his wife as it would be financial suicide. Then she said, "Patty, you just need to make the best of a bad situation."

It was hopeless. I began thinking I was my mother's daughter, following in her footsteps. The song by Peggy Lee "Is That All There Is?" became my song.

I continued seeing Ed, hoping that he would one day leave his wife. I stopped going to church. Sometimes I felt dirty. I didn't think I could ever be loved by anyone again as I was "used goods".

It was almost graduation time. Dad surprisingly said that I could go to the all-night party. Ed and I had other plans. He was going to celebrate my graduation with me in style. He said it was a surprise. I had talked myself into thinking our relationship was OK and we would eventually be together for the rest of our lives. Dad wouldn't expect me home until late morning the next day. Ed and I would have the whole night together. It would be the first time I would spend the night with a man.

Ed bought me a nice watch for graduation. He had also gotten a very nice hotel room stocked with liquor. That was his big surprise. I wasn't happy. I didn't drink; I was only eighteen. About 2 a.m. Ed

40

said he would take me home. He had made me a few drinks, and I felt a little woozy but good.

I said, "Why? I am supposed to be at my all-night party! I can't go home in the middle of the night! I thought we were going to spend the night together."

Ed asked me to be reasonable. "How can I explain to Carol and my kids where I was all night?"

Even though slightly inebriated, it was like a light clicked on in my head. This man didn't love me! He would never leave his wife. All he wanted was sex from a young girl!

I cried and demanded he tell me if he had even filed for a divorce. I knew he would probably lie to me, so I begged him to tell me the truth this time as this was my graduation night. It should be a time for hopes and dreams. It should be a time when I should be excited entering my new adult life.

He hung his head and said, "No."

I told him to take me home. It was a silent drive. He dropped me off down the block from my house and said, "When can I see you again?"

I just stared at him. Shaking my head, I told him not to call me again. It was 3 a.m., and I was exhausted and sad. The door was locked. I didn't have a key, so I had to knock and wake up my brother Richard, who was now home from the service. He asked me what I was doing home.

I simply said, "I wasn't having a good time. I wanted to come home."

I cried in my pillow so no one would hear me. For the first time in many months, I prayed and asked God for forgiveness and to give me strength and hope. I didn't want to be like my mother. I wanted to be happy. I wanted to find someone who would cherish me and not screw around — someone I could spend the rest of my life with, far away from here.

Chapter Seven

The next five years were years of mental and moral growth for me. Several months after I graduated, I started seeking full time work. I didn't know what type of job I could get. I had good typing skills, and I excelled in English. I was offered a few part-time jobs, but I wanted to earn enough money to pay for driver's education and buy a cheap car. My mother called me from work one day to offer me a job in her office. She had now become the office manager. She needed to hire a file/accounting clerk. She offered me a salary that was hard to refuse for just starting out without a college education. My mind told me "no" but my heart said "yes", thinking of the possibilities of getting my own car and driving. Dad said I should take it. Once I took the job, he wanted me to be his spy and report when my mother would leave work.

I did learn a lot on the job, and after a few months, I was able to enroll in a behind-the-wheel driving course. I did well, and Dad helped me find a cheap car. It was an old white rambler that had push buttons for gears. Once I had my license, LeeAnne and I had fun driving to swimming pools, shopping centers, and sometimes Como Park Zoo.

Things were going well except I still did not have an adult social life. One day, while I was still at home, I caught my father staring at me. I asked him, "What?"

He said, "You seem so unhappy and lonely for a young woman. You never go out with friends. I think it's time you leave home to find your way in life. I don't want you to move far away, but maybe get yourself a nice small apartment and start going out with people from work. Make new friends."

I was shocked! First, because he finally acknowledged me as a woman. Secondly, that he must be aware all my friends were off to college, and he actually wanted me to go out. Third, Dad was telling me to move out!

I found a cute studio apartment a few miles from home. It was right on a bus line so I didn't need to drive each day to work. Dad advanced me money for the damage deposit. The most difficult part of getting my own place was leaving LeeAnne at home to cope on her own. I promised her she would never be alone. I would always be there for her, and I wanted her to stay with me from time to time. We had fun shopping for dishes, pots and pans, towels, and other items for my new apartment. My Dad still insisted I eat dinner with him and LeeAnne each week night to save money on groceries. He also wanted to know what was going on with Mom and work.

Mom and I worked in the office of Flour City Brush Company. The factory for making their industrial brushes was upstairs. One of my duties was to distribute mail to the supervisors on the factory floor. I had to literally walk through the factory, wearing protective glasses, three times a day. Ninety-eight percent of the factory workers were men — men who liked to stare, whistle, and flirt. It was degrading having to be subjected to that three times a day. Several of them asked me out, but they didn't appeal to me. My Dad told me I was too picky. After my experience with Ed, I figured if I had to spend the rest of my life with someone, I was going to be picky. One factory supervisor, Glenn, was nice looking and spoke like he was well educated. I went out to lunch with him one afternoon. Later that same night, the buzzer in my apartment sounded. I asked who it was. Glenn's voice said, "Hey, just wondered if you wanted to go out for dinner too. We could get a casual bite to eat so you don't have to get dressed up."

I went out to his car, and we drove up the street to Elsie's Restaurant. They served food and liquor. We both had a burger. I still wasn't twenty-one, but I did sip on a beer while Glenn downed several. It was getting late. I asked him to take me home as tomorrow was a work day. While driving the short distance to my apartment, I could tell he was a little drunk. When he dropped me off, he asked if he could use my bathroom, saying that the beer was going right through him.

I think a woman should always trust her intuition. I was leery about letting him into my apartment, but we worked together and I knew he had a long ride home. So I let him come in.

After using the bathroom, he kissed me goodnight. Then he wouldn't leave. I said, "Come on, Glenn. We both have to get to work early tomorrow."

He smiled and said, "It has been so long since I've had sex. I thought you would be willing."

"Whatever gave you that idea?" I yelled. "Just like that, you bring up sex after one date?"

He replied, "You went out with me, a married man."

"You're married? How was I to know? You aren't wearing a wedding ring!" I was so upset I was pacing. My mind was reeling.

"Your mother is married and so is Ray. Everyone knows they are sleeping together. I thought maybe like mother, like daughter."

"I don't care! I am not my mother!" I screamed. "Please leave."

He then told me his wife was expecting a child any day now, and he wanted to get lucky while he could.

"Get out of here now or I will call the cops!" I yelled so loud I was sure the neighbors heard me. "Your poor wife! I feel sorry for her. Get out!"

"OK, OK, I'm leaving. See you at work tomorrow," he smiled and winked as I slammed the door on him.

I was literally sick. I vomited in the bathroom. Then sat on the couch and wondered what was wrong with people! Was there no respect, no true love, no sense of right or wrong? The miracle of a new life, a little baby, about to be born, and he was like this! I didn't know how I could go to work the next day. I seriously wondered if there was some mark on me like a scarlet letter, or some bad aura surrounding me that attracted these jerks.

I did go to work the next day. I was very quiet and subdued. I felt defeated by life. I knew I had to leave this job. It was a mistake working with my mother.

I was so nervous doing my rounds in the factory that day. I could hear the whispering and whistles as I walked by. I was getting sick again. I ran to the bathroom not even finishing my rounds and threw up. After a while, I went into Mom's office and told her I couldn't do the job anymore. I explained to her what happened the night before. She asked me what I did to encourage Glenn. I got up, picked up my purse, and walked out. Just like that I left the job. I jumped on the first bus that came by. I didn't know where I was going. People were staring at me as the tears rolled down my cheeks, but I didn't care. I knew by my walking out, it would look bad for Mom. I needed to escape from my family. I needed peace.

After a while, I realized the bus was on the Nicollet Mall in downtown Minneapolis. I knew my mom would have called Dad, and he would be worried. I got off the bus, found a pay phone, and called Dad. As soon as he answered, I burst into tears. Mom had called him. He told me it was all right, and I should just come home.

"Dad", I said, "As long as I am downtown, I'm going to find a bathroom, wash my face, and look for a job here."

"Why would you do that? There are all kinds of weird people downtown. Don't get a job right now. Take a break," he pleaded. "I think you should apply for unemployment and move back home to take care of me."

Oh my God, that would be all I needed! I couldn't get pulled back in. I had to be strong. "No, Dad, just let me try this. I will stop by the house when I am done." And I hung up.

I went to a few retail stores and put in applications. One store, J.C. Penney, suggested I apply at their Regional Credit Office a few blocks away. I walked over and had an interview right away. One thing I had going for me was that I could be available immediately. They hired me on the spot, and I would start the following week. I had a tour of the office. It was huge with offices on four floors. I noticed many people my own age. I didn't know anyone there, and I had a good feeling about this.

Dad couldn't understand why I wouldn't want to stay home and collect unemployment. I was excited at the thought of working downtown. The following Monday, I took the bus downtown and started my new job. To my amazement, the week before a woman put in for retirement. She worked in Commercial Accounts, and my boss asked if I would be willing to be trained in on that job instead of the clerical one they originally offered me. It would be a level higher and more pay. Of course I would! On my first day of employment, I got a raise. A very good sign.

Chapter Eight

It was early 1970's, and I had a cute little apartment, a job I loved, and had made many friends at J.C. Penney. It was fun to go out after work and socialize on weekends with people my own age. I tried to wean myself away from most of my family, however, the turmoil that existed was hard to ignore.

My sister Kimberly had a precious, beautiful daughter. Her name was Sara. She had long dark hair. When Sara was two and a half years old, she developed an ear infection. The doctor had given her penicillin. No one in my family realized that most of us were allergic to penicillin. Kimberly and David had taken Sara to General Hospital Emergency as they could not get her fever down. Once admitted, the nurses and doctors also had difficulties getting the fever down. The poor little girl was actually blistering from the high temperature. She died that night with a diagnosis of Spinal Meningitis. It was the saddest tragedy. Just looking at that small child-size coffin tore most people apart. Her skin had to have so much makeup on to cover the purplish tinge and blistering. I don't know why Kimberly insisted on an open casket. After the funeral, that same night, David packed his bags and told my sister the only reason he stayed with her was for their little daughter. Now she was gone, so there was nothing left. Kimberly was devastated. We couldn't believe he would do that the night of their daughter's funeral.

My brother Bill was also having a tough time. I remember when he was in school, the girls flocked to him. He was extremely good looking and resembled James Dean. Bill had many girlfriends. My brother Curt looked up to Bill. He idolized him. When we lived in the projects, after Bill quit school, he got a job. He worked in a restaurant and later at a hotel in downtown Minneapolis. He took a break from having girlfriends for quite awhile and seemed to be staying out of trouble. One day, Dad was looking in the closet the three boys shared. He found a satchel that Bill usually took to work. For some reason, Bill had not taken it that day. What Dad found inside changed how all of us looked at Bill. The satchel contained different colors of nail polish, lipstick, and makeup. When Bill came home, Dad was waiting for him. You could hear Dad screaming all over the house and outside. He wanted to know why Bill had these things. He called him names like "fairy", "queer", and "fagot". Dad told Bill if he was going to behave like this, he wasn't welcome in the house. Bill remained silent. That night while we all slept, Bill left. He never lived at home again.

In 1972 he came to our house with a woman. He wanted to introduce her to us as they planned on getting married. Jane was older than Bill, not good looking, and was extremely overweight with teeth missing. Bill said she was good to him and good for him. Dad said nothing. The rest of us wished them well. A few days later, Dad told us he did some checking on Jane. He claimed both Jane and Bill were homosexuals but decided to get together to see if they could make it work. They both wanted children.

My brother Richard married Terri, a girl who already had two children. She was also not attractive and had a horrible reputation. Dad said when you looked at her she looked like disease. Richard and Terri had two children together. They divorced after Terri was arrested at a bar with her children. Richard was working at night, and Terri was soliciting herself and her oldest daughter. Her daughter, my brother's stepdaughter, was only ten years old. It was very embarrassing for all of us because the story of her arrest appeared on the front page of the Minneapolis paper. Later there was a follow up story about finding child pornography at their house, and my brother was questioned as to being an accomplice.

Then there was Curt and his wife Linda. Together they had the one son who was three years old. Linda had given birth to two adorable twin girls the year I graduated from high school. They were premature and had to stay in the hospital a few weeks. Back then, they must not have done all the ultrasounds because Linda didn't know she was having twins until they were born. I remember Curt was working hard at the foundry and was sober (again). Trying to make extra money for the unexpected mouth to feed, he took on extra shifts and could not leave work once the babies were ready to come home. I went with Linda to the hospital to pickup these precious babies. Dad drove but waited in the car, and Linda and I went to the nursery. I was so excited! I didn't know anyone who had twins. While riding up in the elevator, I asked Linda, "Which baby do I get to hold?" I was just giddy.

Linda deflated my mood as she responded, "I don't care which one you hold. When I was on that delivery table, and the doctor said another one was coming, I just prayed it would be born dead!"

The elevator doors opened then, and she walked out as I stood there with my mouth open not believing what I just heard.

Once we got the girls settled in their apartment, we left. Their son was at Linda's mother's house. I thought we should stay until Curt came home, but Dad said that wouldn't be until morning and Linda needed some alone time with her new babies.

When we got into the car, I told Dad I was worried about the twins. I told him what Linda said in the elevator. He told me to keep it to myself. To this day, I don't understand why.

Veronica had a cute little boy, Michael. Fortunately, he did not inherit any of the albino genes. Unfortunately, Veronica was too young to have a child and so was her husband. The marriage didn't last. After the divorce, Veronica started dating a friend of Curt's. Roger was of American Indian descent; his skin was quite darker when seen next to Veronica's albino features. He was in and out of trouble and had recently been released from jail. The following year, Curt, Linda, Veronica, Roger, and their children all lived together in a house they rented in south Minneapolis. During the summer, they brought all the kids to the Northeast Parade. LeeAnne and I had gotten there early with a few blankets to save places for them. We were sitting

52

right on Central Avenue across the street from a gas station. Linda kept whispering to Curt. They were drinking beer. I asked Linda what the big secret was. She put her finger to her lips indicating not to say anything and opened her purse to show me a handgun! She whispered to me that gas stations had lots of cash, and getting it would be easy, especially with so much noise outside and so many people busy watching the parade. As the band marched by with the booming of the drums, I could feel my heart beating in my throat. She warned me not to say anything to anyone, especially my dad. I turned and stared at Veronica. She said, "I want nothing to do with this. I am not involved." The next thing I knew Curt stood up and was kicking Linda, telling her she was stupid as I would of course tell Dad. The babies were crying, and the music from the parade was loud. Veronica was silently crying, and I promised them I wouldn't say anything, but I had my fingers crossed.

Chapter Nine

Anyone can say what they want. Call me a tattle-tale or a snitch, but I had to do what I knew was right. As soon as I got LeeAnne home, I told both my mom and dad about the gun in Linda's purse and the plan to rob the gas station. Mom didn't believe me but Dad just shook his head. He wanted to call the police, and Mom yelled at him that he couldn't report his own children. Dad said, "Oh, yes I can! But I am more worried about any consequences that would come Patty's way." I stayed at the house that night instead of going to my apartment. I had already seen what Curt did to his own wife. We didn't need another drunk with a gun coming to the house.

The next day was Sunday. Dad made breakfast. He asked me to sit down and eat as he had something to discuss with me. Mother and LeeAnne were at the table too.

Dad had seen a four-plex six blocks away from the house. He had mother check it out. It was fairly new and had a nice laundry room. My parents were still using an old wringer washer in the house and hung a clothesline outside or in the dining room during winter to dry clothes. I was happy when I moved out to have modern conveniences like washers and dryers in the apartment laundry room. In this newer four-plex, there would be four steps Dad would need to climb to get into the building and another four steps to go down to the unit that was available. There was a bedroom for Mom and a bigger bedroom that LeeAnne would get. Dad would continue sleeping in the living room. It was new and modern, and I just knew before they asked they wanted me to move back home! LeeAnne's bedroom would be big enough for us to share.

"Dad," I said in a somewhat raised voice. "Remember I signed a year's lease. I can't just break the lease. They would make me pay additional rent." I was hoping I could come up with some reasoning for them to see it would be best for me to stay in my own apartment.

"Tell you what," Dad said. "I will write a letter to the apartment manager telling them about my illness and that you are needed back at home."

I stood there unable to respond right away. I felt stuck again.

Dad must have sensed my hesitation. He urged, "We won't charge you any rent. You can buy groceries occasionally, but think of the money you will save. I won't be around forever. I don't think I have that much time left."

Then LeeAnne pleaded, "Please Patty. I miss you so much." I felt that I had no choice. The guilt set in and I agreed.

Once I moved back in, I continued socializing with my friends, however, I was more available once again to be caretaker, chauffeur, and stand-in mother. Kimberly, who was ten years older than I was, had never learned to drive and didn't want to. She was having a tough time emotionally since David left her. I was the most logical one to take her grocery shopping and on other errands. Kimberly's divorce was still not filed after six months. She started meeting David to discuss the terms and to file. Those meetings ended up with Kimberly once again pregnant. They decided not to divorce. David moved back in, and six months after Kimberly gave birth to a healthy boy, Shane, David once again left.

Bill and Jane eventually had three children, two girls and a boy. Not long after the birth of their third child, Jane called my dad sobbing about a fight she had with Bill. She said his mental state was not good, and he had been taking drugs for sometime. Dad, mother, LeeAnne, and I got into the car and drove over to their apartment to see if we could help with anything. Jane was sitting at the table crying. She told us some crazy things Bill was saying to her. He told her he loved her and the kids, but he wanted to experience what she felt as a woman...he wanted to become a woman!

Jane told us this had been going on for a while. Their grocery money was gone because Bill had taken it to buy drugs. She wasn't sure what kind of drugs. Jane intended to file for divorce the next day. There really wasn't much we could do. Mom gave her some money for groceries. Jane's sister was on her way over to help with the kids.

Richard and Terri got divorced once Terri was out of jail. All of her children, as well those with Richard, were put into foster care. Although not charged with anything, the police made it clear to Richard they would be watching him. They did not understand how Richard could be unaware of the child pornography that was found in his house. For now, his punishment was having his children put into foster care. Richard had the same job at Electric Machinery since he got out of the army He decided to work harder, get a house, and get his children back.

Curt and Linda had a tumultuous relationship. Curt was working at a Holiday Station He seemed to have a great job as he was promoted to Night Manager — a perfect setup for his already experienced thievery. This Holiday Station not only sold gasoline and had a small convenience store, it also sold small electronics. That year for Christmas, we all got such expensive gifts from Curt and Linda. Our family was not accustomed to that. Mom and Dad got a big TV, Veronica got a stereo system, I got a clock radio, and I can't remember what everyone else got. I heard Dad talking with Curt in the kitchen after we opened our gifts. Dad was warning Curt he better be careful. Curt told him he was. After Curt, Linda, and their kids left that Christmas evening, I asked Dad how they could afford such gifts. Dad said, "They can't. I am sure they are stolen."

"We aren't going to keep them, are we?" I asked.

Dad replied, "For now. We'll see what happens."

I hated that clock radio. I felt dirty keeping it. I couldn't understand why it didn't seem to bother anyone else in my family.

Months later. Curt was caught and arrested as he had been stealing for sometime. He was sent to St. Cloud reformatory but eventually ended up at Stillwater State Prison as it wasn't his first offense. He was gone over a year, and during that time, Linda divorced him. We never saw much of their children after that. Their son started getting into trouble with the law at a very early age. At ten years-old he was fighting and stealing. The twins were living with their physically abusive mother. Their mother, Linda, was never smart. She didn't do well in school, and her mother didn't care that she just quit going before starting high school. I remember being shocked when I realized that she couldn't add, spell, or even read. After several years, all their children were put into foster care. Curt didn't seem to care. Once he got out of prison, he still didn't attempt to get them back. Quite a difference from Richard's plan. I really missed those twin girls, but no attempt was made by my parents to find them.

Veronica gave birth to her second child, a girl that she named Patsy, after me. Patsy's father was Roger. Patsy had the dark features of her American Indian father. Veronica and Roger never married. Roger spent the first ten years of Patsy's life in prison for armed robbery and attempted murder.

LeeAnne and I continued to live day by day. LeeAnne liked the school choir, and she played drums. As we lived in an apartment, she could only practice on a drum pad. I helped her with costumes and went to her school programs. If Mom showed up, she usually came late and drunk. LeeAnne was embarrassed by Mom's boisterous demeanor when she was drinking. I got so mad at Mom one night during LeeAnne's school play, I told her to leave. She did. After LeeAnne's performance, we walked home. Mom hadn't come home. It was dark, and I went outside to retrace our steps to see if I could find her. As soon as I got outside our apartment, I noticed something on the side alley. There was Mom, laying on the ground, passed out drunk, with vomit down the front of her coat. I shook her and shook her to wake her. She finally stirred and said, "What do you want?" I got her to sit up until she could get steady enough for me to help her walk inside. She had no idea where she was. Dad had me take her clothes off and shove her in the shower. At that moment, I hated my mother. I was so angry I didn't know how to control it. The thought even crossed my mind if I could kill her, would I be able to live with myself.

Dad sensed my anger. He wanted me to go to Al-anon but I wouldn't go. He thought it would help me, but I was too angry and embarrassed by her. Maybe I didn't want to understand her. I felt for my own sanity I should not be living under the same roof as my mother. I started looking for apartments again.

One night I came home from a date. It was about two in the morning, and the lights were on in our apartment so I knew something was wrong. I walked in, and Veronica was there with Mom. Veronica told me Dad was taken by ambulance to the hospital. He was having pains in his chest and had asked Mom to call for a doctor. Mom did, but right now she was sitting at the kitchen table looking sad, drinking an amber colored liquid that I knew was her rye whiskey.

"Why didn't you go with him, Mother?" I asked. She just shook her head and said there was nothing she could do to help him, and besides he didn't want her there.

Veronica said Dad started crying as the paramedics carried him out on the stretcher into the ambulance. He kept yelling, "Where is Patty?"

The next morning, LeeAnne and I went to the hospital. We told Mother she needed to come with us. It was morning, and she was sober, so she had no excuses.

Dad was in a ward at Hennepin County General Hospital. The ward was filled with cots holding men of all ages but mostly elderly. A thin blue curtain is all that separated these men from each other and from the privacy of strangers like us. Dad, being such a large man, was in a special rotating bed in the center of the ward. No sheets hid him; no privacy was given him. He smiled when he saw us and said he was doing better. The nurse approached us wanting to know what relationship we were to the patient. Dad introduced us. The nurse told us Dad had a buildup of fluid in his chest resulting in a mild heart attack. The rotating bed helped break up the fluid. His diabetes was not under control, and he had also developed a few bed sores on his buttocks and the one leg. He was under observation for now and may need to stay in the hospital several days.

As I worked downtown, the hospital was within walking distance so I visited Dad every day during my lunch hour. After three or four days of my usual visits, I could not find him. The nurse said he had to be moved to a room away from everyone as the bed sores on his remaining leg had gotten infected with gangrene. My dad had told the nurse that I would be the main contact, and she could tell me everything. She wanted the doctor to talk to me before I saw Dad. She paged the doctor, and once he came into the ward, he told me the severity of Dad's condition. The second leg needed to be amputated. He had explained this to Dad earlier that day, and Dad had not taken it well. He did not want to lose his other leg. The doctor wanted me to be prepared as the room Dad was secluded in had a hot lamp over the festering leg, and the gangrene smell was unpleasant. If there was anyway I could convince my dad to go ahead with the surgery, they would schedule it for the next day. The longer he waited, the worse it would get as it could possibly spread all over his body.

As I entered the closed room, I remembered the horrific gangrene smell when Dad had the first leg amputated. This smell was much worse and stronger. I tried not to, but I gagged. Dad was lying in the bed and when he saw me, he sobbed. "What kind of father can I ever be?" he cried. "I went through the army during World War II and never had anything like this. I just want to die."

"Don't say that Dad", I begged him. We were both crying now. "You can't leave us now. LeeAnne and I need you. If it weren't for you, I think I would have killed Mom."

That seemed to trigger something in him. "That bitch of a mother doesn't care. She would like it if I died. Do you think I should let them cut off my other leg?" he asked.

"I don't think you have a choice, Dad. You need to get this infection out of your system."

The next morning, Dad had the surgery. Kimberly, Richard, Veronica, LeeAnne, and I were there with Mother. Dad came out of recovery and had a quiet sense of acceptance.

I didn't go back to the hospital until evening the next day. I wanted to go home and pick up LeeAnne. Dad was back in a ward. He smiled when he saw us, and all I could think of was how he used to be such a large, mean man. Now, without either of his legs, and because he had lost some weight, he looked so small and docile.

We continued to visit him every night for a few weeks until one night when he told us to leave. He was depressed and didn't want to see us for a few nights. He said his own wife wouldn't visit him, so why should we? He told us to go out and enjoy life, and not come to a hospital every night to see sickness. I knew the hospital chaplain had seen him a few times. I reluctantly left with LeeAnne and went to seek out the chaplain. He was unavailable, and we left to go home. We stayed away for two days, and when we came back to the hospital, Dad seemed to be in a better mood. He told us he had been talking with the chaplain and wanted us to meet with him sometime.

The next day was Saturday, and I was getting ready to take LeeAnne to her morning eye doctor appointment. Mother had left already and was supposedly at work. We were just about to walk out the door when the phone rang. It was one of Dad's doctors at the hospital. He asked to speak with Mom. When I told him she wasn't there, he wanted to know how old I was. I said twenty-one. He then told me that Dad had a staff infection in the recently amputated leg.

He still had bed sores on his buttocks from being in bed all the time, and those were appearing to show signs of gangrene. They wanted to do surgery to see if they could flush his system out. I really didn't understand what they were going to do. The doctor told me to gather the family together, and we should all come to see Dad as this was very serious.

I got on the phone, cancelled LeeAnne's eye doctor appointment, and called Mother at work. No answer. I called my sisters. Veronica gave me a few names of bars to call to see if Mom was there. She would also call a few. It was only eleven in the morning. How could she be at a bar? The doctor had also mentioned Dad may need blood. Both Dad and I had B+ blood, the rarer kind. I called the in-town aunts and uncles for blood donations. Only one uncle had the same blood, and he was out of town on vacation. I then started calling the bars. They were mostly located on West Broadway in north Minneapolis. Most of them knew exactly who I was talking about but said she wasn't there. I gave up trying to locate Mom. LeeAnne and I needed to get to the hospital.

Chapter Ten

It was early afternoon when LeeAnne and I arrived at the hospital. The door to Dad's room was closed with a "NO ADMITTANCE" sign. The nurse told us the doctor was on his way to talk with us. Dad had already been sedated in preparation for surgery. When the doctor got there a few minutes later, he told us how grave Dad's condition was. He said we could go into the room, but Dad most likely would not come to, and if he became conscious at all, he would not make much sense.

LeeAnne and I entered the room. We each stood on a side and held Dad's hand. Dad opened his eyes! He looked at both of us and smiled. Then he said, "Well girls, this is it! I'm going up to that operating room, and I'm not coming back down."

"Dad, that's not true. You're going to be fine." I started crying. LeeAnne did too as she reached over to hug him.

Dad said, "Listen to me now because I won't be here in a few hours. Patty, please try to get along with your mother. I know she's a drunk, but promise me you will try."

I nodded and said, "Yes, I promise."

"Patty," Dad pleaded. "I don't want you to cry anymore. You always cry too much. You've had too much to cry about your whole life. This is for the best. You can have your own life now, both of you. Promise me you will be happy. I love you both very much."

That was hard to take as I can't remember my parents telling any of us kids that they loved us. Even today, whenever I hug one of my siblings or tell them I love them, they look at me in a confused way and want to know if something is wrong.

After a few moments of silence, Dad closed his eyes and quietly said, "Now go."

LeeAnne and I looked at each other not sure what to do. I told Dad we would leave him alone for awhile but wouldn't leave the hospital. We were staying throughout the operation. He didn't say anything. He stretched his arms upward for a long time like he was reaching up to heaven. He seemed to be whispering something to someone who wasn't there. We left the room.

The chaplain and doctor had been outside Dad's room when we came out. I told them how Dad was alert and spoke with us. The doctor said he was surprised as he was under sedation just before we got to the hospital. The doctor said he was going to have the nurses further prep him for surgery, and they would be taking him up shortly. The chaplain wanted to spend a few minutes alone with Dad and asked us to stay in the waiting room so he could speak with us after.

It wasn't long before the chaplain came out. He asked us to pray with him for Dad's peace and the best possible outcome. Then he took my hand and told me my dad had asked the doctors for peace. He had asked them to let him die. Dad had confided in the chaplain telling him I needed to have my own life. If he didn't die, I would put the responsibility of taking care of him on myself. The other kids wouldn't, and his wife was useless. The chaplain further said Dad was sure the reason I wasn't yet married was because of him.

I told the chaplain, "I'm only twenty-one." Then he told me Dad had confessed to him and was ready to die. He would never divulge the confession but wanted me to know Dad blamed himself for holding me back from college, dating, and life in general. He had made many mistakes and wanted me and LeeAnne to move on.

There wasn't much I could say. Was I to blame if Dad died? Would he actually die because of me?

Later, Kimberly, Veronica, Richard, and Curt showed up as well as Dad's sister Diana. Mom finally showed up too. Veronica told me she found her in one of the bars she had contacted. Shortly after they all arrived, Dad was wheeled on a gurney up to surgery. All of us ran to his side. We told him it was going to be OK. He smiled, said goodbye, and told us again he loved us.

He wasn't in surgery long when the doctor came down and asked Mom if she would please gather the family together. We went into a small conference room. The doctor simply said, "He has died." Most of us were shedding tears, but I thought it was so strange that Mom turned to me in front of everyone and simply said, "Patty, I am so sorry."

Veronica demanded to see Dad's body. Mom didn't want to. Kimberly and I told Veronica we would go with her. The doctor asked if we were sure. We were. LeeAnne wanted to go, but Mom said she was too young.

Dad's body was upstairs outside the operating room. He wasn't covered. He was laying on a gurney, and as nurses and doctors were whizzing by him, they would set things on the foot of his gurney like it was a table. Some were standing there chatting and laughing like they just told a joke! Our father was laying there dead and naked; they were acting like it was no big deal. Veronica freaked out! She started screaming at them.

"Do you not have any respect for someone who has just died?" she accused. "What is wrong with you people?"

I stroked Dad's hair, kissed him on the forehead, told him I loved him, and said goodbye. Kimberly did too. I told Veronica we should leave. Sobbing now, Veronica went with us downstairs. The doctor was still talking with Mom. Veronica approached him, looked him in the eye, and demanded, "Tell me you didn't just kill our father! Tell me you didn't let him die because he asked you to!"

The doctor and Mom tried to calm Veronica down, but it was useless. It took both Richard and Curt to get her out of the hospital, into the car, and home.

Mother, Kimberly, LeeAnne and I stayed to hear the explanation of how and why Dad died. The doctor explained that Dad's heart stopped early during surgery. Apparently, the gangrene infection was spreading to the bed sores on this buttocks. Due to Dad's condition, he was in bed all the time at the hospital and with his diabetes, it was difficult for the bed sores to heal. The infection had spread up inside the rectum so the doctors were trying to perform a colostomy to stop the gangrene from spreading. The doctor explained as soon as the incision was made, the infection immediately spread throughout his entire body. It was too much for his system to handle, and he went into cardiac arrest. He was in such a weakened condition due to the recent amputation and previous heart attacks, he was not strong enough to fight any longer.

Dad died on September 2nd, and because it was the Saturday before Labor Day, it took longer for arrangements to be made. As Dad was a veteran, he would be buried at Fort Snelling National Cemetery.

During the week prior to Dad's funeral and burial, LeeAnne and I clung to each other revealing and sharing our fears of living with Mother. I was worried Dad could now see all my sins made by my past bad choices. I confided this to my sister Veronica. She smiled and said, "Patty, don't put that pressure on yourself. Dad knew you weren't a virgin. When you went to work, he snooped in your dresser, like he did with all of us. He told me he found your birth control pills. For God sake, girl, you are a human being and not perfect. Do you really think he is looking down with God and judging you! Besides, there is no God anyway."

So Dad knew my faults? He still loved me. He searched through my dresser drawers. Did he not trust me?

Another task we had was to locate my brother Bill. He had been staying at different shelters like The Harbor Lights and The Salvation Army. He wasn't at any of those. We left messages in case he wandered into one of them. He did. He called home and spoke with

Mom. When she told him Dad was gone, and she wanted him at the funeral and sober, Bill went off the deep end. In the middle of the night, Mom got a phone call from the police. Bill was found laying in a gutter off Hennepin Avenue in downtown Minneapolis. He was alive but in bad shape. He had ingested rubbing alcohol, vanilla extract, and the worst thing, a bottle of Lysol. The police explained that severe alcoholics go to such extremes in drinking these things because they all have some percentage of alcohol in them. The percentage may be small but it works for a temporary fix, and they are cheap in comparison to a bottle of booze. Bill had to remain in the hospital, and once he was better he would need to be transferred to detox. This was due to a court order. He would not be able to attend Dad's funeral as he was in no shape to go, due to his singed esophagus and stomach from what he ingested.

I had promised Dad I would try to get along with Mother. I tried. We were incredibly civil to each other that entire week. It bothered me that I never saw her cry for Dad, but I tried not to think about that. It was especially worrisome as Curt suddenly made an appearance and seemed to be "a caring brother". He even spent nights at the apartment helping Mother get social security benefits. Mom was still working but as LeeAnne was only eleven years old, she was entitled to monthly benefits through Dad's social security.

Dad had an impressive funeral. Everyone from the old neighborhood seemed to attend. For those who were no longer with us, their children came for at least the prayer service the night before the funeral to remember and honor Dad. There were many envelopes with money people had given, saying Dad helped them out when he had his grocery store.

It was a long day from the funeral home, to St. Cyril's Catholic Church, to Fort Snelling Cemetery. We were drained. Once we got home, LeeAnne and I changed clothes. We came out of the bedroom to find Curt with Mother sitting at the kitchen table and of course both of them had already poured themselves a drink.

Mom said she needed to discuss a few things with us. Curt told us to sit down. He was going through all the memorial envelopes and taking the money out. Mom said there would be some changes made around here. I was no longer to be disrespectful to her. She said she was my mother and she was LeeAnne's mother — I wasn't. She told me if I didn't abide by her rules, I could move out. If she had any problems with me, she would have Curt resolve them. LeeAnne was so mad. She started yelling at Mom. Curt told her to shut her mouth and be respectful to her only surviving parent. I was terrified. I just stood there going over in my head the last conversation with Dad promising to get along with Mom. How can you get along with a drunk?

"Why are you being so mean? We just buried Dad. Why are you doing this today?" I cried at both of them. "Mother, we have been getting along all week. Why all of a sudden are you doing this?"

Curt spoke up then, and it was obvious he was getting inebriated, "Because little sister, Dad is gone. Daddy's little girls are all alone now."

I was petrified! I could remember the time he pulled his penis out and wanted to show me what it was all about. I was so fearful he would do something to my little sister. He was evil!

The next day I rented an apartment. It was about a mile away from LeeAnne. I still worked at J.C. Penney, so I took LeeAnne to the downtown Minneapolis store, used my discount, and bought both of us bikes. I wanted to be sure we both had some sort of transportation to get to each other if need be. I warned her about Curt. I gave her a key to my apartment and told her she could come over anytime. I advised her to be extremely tolerant of Mom and get along with her no matter what. I didn't want Curt involved at all and figured if there was no animosity, he wouldn't stick around.

It was tough for awhile. LeeAnne would cry and tell me she didn't want to sleep at home because Mom was drunk. Curt eventually got out of the picture. I was sure once the memorial money was gone he would only stay until something better came along. He was nothing but a gigolo.

My new apartment was across the street from St. Anthony of Padua Catholic Church. It was there I made by First Holy Communion many years before. I invited LeeAnne to go to church with me. We both started going again on a regular basis and joined the choir. It was a positive experience for us. The priest was a good sounding board, and I finally had someone else to confide in. He helped me manage my anger by listening and understanding. He gave me books to read on grief and taking care of myself and my soul. Sometimes LeeAnne would stay over at my place for the weekend. We would bake and bring cookies and cakes over to the church. On Sunday afternoons, LeeAnne would go back home with Mom.

One Saturday afternoon while LeeAnne and I were baking, there was a loud banging on the door.

"Police, open the door," a man's voice sounded so demanding both LeeAnne and I jumped.

I unlocked and opened the door. My mother had called the police saying I had kidnapped her daughter. The police were going to take me in and return LeeAnne to Mom. LeeAnne adamantly told them she was at my apartment because she wanted to be. I explained Mom was an alcoholic and our dad had recently died. I also told them Mom knew LeeAnne was here as we were together doing work for the church. The police could see we were baking, and I was not a danger to my little sister. They didn't arrest me but explained they couldn't get involved in such domestic issues. LeeAnne had to go home to her mother, and maybe I should check with child services for some kind of intervention. LeeAnne started crying and wanted to stay, but the police said she had to go home.

After LeeAnne left, I didn't even finish the baking. I sat on my couch and just stared into space. She had broken me. My mother had finally broken me. I had failed. I failed Dad, and worst of all, I failed

LeeAnne. I can't remember how long I sat there. I recall getting up to go to the bathroom and then lying down on the cold tile floor. I woke up to the sound of the phone ringing. By the time I got up and made it back to the couch, whoever called had given up. I sat back down on the couch. It was dark outside now, and the only light in my apartment was the light in the bathroom I forgot to shut off. I wasn't hungry. I didn't know if I was even tired. I just sat there and stared into space. After awhile there was knocking on my door. I recognized my aunt Diana's voice coming from the other side of the door begging me to let her in. I got up and let her in. She had just spoken with LeeAnne and came over to see if I was OK. I didn't know. I didn't know if I was OK. I didn't know anything anymore. She recognized sorrow and grief was playing a part in my quiet, subdued demeanor. I had given up. She asked if I would come with her to the hospital to be checked out. At first I refused, but eventually agreed to go with her. I didn't care. That evening I was admitted to the hospital with the diagnosis of depression and a possible nervous breakdown.

Chapter Eleven

I stayed at the hospital for five days. The second night I was there, Mother, Kimberly, Richard, Curt, Veronica, and LeeAnne all came to see me. It was too much. I didn't mind the others there, but I was afraid of Curt. Mom seemed sober and genuinely concerned. I was sure Kimberly and Veronica insisted if she came to the hospital she needed to be sober. All of them seemed to talk at once about everything in their lives, and it was not what I needed. I also had a roommate, and it was distracting for her. My family knew I was sad and unhappy. They told me it would just take time for me to get past Dad's death. They thought that was all it was. I told them I was just tired and wanted to sleep. I was getting more stressed thinking about LeeAnne under Mom and Curt's thumb.

After they left, the nurse came in and told me it may not be a good idea to have so many people visit at the same time. I agreed. The doctor would be in to see me the next day, but for now I should just rest. She gave me some anti-depressant medication and something to help me sleep.

The next day the doctor ordered blood tests and an imaging of my brain. My blood count was a little low but the scans were normal. He then had me take a five-page test called an MMPI, the Minnesota Multiphasic Personality Inventory. It was boring. I could easily tell the test was geared to ask me the same questions but in a different manner, probably to see if I was telling the truth or if I was in the real world. The outcome of the test showed I was depressed and had many hidden hostilities and anxieties. I just wanted to scream, "No Shit" at the doctors. How many of them could endure everything I had by age twenty-one? I wondered how many of them had come from a privileged family and never had a reason to worry. They were probably busy drinking and socializing in college while I was trying to deal with my dysfunctional family. It made me angry. My saving graces were LeeAnne and my oldest sister Kimberly. They visited me at the hospital everyday. It was Kimberly who talked to the nurses and doctors with me, not my mother. It was Kimberly who sought out my priest, Father Garvey, to voice her concern, not my mother.

Father Garvey stopped by the hospital a few times, prayed with me, and left books for me to read. We talked about alcoholism being a disease, which was hard for me to accept back then. We talked about unrealistic expectations made on people from those dying. We talked about how God wanted everyone to live their own life, to take away the complications of life by surrounding ourselves with positive people. We talked about letting people find their own way. I was getting the picture. One day he asked if I wanted him to hear my confession. I was reluctant to do so as my roommate was there, but behind the closed hospital curtain, once I started, it all came pouring out. I told him about my previous relationship with Ed and others, about the guilt I felt, the lying to my dad, and the fear that Dad knew everything about me. I knew I was starting to cry. Once I started, I couldn't stop. I wept harder than I could ever remember. He just sat there and held my hand for a long time. Once my emotions had somewhat subsided, he stroked my head and reminded me if we are sincerely sorry for our sins, Jesus always forgives us. He even forgave Mary Magdalene, and I was no way near her sins. That made us both laugh. He then gave me reconciliation. For my penance, he said I didn't need any as I had already taken the world on my shoulders. He then spoke seriously to me about talking to God. He said so many people go to church each week and get involved in church activities. He felt many did it out of obligation or they just felt it was the right thing to do. Maybe it made them look good in the eyes of their peers. He said for me, he felt that God was truly in my heart and I should not be afraid to make mistakes or talk about them with God. God created us as imperfect human beings, and He wanted us to go to Him and talk. He needed us to make mistakes, otherwise we would be perfect and wouldn't need Him. God needed us to confide in Him. Somedays maybe He wanted us to discuss the mysteries of the universe or maybe just tell Him we had a bad day, or even thank Him for a good one. He encouraged me to use God as my sounding board. He then gave me communion. After that small, ivory colored host melted on my tongue and Father Garvey gave me a blessing, I felt like the weight of the world had lifted off my shoulders. It was like my life was just starting — a new beginning. I knew my neighbor laying in the bed beside me probably heard most of our conversation, but I didn't care. I no longer wanted to be in this bed in the hospital. I wanted to be outside, to be happy, to live. I was released the next day from the hospital. I wasn't given any further depression medication, only iron tablets. I needed to follow up with my regular doctor in two weeks. There was no way I was going to be labeled with a mental problem. In my own immature way, I felt shame at being labeled with such a condition. Craziness was my family, not me.

I returned to work a few days later. The doctors had been wonderful by simply stating on my return to work form that I had anemia and due to my blood being low it caused tiredness and depression. I was OK to return to work full time.

I made a sincere effort to talk with Mom and tried to understand and accept her for what she was. It seemed easier to do as Curt was not hanging around much. After listening to the priest and reading some of the materials he had given me, one of which was an Al-anon book, I now realized I couldn't expect Mom to stop drinking. She was sick, and she was probably lonely. She was in love with a man who wouldn't leave his wife. Furthermore, both LeeAnne and I needed to not take things personally. The ridicule and sarcasm that came out of Mother's mouth when she was drunk was the liquor talking. It was difficult, but we seemed to give each other latitude and start to respect each other's boundaries. At least sometimes. Mom had been an only child in a wealthy family. When she married my dad, her family disowned her. We never knew her family. Mom had seven kids, and it had to be tough on her. She didn't cook or keep house very well. Her family had hired help to do those chores.

I continued to live close to Mom and LeeAnne. I was starting to feel good about my life. I tried to rise above the turmoil in my family. My brothers and mother enjoyed drinking and gambling together. In the autumn and summer months, they would often drive up north for a weekend. LeeAnne usually stayed with me or Veronica, which was good because on many occasions there were problems. Once it was a bar fight, and another time Curt beat up some Indians when they told him he was trespassing on their land. One time they were all stopped for drinking while driving and having open bottles in the car. Mom was present in all of these situations. It made me wonder why these adult brothers of mine would hang out with their mother? That became apparent when Mom had to pay to bail them all out of jail. She also financed the trips. I thought it was sad that she had to pay for company. She never had any girlfriends that I remember. Mom made a good salary but did not have much to speak of. The last encounter involved paying for lawyers so that my brothers wouldn't lose their drivers licenses. It was the last straw for her. She had to borrow money from her boss to pay all the charges. She was embarrassed. It was quite expensive, and I doubt if the boys ever repaid her.

After that last episode, we didn't see Bill for a long time. Richard never did get custody of his kids, but he did honor the visitation he had with them. It was sad that his ex-wife's daughter, Shannon, ran away from the group home and by fifteen years of age was a prostitute. The worst part was that she was proud of it. She stopped by my

78

mother's house one day while I was there. I didn't even recognize her. She had tons of makeup on, high heels and wore an extremely short skirt. She wore a tight, low-cut sweater showing off her breasts. At fifteen years-old she looked like a whore and was one. She stopped by to see if Mom knew where Terri (her mother) was. I looked out the window, and a car was parked on the street. Her pimp sat inside. He was black and wore gold chains around his neck. I asked Shannon if she needed help, if we could call the police and get her away from the guy in the car. She laughed at me and said she loved her life. I asked her where she was staying, and she wouldn't tell us. She didn't want us to notify her parole officer. Fifteen years-old and she had a parole officer and a pimp. Mom did call Richard to alert him about Shannon. He said there was nothing he could do. She wasn't his daughter, and he had never adopted her. Richard had moved on.

Richard had been overweight like my father. After his split with Terri, he topped the scales at 400 pounds. Trying to turn his life around, Richard underwent surgery. Back then it was called "stomach stapling". He was quite successful with his weight loss and got down to about 170 pounds. He looked great! He was also attending Alcoholics Anonymous. He met a nice, attractive woman there. Her name was Rose, and she had a son of her own. They married and had two boys together. They both had good jobs and bought a house.

Kimberly, too, suffered from being overweight all her life. She promised Richard she would follow in his footsteps and have the same surgery. Kimberly was petrified of going under the knife, but she did

79

it. Her surgery was not successful as the staples caused internal bleeding. After she recovered, she remained overweight, but at least she tried.

Curt married again. I remember Ramona had very long, red hair. She did not have any children, but together Curt and Ramona had four daughters. That was seven children for Curt. A lot of child support when you divorce, and they too did divorce. All four of their children were close in age, so I would guess they remained married for about seven years. We thought they had seemed to be doing well. For Curt, doing well only lasts a few years. Both became involved with drugs, and Curt was physically abusive to Ramona.

Curt had crafted all kinds of schemes. He moved into a house in South Minneapolis that he rented with some friends. They had many parties. My sister Veronica told me how disgusting Curt was at one party she attended. Music was playing, and people were getting drunk and high. Curt loved James Brown and when the song "I Feel Good" came on, she said Curt came into the living room in front of everyone, dancing naked with his penis inserted into the hole of a 45 RPM record. What a way to ruin a good song as whenever I hear it, I have to push that picture out of my mind. Why in the world Veronica sometimes still associated with him, I will never understand.

Curt was being pressured for child support. Veronica told me that for all his financial troubles, he seemed happy that night and said everything would be OK in a few days. He was expecting to get a settlement that would take care of his problems. That night after everyone left the party, in the middle of the night, the house burned down to the ground. Surprisingly, or not, no one was injured. Curt had taken out a larger than usual renter's insurance policy one month before the fire. He didn't have any furniture or anything valuable. Within a few weeks, he had received the settlement he planned.

Chapter Twelve

Mom had increased her drinking. It was getting worse than ever. Some Mondays, after a drunken weekend, she either missed work or was late, as she couldn't get going in time. Mom and I often took the same bus to work, so if I was early, I would stop by her place and pick her up. She always brought her lunch and a large thermos of coffee. One morning I thought I smelled liquor. It was only 7:15 in the morning, so I thought I must be wrong. As Mom put on her coat, I turned my back to her and opened her thermos to smell. Sure enough, there was whiskey in her coffee. I didn't say anything. It wouldn't have done any good.

I did well working at J.C. Penney. After less than a year, I was put in charge of the Commercial Accounts Department. Not a manager, but I did supervise two employees. I enjoyed my job so I was not happy when my boss told me I had reached the top of the pay scale for the position. He was moving me to a new department, New Accounts and Collections. I didn't want to move but didn't have any choice.

I relocated to the floor below and started training. The New Accounts duties were kind of fun. I would get credit checks on people and recommend lines of credit. Once approved, I would set up their account in the computer, issue credit cards, and notify them. I would also do address changes and name changes whenever a marriage or divorce occurred. The part that wasn't fun was collections. I have never been the type of person who would be a good salesperson or ask someone for money. I had to listen to a lot of sob stories, and it started depressing me. I was not good at this part of my job. My numbers for collections were down. My boss discussed this with me. I was honest with him and told him that I did not like the collections portion of my job. I wanted to go back to my old department. He said he understood, but I needed exposure in all departments.

I asked, "Why are you saying I need to spend time in each department? Are you prepping me for a managerial position?" He told me he would like to. Unfortunately, I only had a high school diploma. Company policy for management required a college degree. I felt let down after finally being on a high for awhile.

My performance reviews had always been very good. I wondered if all companies had this policy. I decided to check out the want ads in the paper. I went on several interviews. One was to St. Paul, and I had to catch two busses to get there. I prayed I didn't get a good offer from them.

I hadn't heard back from any of the others. I had one more place to go. It was in the next building from where I was currently working, so I arranged an interview over my lunch hour. That company was Cargill. I thought Penney's was large, but Cargill was huge! I was applying for an entry level position and was worried the pay would be a lot less than what I was making. I was given a typing test and a math test. I then had an interview with a man who was very nice, but I thought it was strange he had such long curly hair. Cargill seemed conservative, but here was this manager, named John, with shoulder length curls. I felt the interview went extremely well. The only thing I was worried about was getting back to work. John and I had spoken for over an hour. Our conversation drifted off from work to personal things. I found out he had been divorced for some time, and he alone was raising his two sons. I noticed the time and told him I had to get back to work. He told me I would hear from the personnel department in a few days if I got the job.

Under scrutinizing eyes, I hurried to my desk. After only half an hour I got a phone call from Cargill offering me the job, and they would match my present salary. I was thrilled.

The first day of work at Cargill, I looked for John, the manager who hired me. I didn't see him. A woman was training me in. I started at the bottom, opening mail and light accounting work. I asked her where the manager was.

She said, "He's right there at his desk." She pointed across the aisle to a few offices.

I said, "No, that isn't him. This guy had long, curly hair." She laughed and told me that John had finally gotten his hair cut short. He was known as one of the rebels. He got fed up hearing his boss bitch about his hair, so he cut it off. I looked at him again and thought, "You know, he's kind of cute."

Working at Cargill was my greatest move both career-wise and personally. I worked my way up into the accounting department, getting better than average raises. The accounting department was next to Cargill's Internal Audit department. Everyone in the audit department was male, and every one of them were single and good-looking. Most of the girls I worked with were single too. Many friendships were developed, and I had never dated so much or gone to so many parties. I was busy all the time and felt that LeeAnne was starting to resent the time I spent with friends.

Veronica had moved into an apartment with her son, Michael, and her daughter, Patsy. Her apartment was in the same building as Mom and LeeAnne. Patsy was Veronica's favorite. She adored her, and there wasn't anything she wouldn't do or give to Patsy. Michael was often ignored. Michael was timid. Before Patsy's father went to prison, Kimberly and my dad had noticed bruises and welts on Michael. Dad threatened Veronica that he would call the authorities and have Michael taken away from her if the abuse didn't stop. Veronica broke down and admitted it was Roger, Patsy's father, who abused Michael. Veronica never wanted Rob, Michael's dad, around, but our dad said it was time to get him involved and let Michael spend some time with him. After Roger went to prison, Michael spent time between both his mom's and dad's houses. Veronica continued to laden Patsy with clothes, toys, and most importantly time. Michael was mostly ignored by his mother. It was about this time that LeeAnne started getting closer to Veronica. I knew Veronica occasionally smoked marijuana. LeeAnne knew that too, but she had a good head on her shoulders, so I didn't think it would be a problem.

Curt was still another issue. When we lived in the projects, my brothers became friends with a guy named Randy. Although he had grown up in the projects and hung around with my brothers, Randy finished high school and immediately after, joined the army. Curt and Richard always remained friends with him. When Randy got out of the service, he was bound and determined to get a good job, find a nice girl, get married, and have a family. I secretly had a crush on him but would never let it be known as I would never want to associate with my brothers. Eventually Randy did find a nice girl, or so I thought. Cassie was nice but seemed naïve. A few years after they were married, it seemed like Curt was always at their house or with them. They lived in our neighborhood, so we saw them frequently. The three of them were always hanging out at the neighborhood bars. One night on Cassie's birthday, the three of them went out to celebrate. Apparently Curt and Randy got into an argument. Curt left, and Cassie and Randy drove home. The next day Randy was found dead in his garage.

Cassie claimed that once home, she got out of the car and stormed into the house. She was angry about the fight with Curt. Their garage was a detached one, and Randy said he would be in in a few minutes. Cassie got tired of waiting for him and fell asleep on the couch. The next morning when she couldn't find him, she wandered out to the garage and found him dead. It was strange because at first it was assumed he died of carbon monoxide poisoning, but he was outside of the car and there was a mark on his head, like a blow from an object that could not be explained. The police investigated and even attended the funeral. I remember sitting in the pew at the funeral with my sister Veronica. We both noticed how Cassie and Curt were always together. It was like Curt had taken over for Randy. We actually saw Curt shed a few tears but never saw Cassie cry. Veronica said Curt's tears were fake. She knew Curt had killed Randy, but she couldn't prove it. She thought Cassie and Curt were having an affair for some time. If she could prove it, she would tell the police. It was only a week after the funeral, and Curt moved in with Cassie! Unbelievable! The police investigated for a long time; they even came to Mom's house to talk about Curt. The head wound on Randy was thought to be made by a pipe of some sort, but it was never found. Curt's footprints were on the garage floor, but he often was in there with Randy. Of course, Mom wouldn't say anything negative about her son. The investigation went on. Curt and Cassie were both interrogated several times, but no arrest was ever made. The car had been on until the gas ran out with the garage door closed. Carbon monoxide was the main cause of death. Still there was no explanation for the head wound, and there was always the suspicion.

Curt stayed with Cassie for a few years. He was employed here and there on short term jobs. About six months following Randy's death, Curt convinced Cassie to use the insurance money and the military money from Randy's estate to upgrade her house. Curt was good at construction. Not great, but good. He had Cassie give him the money, and he would do all the work. Curt quit his current job and spent all his time fixing up Cassie's house. The house needed a lot of work. It was in an old part of northeast Minneapolis. At first, it seemed amazing how much Curt changed the look of the house. The front porch was now screened in with new support beams, and the sagging roof was repaired. The inside bathroom was updated as well as the kitchen. New cupboards and woodwork were installed, and fresh paint really changed the appearance of several rooms. The house still needed work. The chimney sagged, and the plumbing was a problem. It was about this time that Curt always seemed drunk or high once again. He became physically and verbally abusive to Cassie. One afternoon Cassie confided to me and Veronica that Curt had gone through almost all the money she got from Randy's estate. If she refused to give him any more money, he would become violent with her. We told her she should call the police and file a restraining order. Cassie just got quiet and said, "I can't do that." Veronica and I always suspected that Curt had threatened her with her role in Randy's death. At the end of that year, Curt had left Cassie with her house half done. He had started to dismantle the chimney but just left it. Cassie had no extra funds left. She ended up losing the house, and Curt moved onto his next conquest.

Chapter Thirteen

I admit after a year and a half of partying and dating, it got old. All those young, good looking guys at Cargill just seemed the same after a while. I was tired of it and started to back off. I had had a few boyfriends at work, but the relationships didn't last long, and it seemed eventually everyone was dating each other in that group. I knew I wanted more. LeeAnne and I continued to sing in the church choir and hang out. After work, we would go swimming or ride our bikes if the weather was warm. LeeAnne also continued to get closer to Veronica.

Mom seemed to be sick all the time. She had that cough that I now recognize in people who drink and smoke too much. She seemed the happiest on Sunday nights when she would sit on the couch and watch "House on the Prairie." After all the anger and pain, I had felt toward her, I now felt sorry for her. She would often comment how wonderful life would be if we all lived like the people in that show. But that wasn't my mother either. During her sober moments, and sometimes after she had been drinking, I tried to talk with her. I asked her why people turn out the way they do. I asked her what happened to my brothers and why she always bailed them out of trouble but didn't have enough money for other things. She smiled and said, "When you lose the only family you once knew, you will do anything to keep the one you now have, whether they are good or bad.

It is like the movie, 'The Bad Seed'. I am responsible as I gave birth to them."

"Mom, Dad was responsible too," I said. "Besides, everyone reaches an age of understanding when they know the difference between right and wrong. Why should you always protect them? They're adults."

"You wouldn't understand. I think the main problem was on your dad's side of the family, but your dad always protected you." Then she didn't want to talk about it anymore.

I was more confused than ever. I called my sister, Kimberly, who was ten years older than I was. I told her I wanted to talk about our family. She met me for dinner downtown at the NanKin Café. We both loved their Chow Mein. It's a shame it's no longer in business. Kimberly reminded me that mother was an only child — a spoiled, once wealthy, spoiled child. When she married Dad, that all changed. Kimberly told me that years ago, one of our aunts on my father's side told her that way back in history, a first cousin married a first cousin. That caused some kind of genetic malfunction which resulted in the dysfunction of our family.

"Wait a minute," I spouted with half a smile. "Our aunts and uncles on Dad's side have children too, and they seem normal. Well, most of them."

She just said, "I guess it's the luck of the draw."

So I still had no answers. Then I asked her about me and Veronica. Veronica was born an albino, and I came two years later with a streak of white hair mixed in with dark hair. No one in the family had that. Kimberly explained to me that we never knew Mom's family, so we really couldn't say why. She said maybe we should accept what we have and not question it. She then went on to tell me about her search for her biological father. It was traumatic for Kimberly not knowing until she was eighteen that she had a different father from the rest of us. I never knew until that night that Kimberly had contacted her father. He didn't want anything to do with her. He had a new family and a new life. I was sad for her. Years later, her birth father's son entered politics and was well known in the Minneapolis area. I know that whenever he was in the news, Kimberly felt like she was slapped in the face.

I still couldn't understand how a family could disown their only child, my mother, because she married someone who didn't graduate from school and wasn't rich. It was different times back then. Dad was born in 19 5, and he didn't finish school because he had to work and help his family survive. Many people were in the same situation then. Mom's family was so different being wealthy. My dad's sister, aunt Margie, had been friends with my mother. She introduced them to each other. She used to tell me, for many years Mom and Dad were very much in love, and they couldn't keep their hands off each other. They had so many children and birth control wasn't prevalent then. The stress and expense of having a large family eventually wore down my mother, and she started to resent her life. Margie said my mom dwelled on memories of her prior privileged life.

But how could you condone the shallowness of deserting your only child because of wealth, or lack of? It was a mystery to me, and I didn't want to catch myself living in it and being haunted by it. I needed again to move on with my life.

One afternoon I was working with my manager, John. We were looking up old accounts in the storage room. He and I were the only ones there, and we started joking around. He had such a great sense of humor. His last name was Italian, and he told me his dad was Italian but his mom was Polish. I told him I was Polish too on my dad's side. My mom was Irish. I found out John loved to cook. Although his specialty was lasagna, he loved to cook both Italian and Polish food. Then he asked me if I would be interested in coming over for dinner one night and he would cook for me. I told him I would have to think about it and let him know. I was nervous. He was my boss! I was attracted to him, but he had two children and I wasn't sure how that would work out. By the end of the day, my attraction peaked, and I told him I would come over for dinner, but I didn't want anyone working with us to know. He told me he was going to say the same thing to me if I agreed to come over. I informed him I no longer had a car as I lived on the bus line, and my old beater had given up long ago. He lived in Bloomington, and I lived in northeast Minneapolis. He seemed like such a gentleman as he said he would never expect me to come over and then drive home alone late at night. If I gave him directions, he would pick me up and bring me home.

I was so nervous that entire day. It was a Saturday, and I kept thinking, "Am I like my mother? Dating my boss?"

I asked my sister Veronica and she said, "Hell, no. Neither one of you are married. Don't let our parents' screwed up lives make you question yours. You've always done the right thing, not like the rest of us."

Saturday night arrived, and John was prompt. We both seemed nervous driving to his apartment. Those uncomfortable moments of silence seemed so long. Before we entered his apartment, he told me he had to apologize for dinner.

"Why? I haven't even tasted it yet?" I smiled at his ridiculous comment.

"Here's the thing," he began. "Usually when I am cooking my Italian meals, I drive over to St. Paul to an Italian specialty grocery store and pick out the best Italian sausage, cheese, and cannoli. I had every intention of doing that, but my two boys started arguing and rough-housing early this morning. One of them tried to lock the other out on the patio, and they broke the glass on the patio door. I had to go all over to try to find someone to fix it right away. I ended up putting cardboard over it as I couldn't get the window replaced until Monday. I thought about calling you and cancelling, but I really wanted to see you outside the office and get to know you. I turned the heat up so you shouldn't get cold."

It was December and it was cold outside. His explanation was so truthful and his concern so sweet, I had to chuckle.

"It doesn't matter," I said. "We can order pizza!"

"Oh no, I still cooked. I just didn't make lasagna. I made some rigatoni, but it is made with sausage I bought at an ordinary grocery store. I would still like to make you lasagna another time, if you want."

I couldn't believe how much he had gone through in one day and still had me over for dinner. Right away I met his children. Stephen was fourteen years old. He had dark, curly hair with a stocky build. Gregory was twelve. His hair was dark but straight, and he was tall and lean. They were both good looking boys with dark eyes and olive skin. You could tell they were of Italian descent.

The dinner was very good. Much better than I was used to. We ate Italian salad, rigatoni (which I never even knew what it was), Italian bread, and John and I drank red wine. Spumoni ice cream was for dessert, and I had never had that before either. I kept complimenting the food, and John said if I liked this, I would love his lasagna. We all sat at the table, and by the time dinner was over, I was very impressed by Stephen and Greg's good manners. They wouldn't let me do anything. They cleared the table and did the dishes while John and I visited on the couch.

Once the boys were done in the kitchen, they were instructed to go to their room, in punishment for fighting earlier and breaking the sliding glass door window.

It was still early, so John and I had a good opportunity to get to know each other. We talked about his divorce. I could tell he had really loved his ex-wife. He had taken her back once before when she had been unfaithful. The last time, he had been at work when she left. I think the kids may have been eight and ten years old. When John got home, the kids were home alone. Dinner was on the stove, and the table was set. On the table was a note from his wife saying she was tired of her life. She went further on to say she felt trapped and hated John. She also said she disliked her oldest son as she was pregnant with him when they married and maybe she wasn't quite ready to marry. She thought if she had never been pregnant, maybe they wouldn't have married and she would have had a better life. She had run off with her boss who had been a mutual friend of both her and John. She was gone for over a year and never attempted to have any contact with her children. After a year, John's parents and sister stressed to him the importance of getting a divorce in case she came back and tried to take the children, as the law usually favored the birth mother keeping her children. It took a long time for John to accept she would not be coming back. He obtained a lawyer, but no one knew where she was. Her own parents were devastated by what she had done. Within the second year of her departure, John was granted a divorce on desertion. She was located eventually but never contacted her children. John told me how difficult it was to observe his children wanting to be the first ones to meet the mailman days before their birthdays and Christmases hoping for some word from their mother.

Once the boys were sleeping, John drove me home. He said the kids would be OK to stay alone as Stephen was fourteen, and they didn't dare pull anything as they were already in trouble for the broken window. I sensed John's kids were sometimes a problem, but he seemed to have control over it.

John stayed at my house for a few more hours. We just talked. It seemed so easy for both of us to talk with each other. He revealed how much he had been hurt by his ex-wife. That had caused him to feel that he would never marry again.

When he left my apartment, we kissed goodbye. It was a long kiss. Then we kissed again and again, with each kiss getting more passionate than the next. John pulled away and said he better get home to his kids and left. I couldn't stop smiling once he left. My phone rang about a half hour later. It was John telling me what a wonderful time he had.

I was so nervous going to work the following Monday. John and I both played it cool but there were times I couldn't stop thinking about him. I would be working at my desk and look up to see him in his office across the aisle from me. He would be staring at me, and when our eyes met, he would smile and wink at me. I knew I was blushing as I could feel the warmth rise from my heart to my cheeks.

The following weekend we went on our second date. We had to be careful where we went as we didn't want any coworkers to see us together. It was still December, but it wasn't too cold out so we took a drive to Stillwater. We walked a few blocks and visited some gift shops. I could not believe how many ornaments and decorations were in the Christmas Shop. We had lunch at a small but nice restaurant right on the bank of the St. Croix River. John told me he was leaving for a few weeks during Christmas break. Every year he took his boys to visit his family. They lived in Branson, Missouri. His only sibling, his sister Marilyn and her family, lived in Nixa, Missouri, close to Branson. He told me how beautiful Branson was. Sometimes his kids would spend a month there in the summer. The kids always had fun at Silver Dollar City and hanging out with his sister and brother-in-law, their cousins, and grandparents. In the autumn, Branson's hills and trees are magnificent in the orange, red, and golden colors. The town referred to this as "The Flaming Fall Review." He said people would come from all over the country to travel the long, hilly roads and spine-tingling curves up to the grand mountain tops to witness the breathtaking views of the area. He thought I would love to see it someday, and if he ever married again, it would be a nice place to go for a honeymoon.

We finished our lunch and headed back to the car. John told me how much he enjoyed spending time with me. He thought he would never date such a young woman as he was fourteen years older than I was, but he said I was different. I was the only younger person he had met who could carry on a sensible, adult conversation with him. He said I had an old soul. I knew he meant it as a compliment, yet many times I felt I had been cheated out of my childhood.

When we reached the car, he opened the door for me. Before I got in, he put his arms around me and kissed me. He wanted to know if I would go out with him when he got back after Christmas. He said he was worried I would start dating one of those young auditors again, and he didn't want to lose me.

I was a little surprised by our earlier conversation. It was only last week John said he didn't think he would ever marry again. It was now our second date, and he said, "If I ever married again." I could tell John had much love to give someone and that type of relationship had been missing in his life. I agreed to go out with him after Christmas and told him, "Those young guys don't interest me anymore." He squeezed my hand and told me he would miss me.

Chapter Fourteen

I spent Christmas that year like I had done for so many years. LeeAnne and I went to Christmas Eve Mass and then had dinner at my mother's place. Dinner consisted of just appetizers and cookies. We usually exchanged presents with each other. We never knew if my brothers would show up, and because we were now all older, any gift exchange was done between only the girls in the family. We always had a few toys wrapped up in case any of our brothers' kids, our nieces and nephews, showed up. We never knew from one year to the next who would have the kids or if they would be in foster care. We always thought of them. It was hardest to feel the absence of Curt's twin girls. It had now been years since anyone had seen them. We knew they were in foster care but did not know where. Curt never discussed them. There was always a sadness thinking where they were and if they were OK.

After the gifts were exchanged, we would watch an old Christmas movie either at my mom's apartment or LeeAnne and I would go to my apartment. It depended on who showed up at Mom's and if there was a lot of drinking.

Christmas Day we all brought a dish to share over to Mom's, and she would bake a ham. Kimberly always made the Polish poppy seed bread that had been a tradition on my Dad's side of the family.

This particular year, Curt came over and brought brownies. He said they were really good, and he made them himself. I thought it was strange he would do that until I found out why. Veronica was there and warned me and LeeAnne not to eat the brownies. She told us they were laced with marijuana. I couldn't believe he would do that without telling anyone. I noticed Mom was extremely drunk and giggly.

Curt said, "Isn't she funny? This is the happiest I've ever seen her. She's eaten half a pan of brownies."

Veronica, LeeAnne, and I went across the hall to Veronica's apartment. Veronica told me Curt was high when he came over. The reason for the brownies was to get Mom so inebriated he could con her out of money. She told me that whenever Curt needed money, he would get her drunk or slip something into her drink. It was so depressing. I asked Veronica if she knew this, how could she let it happen? Did she confront mother and tell her how her own son was using her? She said she had told Mom, but it was useless. Then she asked me if I had ever tried to tell Curt anything. You didn't cross my brother. I could understand what she meant. I knew Veronica smoked pot. Her whole apartment reeked of the smell. I was so naïve, I didn't even know what the smell was. LeeAnne told me. Then I wondered, how does LeeAnne know? I just wanted to get back to the healthy, calm stillness of my own apartment. I only had two dates with John, but I found myself waiting for his return from Missouri. Somehow our short relationship already seemed right. It seemed different from anything I had experienced.

Once John returned, he called me even before he went back to work. We talked for a long time. He told me his mom and dad were upset with him because he was in such a hurry to get back to Minnesota. They asked him what was wrong as he had never been in a hurry to leave before. He told them he had met someone and didn't want her to get away. I laughed and felt so good inside. This man had only dated me twice but made me feel so happy I glowed. Most of all, he respected me and treated me like I mattered and I was really important to him.

On our third date, we had dinner again at John's apartment. This time he made his famous lasagna. It was delicious. I told him if I kept eating like this, I would start gaining weight.

"That's OK, honey," he chuckled. "It doesn't change the person inside you. I love to see you enjoy something so much."

Wow! I wasn't used to such tenderness. Then he really surprised me by saying, "If we ever get married, I would cook for you every night."

I didn't know what to say. Our first date he told me he wouldn't get married again. Our second date he said "if" he ever got married again. Now on our third date, he said, "If 'we' ever get married."

I started telling John about my dysfunctional family. He started meeting them. I looked up to John, and he gave me good advice. He never told me what to do but suggested healthier ways of handling situations. The main suggestion was to distance myself from the negativity and start believing in myself. His own past marriage had been dysfunctional, and he knew how hard it was to separate yourself to create a happier, healthier life.

Three months after our first date, John asked me to marry him. I was thrilled and felt such excitement for this positive turn in my life's journey. Three months after he proposed, we were married.

Chapter Fifteen

John and I were both raised Catholic so I wanted to get married at my church, St. Anthony. I called Father Garvey to tell him the news. Father Garvey asked me questions about John. I told him both of us would like to come in and talk with him to arrange the wedding. To my surprise and disbelief, Father Garvey told me I had better really think about this union. He said if I married a divorced man, I would never see the face of God. He said I could never pass through the gates of Heaven. I was dumbfounded. It was 1974 and the church was becoming more liberal. I explained to Father Garvey that John's ex-wife had deserted him and his two children. He said it didn't matter. I was heartbroken. I always wanted to walk down the church aisle wearing a white wedding dress and veil.

John handled it better than I did. He said we could just go to the courthouse but I didn't want that. Our family was raised Catholic, although my mother never changed from her Presbyterian religion. Occasionally on Sundays, Mom attended a small Presbyterian church by her house. It was across the street from Logan park. I was somewhat amazed when she went to the trouble to ask her minister if he would be willing to marry us. He said he would like to meet with us first.

After John and I met with him, we were given a long questionnaire that each of us was to fill out without input from the other. We were compatible except in one area, "children." I knew John didn't want anymore children. He was thirty-seven years old and I was twenty-three. He often said it would be extremely difficult for him to start a family again. He had a rough time both emotionally and financially raising two children on his own. There was never any monetary support from his ex-wife or her family. His parents, sister, and brother-in-law helped as much as they could, but his sister had her own family of four children. John's sister, Marilyn, was always there for the boys if they needed anything.

This was a problem for me as I dreamed of one day having a child of my own. I prayed a lot about it. I even went so far as to ask my mother about it. That was not a good move as she would continue throughout her life telling me that I would never be a real "woman" until I gave birth to a child. I knew I loved John. He made me feel safe. The boys seemed excited for us and to have me in their lives. John and I agreed to marry but wait a year to discuss having a child. This was good as it would give me the opportunity to be involved with the boys in every aspect of their lives.

The Presbyterian minister agreed to marry us and stressed how important it was for both of us to continue to be open and honest about having children. He was great as he changed words in the ceremony to reflect more of the Catholic rituals. I didn't feel right being married in a church of a different faith. We had good friends through work. Robert and Mary lived in a beautiful home in Burnsville, Minnesota. We asked them to stand up for us. Their home was located on Thoreau Drive, named after Henry David Thoreau. It was a picturesque area with stunning trees and striking bushes along a scenic pathway through their backyard. Mary suggested we get married outside on their large wooden deck. She would be sure to have it covered with flowers and vines. We just needed to pray it didn't rain that day. We agreed.

The night before our wedding, two occurrences took place that brought me to tears. First, my aunt Diana, on my dad's side, called to tell me that she would attend the reception but not the wedding. Since my dad's illness and death, I had gotten close to Aunt Diana. She had met John a few times and really liked him. Diana told me she could not attend my wedding because I was disrespecting my father. I couldn't believe it! She told me my father was most likely turning over in his grave because I was not getting married in the Catholic church. I should have just gone to a Justice of the Peace. Furthermore, she was upset that I was having my mother's minister perform the ceremony and that was totally disrespecting my father.

I asked her, "Don't you think my dad would be happy I was getting my mom involved and trying to get along with her?"

She said, "No, and I can't believe you are doing this. I will come to the reception to wish you and John luck."

I said, "I can't believe you are doing this to me the night before my wedding? Why bother coming to the reception?" I hung up and burst into tears.

My sisters tried to console me. John called me, and I told him about it. He thought it was cruel and told me we did not need those people in our lives.

It was a good thing we were busy making food for the reception that night. I was grateful my sisters were all there to give me the support I needed. I think we were all getting tired, and I developed an attitude that I didn't give a shit what my aunt thought.

Then, at the end of the evening, LeeAnne started acting differently toward me. I knew she was tired. She broke down in tears and yelled at me, "You're getting married and leaving me. Now you're going to have Steve and Greg. What am I supposed to do?"

Bam! Another blow to my chance of happiness. I was devastated. LeeAnne meant everything to me. Yes, now I had John in my life, but LeeAnne would always be important to me and always be a part of my life. Veronica said she knew that was coming. She said she would talk to her.

On July 20, 1974, John and I were married. I stayed at my mom's the night before. In the morning, I woke up to rose petals on my bed, the floor leading to the bathroom, and more petals sprinkled in my already drawn bath. This was the nicest gesture I had seen from my mother. LeeAnne seemed to be better. I told her how much I needed her to help me. I also told her when I got back from our honeymoon in Branson, she could come over for the weekend and hang out with Steve and Greg. John and I decided to go to Branson as his parents were older and didn't want to make the trip. They planned a big celebration for us down there.

We had a small wedding. No bridesmaids or groomsmen, just our friends Robert and Mary standing up for us. Couch cushions served as our kneeler for the blessing. The deck was absolutely beautiful. Mary's neighbors were so excited about a wedding in the backyard, they brought over most of their potted plants and vines to decorate. LeeAnne was my personal attendant and helped me get dressed. I felt like I was in Hawaii and how appropriate that I had chosen, without knowing how the deck would look, "The Hawaiian Wedding Song" as the song to walk out onto the deck. The day was sunny and warm without a cloud to be seen. John didn't wear a tuxedo but a blue and white pinstriped sports jacket with gray slacks and a blue tie. His two boys were all dressed up and even had ties on. John told me he had bought them ties, and they were so long he had to take a scissors and cut them down just before the ceremony. I didn't have that church wedding, but I did buy myself a long, white wedding dress with lace and pearls. It was complete with a train and veil. Mom was upset I picked out my dress without her. It was just LeeAnne and me, but Mom was usually drinking at night. I ordered two bouquets of flowers for myself and Mary. I didn't have any color scheme, so I used favorite flowers of mine, my sisters', and my dad's. A cluster of red and yellow roses, blue carnations, and baby's breath made up the bouquets. My sisters all had corsages of their favorite color, and Mom had one with all the colors. Mom was sitting in a chair on the deck.

She always liked to play a martyr. After we were pronounced man and wife, everyone cheered and clapped except Mom. She sat there looking sad. I went over to her, gave her a kiss on the cheek, and presented my bouquet to her. She was not going to spoil my special day. This day was finally for me, not her. Mary, my maid of honor, gave me her flowers. I planned on placing them on my father's grave the next morning before we left for our honeymoon.

After the ceremony, we all drove to the Presbyterian church. We had a luncheon in the basement of the church, and it was not air-conditioned. We served the ham sandwiches and potato salad that Mom, Kimberly, Veronica, LeeAnne, and I had stayed up late the night before making. We also had cake, mints, and coffee. The wedding cake I had ordered started tilting to the side from the heat, so we had to cut it right away. After the luncheon, everyone headed to my mom's house for, of course, liquid refreshments.

My brothers Richard and Curt were at the wedding. Bill was not. At my mother's house, Curt came up to me and John to congratulate us. He said I looked beautiful. He turned to John and said, "Let's get drunk." John laughed and said, "No, I have to drive seven hundred miles in the morning to Branson, and it's my wedding night."

Curt had a funny smirk on his face and said, "Yeah, my little sister." He laughed and walked away. It wouldn't be for many years later that my sister Veronica told me the night of my wedding Curt had talked her into going across the street to Logan park, and he attacked her. He forced her to the ground, kissed her on the mouth and starting ripping her clothes off. She kicked him in the crotch and ran back to the house. Her own brother tried to rape her on my wedding night.

John and I were the first ones to leave our reception. The only alcohol we had was our champagne toast. People were getting drunk. Thank God John's boys, Steve and Greg, were going to spend the night with our friends, Robert and Mary. We would pick them up the next morning to go to Missouri. I was worried about LeeAnne, but she told me not to worry and have a good time. While John and I were getting into the car, my brother Bill suddenly arrived with some friends. He was so drunk he could hardly stand up. He had never met John. As Bill stumbled to our car with my brother Richard's help, he took his finger and kept stabbing it into John's chest saying that he was the oldest man in the family and his dad would want him to be sure I was taken care of. Then he threatened John saying if anything happened to his little sister, he would come after John. Then Bill looked at me. I had changed from my wedding dress into a short dress. Bill said, "Look at my little sister all grown up. She's built like a brick shithouse."

Richard said, "OK, Bill, we have to let them leave." Richard dragged Bill off. I was shaken but John laughed and said Bill was so drunk he wouldn't be able to hurt anyone.

John and I drove to his apartment. He had bought candles and prepared food ahead of time. We had a drink and toast to each other and were thankful to be away from the craziness.

109

Chapter Sixteen

I think the first year of marriage is always tough, especially when you are twenty-three years old and overnight became a stepmother to boys twelve and fourteen years old.

The day after our wedding, John, Steven, Greg, and I packed up the car and left on our honeymoon. John's family wanted to have a celebration dinner for us. His parents and sister would take care of the boys while we spent a few days alone for our honeymoon in Eureka Springs, Arkansas.

John's family welcomed me with lots of hugs and kisses. Everyone in that family greeted each other with hugs, and when they said goodbye to each other, they said, "I love you," even if they were going to see that person the next day. I wasn't used to this. I thought maybe it was a "southern thing" but soon realized many families do this. My family just didn't.

The night after we arrived, John's family had a huge steak cookout on their patio in the backyard. I've never seen such huge steaks, and so many! Relatives from all over Missouri, Arkansas, and even Chicago showed up. It was a beautiful celebration of love.

The next day John and I left for Eureka Springs, Arkansas, where we could finally have some time alone. It was a beautiful drive with all the mountains and clusters of trees. The rock formations along the highway were variegated with rich, earthy tones. I had no idea this part of the country held such natural beauty.

We were almost at our hotel when rain started coming down. Once we arrived, John told me I could stay in the car while he went to check us in. The sky soon became a cloudburst of heavy rain. I sat in the car while the monsoon-like downpour continued. I was starting to get worried as it seemed John had been gone too long. After what I thought was thirty minutes, I braved the rain and ran into the hotel lobby. John was on the phone and indicated he would be off in a minute. He thanked the hotel clerk, and we ran out to our car. We were both soaked. He told me that his mother had been leaving messages at the hotel for me to call as soon as we checked in. There had been an urgent call for me from Cargill. Apparently, the girl I was training in to cover for me during my honeymoon had been diagnosed with infectious hepatitis. I had to immediately go to the hospital and get a shot to prevent any chance of contracting it. John and I checked into our room and proceeded to the emergency hospital so I could get the shot.

After getting what seemed to be a larger than usual needle shot into my butt, we left and the rain had also stopped. The sun came out and there was a beautiful rainbow highlighted over the mountains. We decided to get some lunch and do a little sightseeing. We drove up the winding roads into the mountains. It was beautiful. We stopped at a scenic rock point. Once I got out of the car, I seemed a little dizzy. We were up quite high and as soon as I looked out over the scenic point, my lunch decided it wanted to escape from my body. I was grateful we were the only observers there to witness my puking. I became lightheaded and warm. We went back to the hotel, and my butt started itching where the shot was. WHOA! There was a huge lump on my rear end! John called the clinic and was told I was having an allergic reaction to the injection. After getting more medicine to counteract the shot, I ended up spending the rest of my honeymoon in bed, but not like I thought.

Once back in Branson we had a few more days left to visit. One night the adults headed to the Holiday Inn Bar. There was a country western entertainer there who was great. John's mom and dad knew him, so they had him announce our wedding to the audience. He then sang "For the Good Times" as we danced. After the music ended, there was some commotion on the other side of the dance floor. A man who was obviously drunk, took the microphone. He blurted out that he was proud to be John's father-in-law! John put his head down and told me he was sorry. The man was his ex-father-in-law, obviously upset that John had moved on and remarried.

There were difficult moments like this during my honeymoon. Maybe they seemed so difficult because I was only twenty-three. I was often mistakenly called by John's ex-wife's name, which I know is an honest mistake. My most difficult moment was when we were leaving early in the morning to head back to Minnesota. John's two boys were very much loved by John's family. John often told me how his family maybe coddled them too much because their mother had left. They had offered many times to let the boys live with them, but John was adamant about it because he was their father and was perfectly capable of taking care of them. Whenever they spent several weeks in Missouri during the summers, John said they would come back spoiled worse than the last time. On the morning we were leaving, Greg, then twelve, was reluctant to leave. He hugged his grandmother tight and started crying saying he was afraid to go home and wanted to stay with her. I felt awful, but John got mad. He yelled at Greg to get in the car. John had to grab him away and just about carry him into the car.

John's mother asked me to wait as she wanted to talk to me. She told me that I was young and maybe didn't have the patience needed to take of the children. I will never forget her words to me, "If you ever touch my grandchildren or do anything to make them unhappy, I will come after you with everything I have." I just stood there. She had been so nice to me during our visit and now this. Just then John came back inside to tell me we had to get going. As we said our goodbyes to her, she very firmly said to me, "Patty, don't forget what I told you. I'll be checking up with the kids."

When we got out to the car, John asked what that was about. I didn't want to tell him in front of the boys so I waited until our first rest stop when the kids were in the bathroom. He told me to let it go. His entire family was a little over-protective of his kids. They thought he was too strict with them. He said, "They live seven hundred miles from us. We don't have to worry about them."

113

Once we got back from Missouri and settled into our apartment, it was even more challenging. I had lived alone for a while, so I had furniture that we moved into John's place. He already had furniture, and we didn't know what we would keep. My furniture was newer, but the kids were rough on things, so we decided to wait. Our living room now had two couches, two coffee tables, and four end tables. We folded up John's kitchen table and used mine as it seated more people. It was awkward getting around in the small two-bedroom apartment with four people and two houses of furniture. The boys had my old TV in their room and an extra dresser. I had an old sewing machine in our bedroom and when I used it, you couldn't get around anything else. I had no place to put my makeup. Sharing one bathroom with three men, well, I can't think of one advantage to that. The kids constantly complained I took too long in the bathroom and wanted to know what I did in there for so long.

One Saturday afternoon, I was trying to pick up around the apartment. John was doing the laundry. There was a laundry room two floors below us. The boys were arguing with each other and getting under my skin. John told me not to be afraid to yell at them or discipline them if they were doing something wrong. Of course, my mother-in-law's words kept creeping into my mind. I decided to do some mending and went into the bedroom and closed the door. Silence finally, but before I knew it, the door flew open and the boys were arguing again and asking me who was right. They both just sank into our bed and said they were going to stay in there and watch me.

I couldn't take it. John was down in the laundry room, and I told Steve and Greg to tell their dad I would be back in a little while. They wanted to know where I was going. There was a strip mall across the highway from our apartment. I said I was going to the store. They wanted to come with me. I snapped at them and said, "I want to go alone," and left.

There was a drug store in the mall that had a fountain. I just sat there drinking a Coke and tried to hold back the tears. Did I take on too much?

After about a half hour, I heard Steven yell, "There she is." I looked up, and John hurried over to me with the boys. The look on his face was that of fear and anguish. He could tell I had been crying. He told the boys to go back home. He then sat next to me and asked me what happened.

After I explained, he said he should have realized it would have been difficult for me living with three guys. I told him it was alright; I was over it now. I just needed some time alone. He promised me he would work on making things better. Then he said, "Please don't ever leave me. I was so scared." I felt so selfish. How could I have worried him so much? The look on his face told me how much he loved me.

The next weekend we went out looking for bigger places to live. We found a nice rental townhome in Eagan. It had four floors. The top floor consisted of only the master bedroom and bath. It was so big it even had a walk-in closet. The floor below had two bedrooms and a second bathroom for the boys. The ground level floor was the living room, dining area, and small kitchen. The living room had a stone fireplace and the dining room had a walkout level to a small yard. I could live with a small kitchen. The basement level was unfinished but would be a perfect recreation room for the boys. It had hookups for our own washer and dryer that we would buy. It felt like heaven! I had never lived in such a nice place. I had never had a fireplace. It was more expensive than the apartment, but our happiness meant more.

Chapter Seventeen

Privacy. Having privacy made all the difference in the world not only to me but to everyone. Steve and Greg soon made many friends and loved where we lived. There were two outdoor swimming pools and tennis courts within the complex. All of us took advantage of them, and it gave John a chance to spend some quality time with the boys by teaching them to play tennis.

John had an older pool table that he had stored at a friend's house. We now had room for that and put it in the basement. That year for Christmas, we bought the boys a ping pong table top to set on the pool table. We had fun with tournaments. During that Christmas season, I baked all kinds of cookies. After the first few dozen, the boys wanted to help. I think every weekend in November and December we baked and decorated cookies, bars, and breads. We would sample some and then freeze the rest so that by Christmas Eve we counted forty-two dozen different kinds of cookies along with an array of bars and breads. It was a good bonding experience for me with the boys. They asked me about my Christmases past, and they shared stories of theirs. I was so inspired by our weekend baking get-togethers, I wrote a short story about it and sent it into the Christmas writing contest for *Woman's Day Magazine*. I won "honorable mention" and was sent a silver medal that I treasure to this day.

My life seemed to be going in the right direction. John and I were very happy. I invited LeeAnne over to spend the week-ends, and sometimes she did. LeeAnne was starting to slim down. She had often been harassed in school for being overweight, but now that she was in high school she was losing weight and didn't seem to want to spend much time with me. John told me he thought it was normal. She was now in high school and should be spending time with her friends; however, John suspected she had "help" with losing weight. He said marijuana usually made you hungry, so he was concerned she may be taking some kind of pills.

It was about this time that my mother, LeeAnne, and Veronica were constantly fighting. Veronica thought living across the hall from mother was no longer a good idea. Before I even knew about it, Veronica and her kids had moved to another apartment about ten miles from Mom. LeeAnne was unhappy that Mom never had money for her school things, yet there was always liquor and cigarettes for Mom. LeeAnne was getting my dad's social security, but as she was not yet eighteen, the checks went to Mom.

LeeAnne was getting rebellious. One day, Mom called me crying. She had walked into LeeAnne's room and there was a boy in bed with her. They were both naked. Mom also told me that LeeAnne smoked pot with Veronica and was getting way too wild. She couldn't handle her anymore. She wanted John and I to talk to LeeAnne. I didn't think that was such a good idea. I felt LeeAnne would be embarrassed if John spoke with her. Mom was crying so hysterically, we drove over to her apartment. It was obvious LeeAnne was embarrassed and had also been crying. John didn't want to get involved, so he simply told both of them that LeeAnne was a normal teenager. She should be careful as she didn't want to get a bad reputation in school or get pregnant. With tears streaming down LeeAnne's face, she just nodded and said, "I know." But I could hear the ache in her heart. Somehow, I felt responsible as I remembered what LeeAnne said to me the night before I was married. She thought I was deserting her. I felt awful. John tried again and again to convince me that LeeAnne was old enough to know better. She just made some bad choices, but she would get through it. I tried to call LeeAnne more often, but she usually wasn't there. Actually, I was surprised Mom cared so much until I found out later that Veronica and LeeAnne had talked Mom into signing over the social security payments to Veronica and that LeeAnne had moved in with Veronica. LeeAnne continued to live with Veronica, moving multiple times and going to different schools. Veronica was usually getting evicted for some reason or another, but she made sure LeeAnne went to school. Once LeeAnne graduated from high school, I saw her even less.

Not long after that, LeeAnne and Veronica, along with Veronica's children, moved up to Duluth. They always liked being "up north", and they somehow found out that our brother Bill was now living on the streets in Duluth.

It seemed like I had lost LeeAnne. Veronica occasionally called, especially when she was fed up with LeeAnne. I was filled with fear but felt hopeless to do anything once Veronica informed me that Bill and LeeAnne regularly sold their blood for drug money. I tried to reach out to LeeAnne, but she didn't seem to want anything to do with me. She had a boyfriend, and she soon even lost contact with Veronica.

Mom seemed worried about LeeAnne but said there was nothing she could do about it. Mom's coughing was getting worse. John and I would stop by her place on the weekends to visit, and she was either passed out on the couch in front of the television or just about ready to go to sleep in the middle of the afternoon. We invited her over on a few weekends, but it felt like we were constantly babysitting. Steve and Greg had both joined the service after high school. Steve joined the Marines and Greg joined the Army, so we had extra room for Mom to spend the night. She fell asleep one night while smoking. Luckily, I had gone downstairs to check on her and caught the smoldering cigarette butt right before it hit the sheets. An angel was watching over us then. Mom would also be up extremely early in the mornings. John and I laid in bed early one Sunday morning listening to her open and close every cupboard. John said she was probably looking for booze to put in her coffee. After working full time at stressful jobs, both John and I decided it wasn't in our best interests for her to spend the weekends, and she wasn't happy either as you could just tell she was itching to have her whiskey.

One Monday morning at work I received an emergency phone call from someone at my mother's work. They told me she was taken away by ambulance and was at Hennepin County General Hospital. John and I left work immediately. Mom had suffered a seizure. The doctor explained that it was caused from sudden alcohol withdrawal. If an alcoholic is at this point and ceases their intake or stops cold turkey, the body goes into shock causing a seizure. Mom had just been at our house for the weekend, so of course I felt guilty. I could have let her drink more.

My siblings all knew Mom had been at the hospital. Once she was released, we all took turns stopping by the house and spending time with her. That changed when brother Curt entered the picture once again. Curt decided he would move in with mother and help her. We told Mom she certainly did not need that kind of help and begged her not to let him do this. Of course, she was all for Curt moving in. She said he could take care of her, but I knew she would just be getting a drinking partner. It was useless to persuade her otherwise. At first it seemed to be going well. Mom returned to work. We would still stop by her house on the weekends. Soon it seemed like Mom slept a lot more. The problem was that Curt had been arranging poker parties at the house until all hours of the morning with lots of drinking and drugs. Who knows what he had been feeding my mother? I contacted Veronica in Duluth. She said she would come down and stay with Mom for a while, and maybe Curt would leave. I didn't like that scenario either.

Surprisingly, Curt and Veronica seemed to get along again. Curt stayed at a friend's house for about a week while Veronica tried to nurse Mom.

At Mom's work, another seizure occurred and another trip by ambulance. This time it seemed much worse. Tests showed Mom's liver was badly infected. Mom was afraid. It seemed like Kimberly and I were the only ones who made time to stay with her for very long, and we were the only two with full time jobs.

I had a problem with one of the doctors. He was young and had an athletic build, so you know he exercised and lived a healthy lifestyle. He was so mean to Mom. He yelled at her for destroying her body with alcohol. I asked him to come out to the hall with me.

I told him, "I know my mother is an alcoholic. Why do you have to be so mean to her?"

He said, "It makes me so mad to see people ruin their bodies like this."

"But you are a doctor and have no idea what kind of life that woman has lead and what hardships she has had to live through. Can't you have some compassion?"

He replied, "I'm sorry, but that is the way I feel. I am sure she has cirrhosis of the liver, but I am running some more tests and will be back tomorrow."

What an ass, I thought. I went back into the room, and Mom was laying there. I was sure she heard our conversation.

The next day I was there again when this jerk of a doctor came in. He told us that he needed to perform a biopsy of Mom's liver. Tests had shown serious readings not only involving the liver but other areas. The biopsy was done right in the hospital room. I held Mom's hand while a large needle was inserted into her back. To get at the liver, the doctor had to push the needle in deeply, and when he did, it was like a huge jolt that nearly moved Mom off the bed. I knew it had to hurt as she cried and screamed in pain.

Next, this doctor put his hand on Mom's shoulder and said, "I am so sorry, Betty Lou, I know that had to hurt. Unfortunately, it is the only way I could get a good biopsy. I believe now that you are very sick and it is something that was no fault of your own. I should have the results in a few days." Mom just nodded. The doctor motioned for me to come out into the hall. He informed me that it was most likely liver cancer, but they were unsure if it started in the liver or metastasized from another source. He said once she was diagnosed she would need to have someone live with her.

The only siblings that would live with her were Veronica and Curt. At this point, this would not be a good idea for anyone as Veronica seemed to be getting closer to Curt. Mom said she wanted to live with me and John.

As I sat with her one afternoon in the hospital after she had been given the diagnosis of liver cancer, she seemed in deep thought. The doctor said an oncologist would be in contact to discuss any possible treatment, but Mom's liver was beyond repair. The outlook was bleak. Mom asked me to contact her minister, the one that married me. Then she said, "Patty, I like it when you are with me. You are quiet, and it is peaceful to be with you. The others all talk loud and about their own lives. I know that I never treated you fairly. I know you thought I always did more and gave more to the others; but you didn't need it. They always needed more but I knew you would always survive."

I got teary-eyed and wished she could have told me this years ago when I felt such hate toward her. I then told her not to worry. I would speak to John to see what arrangements could be made to have her move in with us.

She seemed so happy then. She told all my siblings that she was going to move in with me. All of them except Bill. He was back in Minneapolis and had been arrested for solicitation and drug use. He was in the Hennepin County Detox Center.

LeeAnne had recently married her boyfriend and moved to Chicago. No one even knew she was married until after as they went to City Hall. Veronica called her from time to time updating her on Mom's condition. Veronica told me LeeAnne and her husband lived in a trailer house in a not so good part of Chicago. They were in a motorcycle group and were heavily into cocaine.

Now I had to face the reality that Mom believed she was moving in with me. I told her I would speak with John about it but never said it was a sure thing. I wondered where her boss was during all this. After all, they had been having an affair for about twenty years. If they were truly in love, shouldn't he step up to the plate and help?

I told John about the conversation and how Mom told everyone she was going to be living with us. He was not happy. He had visions of her burning down our place and all my siblings hanging out at our house. John and I started looking at places that could take Mom — not nursing homes, but places that could provide her with the treatment she would need. She had good health insurance. We found a place called "Bridging" over by the University of Minnesota. They needed Mom to turn over all her assets to them. Mom had given John and I her Power of Attorney. Mom had nothing — a few small life insurance policies but nothing more. We would have to be responsible for costs not covered by the insurance. The next day John and I went to the hospital to tell Mom about the nice place we had found for her.

She said, "I thought I was going to live with you."

John explained to her that we both worked full time and couldn't give her the care she needed. This place was clean and had nurses full time.

Mom just glared at me and said, "Sorry I'm such a burden to you."

I pleaded with her not to feel that way. I told her we were doing what was best for her.

She simply said, "Please leave, I don't want to be a burden to my family." She closed her eyes and wouldn't speak to us. I thought in time she would get over it, but those were the last words she ever spoke to us.

Within a few days, the hospital called and asked us to contact everyone in the family as Mom was failing. We had to pick up Kimberly and get gas in our car, so by the time we made it to the hospital, Mom had just died. Only my brother Richard was there when she passed. He stood over her with tears in his eyes. Then he looked up at me and gave me this horrible look of hate. He said, "Maybe she would be alive if you would have kept your word and let her move in with you."

I was shocked. We all stood there with our mouths open. Richard walked out of the room. John went after him. I know John said something to him because after a few days Richard seemed civil to me. He never apologized but treated me no differently than when Mom was alive.

I had called LeeAnne as soon as the hospital asked me to contact the family. I tried to contact her the next morning, but she was already on a flight from Chicago to Minneapolis. John and I picked her up at the airport. We stopped for lunch and told her Mom had died. It was tough. LeeAnne took it hard. She stayed for the funeral but then left right after. She didn't have much to say to anyone.

Bill never made it to the funeral as he could not be released from Detox. He called all of us and sobbed about what a screw up he was that he couldn't even attend his own mother's funeral.

My sister, Veronica, also did not attend the funeral. Veronica could never handle death and funerals — even more since she had witnessed Dad's body at the hospital. She could not stand to see anyone in a coffin.

The service was held in the chapel of the funeral home. Mother's minister gave the service. He had visited her in the hospital several times. At one point, he said he asked Mom what she kept thinking now that she was terminally ill. She replied, "I just keep reciting 'The Lord is my Shepherd'."

Kimberly pointed out to me an elderly lady sitting at the funeral. She had white hair and was dressed all in black. She had an old fashioned black box hat with lace that hung down over her eyes. She wore black gloves. She seemed to be from another time long ago.

"My God," Kimberly said. "I think that is one of mother's relatives, but I thought she died."

I didn't recognize the woman because I had not known any of Mom's relatives. Kimberly said we would approach her after the prayer service. She thought she recognized a younger version of her from some old photographs.

Once the service was over we wanted to find out who this woman was before we headed to the cemetery. We turned around, and she was gone! We went out to the hallway and searched the bathroom but couldn't find her. We asked the funeral director if he had seen this elderly woman. He said, "Yes, she had a driver and left just before the service ended." We looked at the guest register but she had never signed in. We never found out who she was, but Kimberly was sure it was a relative and possibly a ghost.

After the burial and luncheon, John and I took Kimberly home. We all decided to stop at Mom's apartment to be sure all was OK. We were very surprised to see Veronica there sitting in Mom's rocking chair. She had been going through some of Mom's things that she wanted. She said Curt was just there, took something, and left. We wondered why Curt did not stay for the luncheon. We had no idea what Curt had taken until a few weeks later. John was trying to balance Mom's checkbook and resolve her bills. After talking with the bank, he found out Mom now had a negative balance in her checking account. Checks were written after Mom had died. Most of the checks were written at a liquor store that Curt usually went to. Eventually we discovered an entire box of checks were taken. John closed Mom's account and called the liquor store telling them what had transpired.

We didn't see or hear from Curt until almost a year later at another family funeral.

Chapter Eighteen

Mom had left a small insurance policy. After paying for her funeral, each one of us seven children would receive $3,000. The exception to that was LeeAnne. In addition to the $3,000, there was another insurance policy just under $10,000 that she was listed on as the sole beneficiary.

I had to have contact with Mom's boss to settle these matters. It was uncomfortable, but John talked to me and helped me realize it was between Mom and her boss. The wisest thing to do was just accept it and move on. After all, Mom was gone, and Ray, Mom's boss, was not a happy person. The times I met with Ray usually ended in tears — his tears. I think he really loved my mother. His life now was miserable, but it had been their choice. I was surprised by the additional insurance policy for LeeAnne. Ray was evasive toward any questions I asked. He was mainly concerned about LeeAnne's welfare. This added more skepticism for me as to LeeAnne's parentage. Years ago, Veronica told me that Ray was LeeAnne's biological father. Mom was working for him before she got pregnant. I had always dismissed this notion. None of us knew for sure, including LeeAnne. At this point in our lives, I don't think it mattered. LeeAnne would always be my little sister. She certainly resembles my dad's side of the family, and what difference does it make now?

The additional money was forwarded to LeeAnne in Chicago. She said it was used toward her mortgage on the trailer home. I didn't care. It was her money.

The only major problem we had regarding life insurance payments was with Bill. Once Bill got out of Detox, he called me and all the other siblings constantly wondering where his money was. He was making daily walks to Mom's office demanding his money. Ray called me often explaining that he didn't want to have Bill arrested, but he was causing a ruckus with his yelling and drunken, disorderly conduct.

A few days after the funds had been disbursed, Kimberly received a collect phone call from Las Vegas. It was Bill. He had taken the money and flown to Las Vegas. He lost all his money, and claimed he didn't have any money to get back to Minnesota. We thought this was weird as you usually buy a round-trip ticket. Kimberly explained that none of us could help him. Eventually Bill came home and was again down at Mom's work accusing them of withholding money from him as he was sure there should have been more. Ray had no choice but to call the police.

It took about six months after Mom's death for Bill to realize there was no more money. I met with an attorney where I worked. I explained the entire situation of Mom's bills, negative account balance, and Curt stealing and cashing her checks. We had already closed Mom's account, so Curt could not write anymore checks. The attorney understood why I would not press charges. He told me that none of us were responsible for Mom's debts. He helped me transcribe a letter to all her debtors explaining there were no funds available for payment. I sent letters to all the debtors along with a copy of her death certificate. We never heard again from any of them.

My brothers and sisters seemed to keep to themselves. I could now concentrate more on my life. John and I worked at the same building for Cargill in downtown Minneapolis. After work one day, we were standing on the corner on our way to the parking lot. The light was red, so we waited with a throng of people all just leaving work. Suddenly, someone bumped into me. I don't even think he realized it as he seemed so out of it. He wore a bright, wildly flowered shirt and was stumbling all over People were staring at him and either laughing or shaking their heads. Once I saw his face, I realized it was my brother Bill. John recognized him too. John put his arm around me and told me not to confront him. We watched him as he stumbled into the IDS Center. At that time, the IDS Center was frequently known as a hangout place for drug addicts and gays. I again thought of Bill's sad life. He had been such a handsome, popular guy in school. His life had taken such a turn. I don't think he even knew what reality was anymore.

Mom had died in April. It was autumn when Bill bumped into me not realizing who I was. We didn't have any contact with him over the winter holidays.

Next year, Easter was early. Although it was celebrated in March, the weather was remarkably warm with no snow remaining on the ground. Every Easter as far back as I can remember, my uncle on my dad's side had all of us over for Easter dinner. This would be the first year that both of our parents were gone. Before we sat down at the table for Easter dinner, my aunt told us that Bill had called her wondering if he could come over for dinner. Of course, she told him he could, but not to bring any of his "street friends". We had just finished eating when we heard the sound of a motorcycle. Bill got off the back of the motorcycle, and the driver took off. Apparently, he had hitched a ride. I had never seen Bill so skinny! He looked like a skeleton. You could smell his bad body odor as soon as he approached. His clothes were ragged and dirty. He wore only a dirty tee shirt and jeans that were torn and smelled like he had urinated in them. No one wanted to be around him. He asked if he could use the bathroom. While he was in there, we decided the weather was so nice we would all sit outside on the deck. I don't think my aunt wanted Bill to sit on her furniture. When Bill got out of the bathroom, my aunt helped him make a plate of food. She carried it outside for him. He ate like he was starving. While he inhaled the food, many of us noticed his scarred and bruised arms. They were so thin, but his veins seemed to protrude out. His veins looked almost blemished through his skin. They were light purple and even yellow in color. He had bumps around his veins that appeared to be black.

Kimberly, being the oldest and most outspoken asked him, "What the hell is wrong with your arms?"

He laughed and said his arms were just about used up. Then he pulled up the legs of his dirty jeans and showed us similar markings.

"Why do you do this to your body?" Kimberly yelled at him.

Bill laughed again and said, "To get that feeling — that high. Have you ever tried it? You would love it!"

No one said a word. I was getting sick to my stomach from the smell and looks of my brother. John and I went for a walk to get away. Eventually my brother Richard persuaded Bill to get into his car so he could take him wherever. Bill wanted to go downtown somewhere on Hennepin Avenue. Once they left, my aunt apologized for inviting him. She had gone into the bathroom, and Bill had missed the toilet and urinated all over her wall.

Richard said before they reached Hennepin Avenue, Bill was begging him for money as he needed a fix. He told Richard he would do anything for a fix. If he didn't get the money from Richard, he would have to trade sex for heroine. He told Richard he was tired of selling his body for a fix to anyone, mostly men. After he said that, Richard told him he was taking him back to Detox to get some help. As soon as they approached a stop light, Bill jumped out of the car, and Richard watched him run down an alley.

A few weeks later, we had gotten a late snowstorm, so the weather was frigid compared to Easter Sunday. Kimberly called me in the middle of the night. I knew it had to be bad news. She told me Bill had been visiting his ex-wife and kids. He left depressed. He walked along Highway 55 with the busy traffic racing by. Instead of crossing the street, he climbed upon a snow mound on 55 and Douglas Drive. He then jumped in front of a passing car. He died on contact.

Veronica and LeeAnne were the closest to Bill. Bill had often called Kimberly too for help. Our family had been through a lot, especially with Mom dying less than a year before Bill's death. In fact, Bill's death was only a few days short of a year after Mom's death. A few days before Bill's death, Veronica received a phone call from Bill. She said that Bill had called Kimberly wanting to talk. Bill said when he called Kimberly she said "You're drunk", and hung up. He then called Veronica. He was sobbing. Veronica told us after his death that Bill had been inconsolable during that phone call. It came out that a few days back he and two of his street buddies went after another street person that had a bottle of whiskey. He wouldn't share it so the three of them started beating on him. They got the bottle and ran after they heard police sirens. The next day, Bill had somewhat sobered up and felt bad. He went to find the man to apologize for his part in the beating. Bill was told the man was dead. He had been beaten to death. Bill told Veronica he couldn't live with himself after what he had done. He just wanted to talk to family members to confess what he had done but was now distraught because Kimberly hung up on him. For that, Veronica blamed Kimberly for Bill's death. So now I was still blamed for Mom's death, and Kimberly was blamed for Bill's death. But none of these people were around when financial support was needed. Bill had nothing. There was no insurance. Kimberly, Richard, John, and I went to the funeral

134

home to make the arrangements. LeeAnne was in Chicago, and Veronica could not handle going to a funeral home. There weren't many options for my brother. He could be given a "county funeral" as many street people were given. He would be buried in a "paupers field". If absolutely no funds were available for a casket, a coffin-sized wooden box would be provided. That is the first time I found out that people could actually be buried like that. It was literally a hardened cardboard box with a lid, a bigger size of what you can get at a grocery store. You could use this for burial in a pauper's field, but a cemetery would not allow it. Bill was still our brother, and we could not handle him being buried like that. We wanted him to receive some dignity for his dark, despondent life. The four of us pitched in and purchased a casket. I remember coming home from the funeral home that night. We got home in time for the six o'clock news. The story leading the news was my brother's death. As the television screen displayed my brother, covered with a tarp, lying dead on highway 55, I finally broke down and wept for his poor, sick life. I prayed his soul would finally find some peace. The news anchor said they did not expect any charges would be made against the driver as the victim had been under the influence and had purposely jumped in front of the moving vehicle.

Kimberly and Veronica found a small cemetery in North Minneapolis that wasn't expensive. Bill would not have a headstone until years later when Veronica arranged for it. The headstone would not have his last name on it. It would be marked only by his birth name "Billy Joe" with the quote, "Free at Last, Free at Last, Thank God I am Free at Last." Bill was only 33 years old when he died.

Bill's funeral was held at the funeral home and was uncomfortable to say the least. Mostly street people showed up in their unkempt ways but their obvious love for my brother. It made me realize how many homeless and troubled people are suffering on our streets.

Curt made an appearance at the funeral, but he did not sit in the pew with us. Veronica was not present. Curt seemed nervous. He stayed in the back and was pacing. Once the service was over and people would leave to go to the graveside, Curt approached my husband, John.

Curt said, "I really like you, John. You are a decent person, so I am going to tell you not to go to the graveside and not to let Patty go as there is going to be trouble."

John didn't know what to say, but he did know my fear of Curt. Just then, Veronica appeared carrying a large black garbage bag. Everyone was gathered in the back getting directions for the gravesite when she arrived. She immediately yelled for Kimberly. Kimberly came forward, and Veronica screamed at her in front of everyone. Veronica told her that because she had hung up on Bill, it made him go over the edge and kill himself. She wanted Kimberly to remember forever what she had done, so she was giving her everything Bill owned. She then hurled the bag of Bill's possessions at her and said,

"That's it, Kimberly. That's all he had in this world, and you didn't have time for a phone conversation with him."

I felt bad for Kimberly as I don't think any of us could have helped Bill. John told Kimberly about Curt's comments, and we would not be going to the gravesite. Kimberly has always been a strong person. She did go to the gravesite and nothing happened. John and I stopped at a bar and had a drink to help calm our nerves, not believing what we had just witnessed.

Chapter Nineteen

LeeAnne and her husband left the day after Bill's funeral. They went back to Chicago. They didn't say goodbye.

Richard's wife, Rose, decided the driver of the vehicle that hit my brother Bill should be sued. I couldn't believe it. She convinced Richard and tried to convince all of us that a person was supposed to be in complete control of their vehicle, no matter what. I argued that it wasn't the driver's fault, and he had suffered enough. The police told us the driver had just come back from proposing to his girlfriend and was happy. He didn't have any record and was a decent person. On that winter night, Bill jumped out of nowhere and landed on the hood of his car. The driver could not get the images out of his mind. When describing it to the police officer, he had broken down saying he couldn't stop seeing Bill's smashed face as he spread out on the windshield before losing his life. That would always remain with him. It would always be the day he proposed. I felt sorry for the driver, and now we had Rose who was just money-hungry trying to cause more conflict. Richard and Rose did get an attorney and had papers drawn up requesting all the remaining siblings sign them. After discussing this with John, I refused to sign the papers as did Kimberly, Veronica, and LeeAnne. Richard's wife was causing so much turmoil in our lives. Rose insisted the lawyer told her that any compensation collected would not reflect negatively on the driver. That's what insurance was for. If we didn't want any money from this lawsuit, we could give our share to Bill's children. After months of arguing and just getting worn down, we all signed it with the stipulation if any funds were to be awarded, they should go to Bill's children. I think that was the final chapter for LeeAnne to have any association with the family. She was angry and completely lost contact with all of us.

I tried to contact LeeAnne many times but could never get a response. Holidays and birthdays came and went with no contact from LeeAnne. After a year or so, her phone was disconnected. I thought maybe Veronica would have had some contact with her. She claimed she did not. She also told me that LeeAnne was deep into drugs. I asked her how she knew if she did not have contact with her. All she said was that she knew our little sister. I continued to send cards to LeeAnne and after a few years they came back, "return to sender".

One weekend John and I visited friends in Chicago. I had LeeAnne's last known address, so John and I went to find her. I figured if I came unannounced, she would not have an opportunity to ignore me. We found the trailer court where she lived. It was not as bad as I had imagined. We rang the bell and knocked on the door, but no one answered. John thought he heard someone inside, but there were no lights on. It was pouring rain, so we sat in the car waiting to see if anyone would make an appearance. John was losing patience with me.

He said, "Patty, she doesn't want anything to do with you. You need to let it go and accept that."

I cried, "She's my baby sister. I think she's in trouble, and I want to help her."

"She is a married woman, and we have no idea of her lifestyle. Let's go. You tried your best. It's now up to her," John pleaded with me.

It was raining hard, but we had come so far. I told John I wanted to write her a note, and then we could leave. As I sat in the car, my emotions took over. I wrote a two-page letter imploring LeeAnne to contact me. I wrote how we all make mistakes in our lives, and it was OK. We had been through so much, and she would always be my little sister. I left the letter in the mailbox by her front door. I never received a response. I tried to move on. I was happily married, and I didn't want to ruin that.

John and I continued working in different departments at Cargill. We saved money and finally had enough for a down payment on a house. Neither one of us had ever owned a home. We were so excited that once the house building started, we would stop by every night on our way home from work. We took pictures of each day's progress even when you couldn't tell if anything had changed.

Once we moved into our new home, John became a fanatic about our yard. We paid several thousand dollars to have it professionally landscaped. It was beautiful, and John read up on every way to have spectacular grass. We had a large ground-level deck built with a matching pergola. The landscapers left an area in the middle of the backyard where we could plant a small garden. After several

140

unsuccessful attempts at both vegetable and flowers, we decided to fill the space with a rose garden. We placed a fountain in the center and planted different colored roses all around. It was breathtaking, and every autumn John would insist on digging trenches and burying those rose bushes. Our neighbors often said our backyard should be featured in *Better Homes and Gardens*. Our backyard gave us peace and much pride.

In earlier years, we had the typical teenage issues with the boys, but they were great kids and turned out to be respectful adults.

Greg, the younger one, married first. He married his high school sweetheart, Rhonda, during a leave from the service. They were stationed in Louisiana. After a year, Greg was deployed to Germany. They had just had a baby, Joseph. Little Joe and Rhonda lived with John and I for nine months before they joined Greg in Germany. Having a baby in our house was so different but loving. Once in Germany, Rhonda gave birth to another son, Bradley. We didn't meet Bradley until he was a toddler when they moved back to the USA. Greg and his family would then be stationed at Fort Leonard Wood, Missouri. They seemed happy, but being away from family and with the strain of moving every few years, the military life took its toll. Greg and Rhonda divorced.

Steven seemed to have a commitment problem. Most things he started, he didn't finish. In high school, he had only a few months left and suddenly just quit. John tried to get him to finish school, but Steven was stubborn. John sat down with him and, in tears,

141

John begged him. John pleaded with him, saying "Son, I have given you eighteen years of my life. Please, all I am asking is for you to give me two months of yours and get your diploma." Steve shed tears then and agreed.

After high school, Steve joined the marines. Again, after he had only a few months left of his military stint, he went AWOL. We didn't know. He came home telling us he had an early discharge. He lived with us and worked at a local restaurant. One night the police were checking license plates after hours at the restaurant parking lot. When they ran Steve's plate, they found a warrant for desertion. He was arrested and sent to the brig in California. He was court marshaled. Steve had a problem with the service, saying they played mind games. He had served almost all his term but was now making this claim. John intervened requesting the service send Steve for psychological testing. After a few months, Steve was freed, released with a discharge that read, "For the good of the service." He had served almost four years but could never utilize the benefits of the service because he could not complete those last few months. Steve eventually married his friend's ex-wife, Peggy. Steve never had children of his own, but together they raised Peggy's two daughters. They are still married today and have two granddaughters they adore. Steve has been a chef at different places for many years. He is an excellent cook but has medical issues. It has been difficult for him to keep a job for any extended period of time.

142

Both John and I had patience for only so long. John's family felt Steven's issues resulted from his mother leaving them. John insisted that everyone has issues, and the boys were raised to be self-sufficient. John never wanted the boys coddled. This caused strong differences of opinion not only between John and Steve, but also between John and his family. Regardless of these differences, John always had great love for his children and family.

I wish, however, my family only had such issues. Besides LeeAnne, Veronica had distanced herself from the family. Kimberly and I had no contact with either of them. My brother Richard saw them occasionally and claimed Curt, Curt's ex-wife, and Veronica were all living together with their kids. They were all into drugs. Veronica's son, Michael, was now living with his father. Veronica still doted on Patsy, giving her anything she wanted.

Richard was also having problems with his second wife, Rose. They seemed to be doing so well after they both met at AA. Now after having two children of their own plus Rose's son, Chad, from her first marriage, Rose was hitting the bottle once again. One night while Richard was working the night shift, I received a call from Rose's son. He was crying and asked if I could come out and pick them up. They were at a gas station, and Rose had no idea where they were. She was now asleep in her car, and the gas station attendant told them if someone didn't pick them up in a few minutes, he would call the cops. I spoke to the attendant, got the address, and told him we would be right down. When we got there, we could not believe how

43

drunk Rose was. She reeked of alcohol and so did the car. Chad, who was about twelve years old, was obviously embarrassed. The two smaller boys were terrified and crying. They were only about six and eight years old. John drove Rose and the kid's home in her car, and I followed in mine to take John home. When John started Rose's car, an open bottle of liquor rolled out from under the driver's seat. He threw the bottle away. Once we arrived at their house, we didn't want to leave the kids alone as Rose was passed out. We had to call my brother at work. My brother Richard loved this woman. He always protected her. He came home and thanked us. You could tell how embarrassed he was.

A few weeks later, the family was again the story of the day on the television. The local news channel reported that Rose had been stopped on Highway 694 after hitting the median. She was drunk, and the two younger children were in the back seat petrified and screaming. Rose had told her children she was going to take them to meet their maker. She was trying to kill them and herself. She was taken into custody. Richard was heartbroken. Rose was sentenced to in-house rehabilitation for several months. Richard loved his children so much. Still, he stood by and supported his wife. Rose's son, Chad, was removed from the home and sent to live with his father. Richard had to jump through hoops to convince the authorities that he would not leave his children alone or with Rose once she was released. He changed his hours at work. Richard got so involved with his children. He got the boys involved in hockey. He spent every available hour he had trying to piece his family back together. Those two boys grew to think Richard walked on water. He never missed a game and often would be at their practice games. Whatever the kids needed for hockey or anything at all, Richard would provide. Richard and Rose's relationship was strained, but they tried again.

After Rose seemed stable enough, she started a new job at an incentive company. It was the type of company that offered employers an array of gifts for their employees to honor them for years of service. I was with girlfriends at a Cargill get-together one night. There were current employees and some previous ones. Jeanette was a gal who worked at Cargill for several years before she left to start her own company with her husband. She knew me when I was single and now married. After a few cocktails, she approached me to tell me what a wonderful man my brother, Richard, was. I asked her how she knew my brother. She told me she hired his wife at her new company. She recognized the last name as being my maiden name.

She then preceded to say, "Most women would love to have a husband like Richard. How he stood up for Rose is unbelievable! You know about it, don't you?"

I didn't but I pretended like I did, "Yes, he really loves her, and she has put him through the wringer."

She continued by saying, "I hope they understand that even though the money was paid back, I couldn't have Rose continue to work for me."

I told her they understood completely. I still had no idea what she was talking about. She then continued. I think the cocktails helped. "I adored Rose. I trusted her so much. One week after I hired her, she did such a good job that I promoted her to my office manager. I didn't mind when the long lunches started, but how could she steal all that money from me?"

I gave in. I told Jeanette I wasn't privy to all the details. She filled me in. Being the office manager of a very small company, Rose was in charge of preparing payroll checks. There were only a few employees, so the checks were simply typed by Rose and signed by Jeanette. It took a few weeks for her to notice that Rose's checks were a few thousand dollars more than they should be. How could that be? Turned out Rose would prepare the checks correctly, have Jeanette sign them, and then Rose would insert her check back into the typewriter, line it up, and add a one or two in front of her earned salary. Jeanette was more hurt than anything. After all, when she first smelled liquor on Rose's breath after one of her long lunches, she only gave her a warning. On the morning Jeanette was going to confront Rose, she couldn't find her. Rose was late, again. After an hour, she called the house. Richard told Jeanette Rose had left on time. He was worried. Jeanette told him about the checks and that she intended to confront Rose that morning. She wanted to hear Rose's story before she called the police to press charges. Richard asked her if she would wait until he got there. Richard found Rose in a bar a block away from her workplace. It was only 10:00 in the morning, and she was drunk.

He called Jeanette and said he would pay back every cent if she wouldn't press charges. He said Rose needed treatment, not jail.

Jeanette told me Richard would come in each week to pay her money against what Rose had taken. She said Richard looked so worn as he was working double-shifts to pay back Rose's crime so she wouldn't be charged. He paid back every cent. Jeanette said, "Now that has to be true love."

The story didn't stop there. Rose was in rehab again, but within that year, she became pregnant with another man's child. Heartbroken, Richard divorced her. Rose gave birth to a girl. Her relationship with the child's father did not last. Within a few years, Rose, along with her daughter, was living in the same house again with Richard and the boys.

Chapter Twenty

It had now been about eight years since anyone had heard from LeeAnne. Kimberly and I also did not have any contact with Veronica or Curt. Someone at work suggested I contact the Red Cross to look for LeeAnne. I was told they not only look for soldiers but also anyone missing. I had a long conversation with the Red Cross giving them details about LeeAnne. They advised me that it sounded like she did not want to be found, but they would make an effort to locate her. After several months, the Red Cross contacted me saying they did not have any leads. I was sinking into depression.

John, who wanted me to stop worrying about LeeAnne, was now concerned. He thought by now LeeAnne would have made some contact. It was hopeless. There was nothing anyone could do. It was about this time I received an invitation in the mail from Veronica. She was inviting me to Patsy's high school graduation. I couldn't believe Patsy was already graduating. She was named after me, and I more or less missed most of her childhood.

John said, "Maybe it's time, Patty. I think we should go."

"What if Curt is there?" I was still terrified of him. I think my life from the time I was five up to this point had always been filled with some sort of fear. I felt cheated out of a childhood. Maybe John was right. Maybe I needed to face the obstacles that filled me with fear. I was so thankful John was in my life. He truly had shown me over the years what love was and what being a family really meant. We decided to go. Kimberly had also gotten an invitation but didn't go.

I was nervous and shaky as we approached the house where the graduation party was being held. John held my hand as we walked to the front door. Curt was standing outside. As we neared, he smiled and said he was happy to see us. He looked the same and seemed sober. While John chatted for a while with Curt, I entered the house. Veronica greeted me. She seemed so happy to see me. She hugged me. Then I saw Patsy who had grown so much since I had last seen her. She was beautiful and was a finalist for Miss Northeast Minneapolis. After some awkwardness seemed to wane, Veronica asked if she could talk to me privately. John was still outside with Curt. Veronica and I went to the only private place, the bathroom.

Veronica told me how sorry she was for every bad thing she had done to me. She started to cry. She wanted to explain to me how she blamed her unhappiness on me for so many years. She now knew it was wrong. Veronica described watching me always trying to please Dad and how unfair it was to me when I started dating. She realized how much more difficult it must have been for me when it was finally my turn to break away. Veronica told me she loved me and wanted to start over. We hugged. I asked her about her relationship with Curt and how she could have anything to do with him after he tried to rape her. She said she had forgiven him as he was drunk, and it wasn't him. He was trying very hard now to remain sober. I told her I would have a difficult time ever trusting him again. I reminded her how he cashed Mom's checks after she was dead. She told me about other horrifying things that Curt had done in the last several years. After Mom's death, Curt befriended a much older woman. In fact, she was as old as Mom and looked like Mom. He played her too. She was an alcoholic and a widow. Curt took her for all her money. Veronica could never get over Curt sleeping with this woman as she was the spitting image and age of Mom. Now Curt was supposedly "trying", but I didn't buy it. Veronica told me she was done getting involved in any drug situations. She just wanted peace and happiness for her daughter. I asked her about her son Michael. She shrugged and said he was with his father.

What really surprised me next was Veronica told me she occasionally was in contact with LeeAnne. I broke down. The last eight years were torture for me wondering if LeeAnne was dead or alive. If it wasn't for John, I might have gone over the deep end. Apparently, LeeAnne was in Chicago, where she always was. I didn't understand. Veronica said LeeAnne did not want me to know this side of her. She was promiscuous and into cocaine. Together we cried and cursed our screwed-up lives and family until someone knocked on the door to use the bathroom.

Veronica and I kept in touch but at a distance. I was drained after that meeting — thankful that I had gone, but bitter, hurt, and angry LeeAnne had put me through all those years of worry and despair. Knowing this, it was easier for me to concentrate on my own life. I decided not to pursue her any longer. If she ever had any love for me, she would contact me eventually.

I now also threw myself into my work, like John. At Cargill I started at an entry level position but had successfully worked myself up to a salaried position as a contract administrator. I was given great opportunities and training. Most people with a similar job had a college education. I was promoted to work in the International Division and excelled working with banks on Letters of Credit. I handled documents with many countries and met many people of different nationalities. I had the opportunity to travel to many countries in Asia.

I remember one banking seminar I attended in downtown Minneapolis. I was an active participant. When the class took a break, a man from the class came up to me and asked what school I had graduated from. When I told him Edison High School, he laughed and said, "No, what college did you go to?"

Meekly, I informed him that I never did go to college. He couldn't believe it. He said, "You are so good at this stuff. You are intelligent and not afraid to speak up. Just think what you could have accomplished if you would have gone to college?"

Hmmm...a compliment? A slap in the face? I wasn't sure. I decided to take it as a compliment, although, in the back of my mind, I thought again, "If I had only been given the opportunity." Then again, I may not have met John. We had a great life, now able to afford things I had only dreamed of. Twice we went to Hawaii. We both had new cars, and our house was almost paid for. I had thrown a 50th birthday party for John, inviting all his relatives. I was tired of people usually getting together only at weddings and funerals. I treated this birthday party like a wedding. I sent out engraved invitations, hired a 50's band, and invited friends and relatives from all over the country. So many people came. It was wonderful! I think we had 26 people staying at our house. John's family from Missouri, Chicago, and Arkansas came for the celebration. People slept on the floor, on blown up mattresses, couches, and chairs, and it was the best time ever. Most people stayed for almost a week. Sometimes we stayed up all night talking. John loved cooking for everyone.

The day of the party, my friend and next door neighbor, Mary Beth, along with Kimberly and I went to the Medina Ballroom where the party was to be held that night. We decorated tables in pink and black. Fresh flowers adorned the tables along with placemats I made listing all the top 10 Rock 'n Roll hits for each year of the 1950's. Everything was going smoothly and John's family and friends were having a wonderful time. They all thanked me for arranging such a celebration. I didn't know that things could ever go so well. I felt so good about what I had done, I broke down crying. Mary Beth and Kimberly asked what was wrong. I told them, "I'm just so happy. I'm waiting for something to go wrong, but I don't think it will. Everything is perfect."

It was perfect. Although the party wasn't a surprise party, I did surprise John with a limo for the night. That was in 1987. We all had a great time, and it is still talked about today.

I could count on one hand the number of disagreements John and I ever had. We knew each other's thoughts and could even finish each other's sentences. Kind of scary. We decided to go back to church. Maybe because we were getting older and thinking about mortality. I never thought John would return after the Catholic Church refused to marry us, but times were changing. I thought it would be nice for us to renew our vows and have a marriage ceremony in the Catholic Church. We discussed it with the priest. He requested we attend classes the church offered for people returning to the church after being absent for years or if they were converting to Catholicism. After several classes, John would then need to request a church annulment from his first marriage. If that was granted, only then could we be married in the Catholic church.

We had a problem with that because John had two grown sons from his first marriage. How and why should that be annulled? Again, I think John did this for me. It's sad how political games are played, even in the Catholic church. We had to pay $350 up front to the Canon attorneys at the St. Paul Archdiocese. If the annulment was granted, another $350 would need to be paid. Then, John needed to be interviewed at the Archdiocese by a panel of Canon lawyers. After the first $350 was paid, John met with the lawyers. The main questions they needed answered were:

Were you in love with your first wife when you wed?

At the time you were married, did you commit to and expect the relationship to be a life-long commitment?

Were both of you Catholic, and if so, were you married in the church?

If you were married in the church, may we contact your ex-wife?

John's response to these questions were:

Of course, I loved her when we exchanged our vows.

Yes, the union was expected to be a lifetime commitment. After all, didn't everyone expect that when they were married?

Yes, they had been married in the Catholic Church, and if they could find his ex-wife, they could contact her.

John explained in detail how his ex-wife deserted the family, committed adultery more than once, and did not have any contact with the children. He further explained he had taken her back after the first time. He had suggested marriage counseling and therapy. They went to a few sessions of marriage counseling. She decided to go to therapy on her own and then had an affair with her psychiatrist. The last time she left, the boys were home alone. She left a note about her feelings of hatred. It had been so long since she had any contact with them that the divorce had been granted on desertion, and no one knew where she was. John never pursued any child support as he cared more that his children were raised in a positive environment.

The Canon lawyers told John he would receive a decision in the mail. It would take about six weeks. We spoke with our priest and he didn't seem to be very positive on what the decision would be.

After a month, John received the letter from the Archdiocese. The request for an annulment was denied. Reasons given were: John should have tried harder to locate his ex-wife and work things out. As they were married in the Catholic Church, the Archdiocese would not rescind the union unless both parties together requested it.

Did they not listen to anything John explained to them? We met with our priest to voice our disappointment. We asked how could John contact his ex-wife without any knowledge where she was? And what about her non-existent relationship with her own children? She was the one who sinned, not John.

The priest was empathetic, but he couldn't go against the Archdiocese. He said we could try again in six months. Maybe by being persistent and showing that we were sincere about wanting a relationship with God in the Catholic Church, we could win them over. The priest would also write a letter of recommendation.

We were discouraged. John actually had a cousin, Vincent, who was a priest and studied in Rome. He was well respected but recently deceased. John had been thumbing through a Time magazine and was shocked to see a picture of his cousin Vincent in Chicago along with Frank Sinatra. Frank Sinatra had just been married in the Catholic church. I think it was his third or fourth marriage with all his previous marriages performed in the Catholic church. We mentioned it to our priest. He shook his head and said, "I bet Frank paid more the $350 to that Archdiocese."

John was angry; I was sad. I knew God wouldn't want faith to be based on monetary or political hindrances, and I knew John wouldn't want to pay another $350 to pursue this again. I was OK with that, but John said he would try it once more. Six months and another $350 later, we received the second denial letter. We stopped going to church after that. John said you only needed church when you were old or dying.

Chapter Twenty-One

John was an accounting manager. Cargill's fiscal year end was May 31st. This meant that anyone working in accounting spent a great deal of their summer working to "close the books." Sometimes, close to the year-end cut-off, John and some of his staff would work all day and night. Those times I would drive out to the office with pizzas or burgers for all of them.

Luckily, I no longer worked in accounting. I worked for a group of traders. That in itself was extremely stressful. I literally was told I could not take a break until the futures market closed each day. Hunger pains and "holding it" when one really had to go to the bathroom caused extreme stress. I finally filed a complaint, and a new policy was implemented. If we could get another contract administrator to cover for us, we could go to the bathroom. If we needed to eat, we would have to do it at our desk — still a problem, as each contract administrator had the same issue. I was getting a good salary but started questioning the worth of it. I was so tired all the time. John was getting extremely tired. He was fourteen years older than I was, and I knew the job was getting to be burdensome for him.

We found great joy in our dogs. They were always happy to see us after a long day at work. We now had three: Shelby, a sheltie; Snow Bear, an abused American Eskimo dog we rescued from Richard and Rose; and Pookie, a black miniature poodle. We always would comment how we loved our dogs more than a lot of humans.

Because of the stress of our jobs, we contemplated retiring early. We brainstormed as we needed to still have income if we did retire early. We thought it would be fun to do something with dogs. John knew someone who had gone to school for dog grooming. They made good money, could set their own hours, and enjoyed the work. We thought that might be fun. So, to add more stress to our lives, we decided to go to school while we were still employed full time. First John would attend evenings and Saturdays as he was older and would retire first. To go to dog grooming school part-time was almost a nine-month commitment with a cost of $2,500. Whenever he could, John would put in extra time at school on Saturdays so he would graduate early and not put a negative impact on his job. The school was located in Blaine. We lived in Bloomington, so it was approximately 30 miles one way at night. We knew the pressure it could cause, but we concentrated on the big picture. John was really good at grooming dogs. He had such patience and especially worked well with the bigger dogs. Once John finished school, it would be my turn.

A few months before John graduated, I received unexpected news from Cargill. The stock market had plummeted on October 19, 1987, and the department I worked in had lost millions in one day. Cargill decided to cut their losses and close the department at the end of the calendar year. Efforts would be made to find jobs for the laid off employees, but there was no guarantee.

I didn't want to go through all the trouble of learning a new job if I was going to quit in a year or so. The manager of my department was looking for people who would stay for a few months to help close the department Everyone wanted to move on if they were offered a job within another department. I was the only one that expressed interest in staying. The manager asked me to sign a commitment letter stating I would assist them through the end of the year. I hesitated, thinking how hard this would be with the upcoming holidays. When he added a $10,000 bonus for the two-month commitment in addition to my salary, I jumped at it. With that money, I would work hard, long hours, but I would be able to take the winter off and attend dog grooming schooling full-time in the spring. It would only take four months. Everything was working out better than planned.

We started our own business in the downstairs of our house. We had a large laundry room that we updated for our grooming shop. The wash basin tub was swapped out for a small raised bathtub so we could wash dogs without bending over. The wall behind the tub as well as the floor was tiled. We had cabinets and counter tops installed. We purchased the dog grooming table, dryer, and equipment with a student discount, and we were ready. We started slowly with a few neighbors' dogs. Our prices were very reasonable as we wanted to bring in clientele. We relied on "word of mouth," and before we knew it, our dog clientele base topped 100! It was such a wonderful feeling to see the happiness on our customers' faces when they picked up their pets. Sometimes we would get dogs that were so matted it seemed a crime their owners let them get that bad. We would work our magic in cleaning them up and transforming them into a much happier animal. We soon realized for us it wasn't so much the money but making the dogs happy. We told their owners if they brought their pets in for grooming within six weeks, we would give them a discount. We enjoyed the grooming business but did it only at nights and on Saturdays as John was still employed full-time. We did not yet have the money we thought we needed to retire early, and we were still way too young to collect social security. Health insurance would be expensive without Medicare. John was 55 years old, and I was only 41, so I had gone back to work at a local company in a customer service position. I didn't make as much money as I did at Cargill, but I made enough and we both had health insurance coverage.

Eventually working full time and then grooming dogs at night was wearing us down. I felt our own dogs weren't getting the attention they needed. I wanted to cut back on the dog grooming to only a couple nights each week, but John was determined. He didn't want to disappoint our many clients.

John had now worked at Cargill for 30 years. Those 30 years included his employment with PAG Seeds in Aurora, Illinois. Cargill purchased PAG Seeds years before I knew John. Part of the acquisition in negotiations was to honor those years worked for PAG as part of the seniority at Cargill. Once an employee put in 30 years of service with Cargill, they had the option of an early retirement package. We decided the first of the year, after the holidays, John would retire and groom dogs. I would continue working at my job full-time. John could handle grooming dogs on his own, and it would open more opportunity as he would be available during the day-time hours. John gave a three-month notice of retirement. We were excited to start this new chapter in our lives.

We started getting some really big dogs to groom: Great Pyrenees, Portuguese water dogs, and full-grown collies. It would take both of us to lift them up on the grooming table and into the bath. John started getting backaches, and we assumed it was from the heavier dogs. His back pain never seemed to lessen. He couldn't get comfortable sitting or reclining in a chair. He went to the doctor and had an x-ray taken. They found nothing wrong. He decided to go to a chiropractor, but that seemed to cause more pain. I would give him back rubs to no avail. After another month, he went back to the doctor. The doctor told John maybe he was a hypochondriac.

John was very depressed. How could he have such pain yet nothing was wrong? One time in the middle of the night, I woke up, and John was not in bed. I called out his name. No answer. I got up and searched the house. No John. Then I checked to see if his car was in the garage, and it was. I could not imagine where he could be. It was early December and cold outside. I was worried and sat up waiting for him. When he finally came home, I saw pain on his face and could tell he had been crying. He told me he was out walking around the neighborhood to see if he could get any relief for his pain. He said he had been going out on walks for several nights while I slept. He didn't want me to worry.

It was time to find another doctor. My girlfriend's brother was a gynecologist. It wasn't his area of expertise, but I went to him and explained the whole story. He told me his friend was an excellent internist. He was young and wasn't afraid to run additional tests. Some doctors won't even mention to their patients the costly tests that can be done as quite often insurance doesn't cover the full cost.

"I don't care how much it costs," I told him. "If insurance doesn't cover it, we will find a way to pay. I just want John to get well."

He made a call to his friend, and the next day John had an appointment. I went with John to the doctor. I didn't want anyone else telling him the pain was in his head. I was witness to it. John was a strong man and usually never complained. The doctor had already arranged for John to get an MRI that day. It was disturbing when the MRI showed nothing wrong. The doctor explained that sometimes an MRI does not show everything. He suggested a bone scan which was done the next day.

The doctor called us the night John had his bone scan and asked if we could both come in the next morning to discuss it. We both knew it wouldn't be good news.

With the images on the lighted board in the doctor's office, he showed us the mass that was on the middle of John's spine. It was most likely a tumor, but there was a possibility it could be tuberculosis.

Chapter Twenty-Two

A biopsy needed to be performed to determine if the mass on John's spine was tuberculosis or cancer. It was the holiday season. John wanted to wait until after Christmas which was only a few weeks away. His early retirement party was also coming up the end of December.

John decided he would have the biopsy on December 31st, New Year's Eve. I begged him not to do it on this day. We had always had a fun time on New Year's Eve, either having a party or going out to dinner at a nice restaurant. I told John I didn't want him to get the biopsy on a holiday because if it was bad news, we would always remember it on that day. John wanted it done by the end of the year, before his retirement, and the only slot open for surgery was New Year's Eve. So, it was scheduled.

The following week was John's retirement party at work. He actually had two parties. He was loved and respected by his staff. They were sad he was retiring but understood. They had a luncheon for him celebrating his "new career". Food was served to everyone in dog dishes with many "pet" gifts bestowed as well. He was given a photo album of his many years at Cargill. It was a fun event. The following day would be the company party. I took off work to go and called Steve and Greg to join me. Greg couldn't get off work, but Steve came to the house to pick me up. Just before we left, I noticed the light on our answering machine was blinking. I told

Steve to wait until I listened to the message. It was for John telling him he had already been set up for a consultation appointment a few days after his biopsy. He was to call the number left to confirm the date. It was from the Oncology Department.

I couldn't understand how they could assume John had cancer as the biopsy hadn't even been done yet. I called the number that was left and spoke to a woman at the scheduling desk.

In a somewhat panicked voice, I asked, "Doesn't oncology mean cancer? Is this an appointment with a cancer doctor?" I was getting almost hysterical.

The woman on the other end waited for me to compose myself then calmly and quietly said, "You need to speak with your husband." That was all she would tell me. I hung up and called John, but there wasn't any answer.

Steve had gone out to the car to wait for me. He came in to see what was taking so long. He noticed I was crying and wanted to know what happened. I told him about the phone call. He wasn't sure what oncology meant. I told him it was cancer. He tried to calm me down telling me it was probably just a post-operative precaution. Then he said, "God, Patty, don't take things so seriously. This is Dad. He's strong. There is no way he has cancer. You're acting like he's going to die or something. He's not going to die! You have to stop so Dad doesn't know you were crying."

With a feeling of doom, I went into the bathroom and quickly freshened my makeup. I went outside and joined Steve in the car. It was a quiet ride to the party. Everyone was gathered in the main atrium of Cargill. They were waiting for John. He had disappeared. Then I saw him through the window as he was approaching the building. He had been walking outside without a coat. I ran to him.

"John, where have you been? Are you OK?" I asked.

"I'm OK. I was just walking and thinking about everything." He looked so sad and defeated.

"There was a message on our phone for an appointment with...."

Before I could finish, John finished for me, "I know, the Oncology Department."

"You knew about this?" I asked.

"Yeah, the doctor called me earlier. He had another specialist read the bone scan, and they are almost certain it is not TB but cancer."

I started crying. He held me and said, "Please don't cry. I haven't told anyone at work about this, and I don't want them to know right now. Let's just go inside and enjoy the party."

How could this man be so strong? But of course, I knew him better than anyone. His face reflected pain, and his cloudy, blood shot eyes showed more than tiredness. They showed worry and fear.

We made it through the gathering, and a few people approached me asking if John was OK. I said, "Yes, he's just got a lot on his mind with retiring."

On December 30th, John wanted us to go out for a nice dinner to celebrate his retirement. He made reservations at Ruth's Chris in downtown Minneapolis. It was so expensive, but John told me not to worry about the cost. We picked out our own steaks, had a few cocktails, wine with dinner, and even an after-dinner drink. Our meal was fabulous. Throughout dinner, I was worried about John's drinking with his procedure the next morning. He reassured me telling me the doctor said it wasn't major surgery, it was just a simple biopsy. He had not mentioned anything about alcohol. I doubted that and told him he had more than enough to drink. Trying to remain upbeat, I told him I would drive home as he had more cocktails than I did. He laughed and said he was just fine as he had eaten so much, the food absorbed the alcohol.

The next morning, we entered Fairview Southdale Hospital. I could not believe the generosity of John's doctor. He had arranged for us to have a "suite" because it was New Year's Eve. I had told him earlier if John was spending the night on New Year's Eve, I would stay with him all night. I could sleep in a chair as I had arranged for someone to watch our dogs. John and I had never spent a New Year's Eve separated since we were married twenty years ago.

Steve and Greg came to the hospital that morning and so did our friend, Mary. We had gotten married at Mary's home and were dear friends with her and her husband, Robert.

Once John was prepped for surgery, he asked me, "Don't you want to kiss me goodbye? It may be the last time."

I told him I would not kiss him goodbye, but I kissed him and told him, "I love you, and I will see you in a few hours." He told me

166

to remember how deeply he loved me, and he had a bad feeling about this. With the anesthesiologist there, I tried to laugh it off by telling him he was scared, but he needed to have a positive attitude before this guy put the needle in him. The anesthesiologist agreed and played along.

Even though the procedure was a simple biopsy, I was grateful for Steve, Greg, and Mary being there with me. We drank coffee, watched TV, read magazines, and shared old stories. I could tell the boys were getting impatient. I was too as this was taking so long. John went into surgery early in the morning. It was now almost 11:00 am. I asked the person at the desk what was taking so long. She said she didn't know, but once he was in recovery the doctor would come out and speak with us. A few minutes later we heard several announcements on the PA system immediately requesting cardiac doctors for a red alert in the OR. I panicked and went back to the woman at the desk. She said there must have been an urgent case that came in, so the doctor may be delayed in getting down to talk with us. The emergency was for a cardiac patient so I need not worry.

Six hours after John went under for his "simple biopsy", a group of four doctors came out asking us to gather together. I immediately started crying as I remembered hearing those same words when my father passed away. I was able to breathe a sigh of relief when the doctors said John was in recovery. Then they told us the bad news. In trying to extract a biopsy of the tumor, they discovered the tumor was wrapped tightly around his spinal cord. All they needed

167

was a little snip of the tumor but in doing so, John's aorta was accidentally severed.

I was speechless. What did this mean? The doctors further explained that in order to save his life, they applied digital pressure with their fingers so he could survive until a heart specialist was called in. Yes, they were keeping John alive literally with digital pressure.

"Was that when I heard the doctors being paged?"

"Yes", they said. With their heads lowered they explained how they had to open John's chest and perform emergency open heart surgery.

I was astounded. John came in for a "simple biopsy" but ended up almost losing his life and needing open heart surgery! Furthermore, they were not sure he would survive the night. He was being admitted to ICU. I was beside myself. I would not leave John's side. We would not be staying in the hospital "suite", but I didn't care. The doctor said he would see what he could do about accommodations for me. Mary told me they would do everything they could as they were most likely worried about being sued. I only wanted John to survive. I didn't plan on staying in any room. I would sit by John's side. I wanted to hold his hand, tell him how much I loved him, and encourage him to survive. That is exactly what I did for most of the night until a nurse told me I needed to get some sleep to be any good for John. He was in a coma, and if he could hear me, the nurse said it could add stress for him knowing how concerned I was. There was a small conference room in ICU across the hall from the family waiting room. It had a

168

small couch, chair, table, and telephone. The doctor had arranged for me to stay there, and it was only a short distance away from John. The nurse said I could be with John whenever I wanted, but it had been such a long day, she thought it was best if I tried to get some sleep.

Of course, I could not get much sleep. It was comforting to have this area where I could close the door, shed tears privately, and pray to God harder than I had ever prayed before.

John survived the night, but his doctor was concerned he wasn't coming out of the coma. Then he asked me if John had any alcohol the day or two before the surgery. I told him about our night before, and he said that may account for John taking longer than usual to wake up.

A few days passed, and John was still in a coma. Many friends and family came to the hospital. They knew John was in intensive care and could not see him. They came to give me support. On New Year's Day, my friend Mary Beth came to the hospital with a "Good Luck New Year's" dinner for me consisting of pork roast, mashed potatoes, sauerkraut, and dessert. I had additional visitors that day, Leroy and Janet. They were such good friends of ours, and Leroy worked with John. Leroy had a manila envelope in his hand. It held John's retirement papers. Leroy told me that he had not yet turned in John's signed retirement papers. Then he shocked me by tearing up the papers in front of me.

"I don't understand!" I exclaimed.

Leroy quietly said, "This way, Patty, John will still be considered a full-time employee with full benefits. By not retiring, he will be on disability with the company and, as a manager, will receive his full salary."

I thought all my tears were shed. I was wrong. Realizing the depth of compassion this man had for both John and myself was overwhelming. If John needed chemotherapy, he would need to change physicians and hospitals as Cargill had changed insurance plans the first of the year. This would all be covered if John was still a full-time employee. I cried as I hugged and thanked Leroy. He was an angel on earth. God was looking out for us.

My sister Kimberly didn't drive but came up with her friend, Ruth, the next day. Together they sat with me for the entire afternoon. They gave me thoughtful gifts and brought cake. I didn't even realize until they came bearing gifts that is was January 2nd, my birthday.

The results of the biopsy had come back. It was malignant. The doctor said once John was awakened and after he had somewhat recuperated from the unexpected open-heart surgery, they would need to run further tests to determine where the main source of the cancer was as the tumor on his spine had metastasized from another source. The doctor also told me when John woke up, he needed to be told the severity of his condition. He didn't want me to sugar coat it if he wasn't present when John woke up.

I had such wonderful friends. Janet and LeRoy, Kathy, Mary, Mary Beth, and many others made themselves available for me if I needed anything. They stayed at the hospital while I went home to shower, change clothes, and hold my confused dogs. Steve and Greg would either be there each day or call me for an update. I surmised they were still in denial. John's mom and sister would call me at the hospital from Missouri at least once a day. Another day passed with John still in a coma. That night I stood by his bedside when he opened his eyes! I couldn't help it. I cried with relief. I called the nurse over. John was trying to ask me something, but his voice was parched and only a whisper. The nurse welcomed him back. She left to get him some ice chips for his throat. I bent my head down to John as he again whispered. With a hoarse, soft voice, he asked me, "What happened?"

I told him how his aorta had been accidentally severed as the doctors were trying to pluck a piece of the tumor. When I explained he had open heart surgery, he shook his head. Then, he asked me, "Benign or malignant?" I couldn't answer. He asked me again.

I tried to hold back tears but couldn't. I whispered back to him, "Honey, it was malignant."

Again, he shook his head, then said "Why? Why?"

He closed his eyes, and didn't wake up for another two days. I was angry the doctor had not been there, and I was the one to tell John of the results.

When John did wake up, he was moved from ICU into a private room. The main concern now was getting his strength back in order to treat the cancer. He wanted that too so he could get the treatment to make him well again.

John confided to me, "I hope they can treat this, and I won't have the pain. Thank God it wasn't in my lung. If I knew this was something I could have prevented by not smoking, I don't think I could live with myself." John had smoked since he was a teenager but quit smoking about eight years before his diagnosis.

That afternoon the oncologist met with us. The tumor itself was inoperable. Once John got back his strength, they would try to shrink it with chemotherapy.

"Do you know what caused this thing on my back yet, doctor?" John asked.

"Yes. The main source is located in the lobe of your right lung. It is lung cancer. I have to be honest with you, John. It is a non-small cell type which is aggressive and difficult to cure. We are going to try our hardest to reduce the tumor with both chemotherapy and radiation if we can."

John remained quiet and when the doctor left, he cursed at himself. If only he hadn't smoked all those years, this would never have happened to him.

I tried to soothe him, expounding on how years ago no one knew that smoking would cause cancer. I told him he was a strong man and so many people loved him. He had to concentrate on getting better. He needed to be positive.

John stayed in the hospital for another week. His ribs, chest, and back were so tender he could only move and turn slowly. I could tell as I drove him home how any little bounce or jerk was painful to him. We lived in a split entry house. There were only six steps up to the main area of the house, and each step took the breath out of him. He sat on the couch in the living room and watched TV for a while. The dogs were so excited to see him, but he was afraid they would jump on his incision. I put the dogs in our dog grooming area. John didn't eat much for dinner. He wanted to go to bed. When he was finally situated in our queen size bed, he asked that I not sleep with him as it would be uncomfortable, and he would be getting up a lot. I told him I would sleep on the couch in the next room. He was adamant that I sleep in one of the boys' old rooms downstairs. He then noticed the baby monitor on the bed stand and wanted to know what it was. I explained to him that I bought it in case he needed anything. When I would be in another room, I could place my side of the monitor wherever I was so I could hear him. He did not like that. He said he didn't need it. I said, "OK", and then pretended to turn it off. I took my part of the monitor with me and put it next to my bed. As soon as I got into bed, I heard John's painful, heartbroken weeping. We were in different rooms, on separate floors, but together we cried ourselves to sleep.

Chapter Twenty-Three

John was a strong man, both physically and emotionally. You never think you or a loved one will be the one who develops a terminal disease. I think for a few months we were both in shock and maybe in some denial. The pain and stress of what we both had been through was a strain on our relationship. John insisted I return to my job full time. I wanted to take a leave to care for him. I hated to argue with him during this time, and we finally reached a compromise. I would go back to work but would come home every day on my lunch hour so we could eat together, and I could check on him.

Thank goodness for wonderful people in our lives. Every few evenings, we would get a visit from Don and his wife Rosalie. Don worked with John, and I had known Don when I worked in the same department. At that time, I did not know Rosalie well. Don and Rosalie came to our wedding years ago, and I often saw Rosalie at company dinners. Once John was ill, Rosalie would bring goodies over for us and sometimes dinner. Her bars were scrumptious and whenever she felt we needed a lift, she would whip up another batch and come over. They became known as "The Bars".

We had other friends who would bring food over from time to time. I don't know if these people realized how wonderful and helpful this was, especially for me. Working full-time and coming home each evening to cook and take care of John was exhausting, but I wouldn't have changed it for the world. Often, I would act cheerful and kiss him goodbye in the morning, then cry all the way to work and at my desk. I put on my positive, cheerful face again when I went home.

Over the next few months, John was on the road to recovering from his open-heart surgery. He never got his strength back to the point it was, but he was now strong enough to start chemotherapy. I insisted on taking him to every appointment, which I did except for one. John's son, Steve, wanted to take him one time, and I felt it would do both of them some good. I wanted Steve to understand the severity of his dad's situation, and I believe he was finally coming to terms with it.

The first round of chemotherapy went well. There was vomiting for a day or two after each treatment, but soon John's appetite started returning. The doctors and nurses instructed us this was not the time for either of us to diet. I was to feed John whatever he wanted and whenever he wanted it. They encouraged me to have snacks and candy all over within his reach. After all, John went in for that biopsy weighing almost 250 pounds and had lost about 20 pounds so far. After a few rounds of chemo, a CT scan was performed. We were ecstatic as the tumor had shrunk, although it was still inoperable. Radiation could not be given as the tumor was too close to the heart. We now just had to wait as the doctor did not want John to have any more chemo for a while as his blood count was getting low. The red blood cells carry oxygen through the body, and when you have a lower than normal number of red blood cells, it results in feeling weak, tired, and short of breath. It is a form of anemia. John was border-line but insisted he felt fine.

A few weeks after that appointment, John walked into the kitchen to take his evening medicine and fainted. He wasn't out long at all, but he had fallen to the floor. I held his head in my lap as I inspected his chest and back for any injury. All appeared fine, and John said he just got dizzy. I called the doctor-on-call. He said to have John come in the next morning for blood work.

The next morning, I noticed that John was looking extremely pale. We went to the clinic, and it was determined he needed a blood transfusion. For cancer patients, the transfusion had to be done in the hospital. We both stayed at the hospital overnight to be sure John would be strong enough to return home. The following day his coloring looked so much better, and he was released. He even insisted on driving home. He definitely seemed to have regained some strength. It was such a good feeling to see John laugh again and have an inkling of hope. How could anything be fatal when you felt you were getting better day by day? As John was starting to feel healthy again, he wanted to keep it that way and said, "I need all the help I can get." So, we went back to church. After all, it couldn't hurt to pray for continued strength and health.

It had been a month since John's blood transfusion. Each month a CT scan and blood work was required before seeing the oncologist. I noticed John started taking more of his Percocet pain medication the last week or two. He was again having trouble sleeping. When I asked him about it, he said, "I've just been having a few headaches, that's all."

When I got to work the next day, I called and spoke with John's oncologist, Dr. Shimp. He was such a kind and caring person. I voiced my concern to him about John's headaches. He said he did not believe a few headaches meant the cancer would have spread to his brain, especially since John had been doing so well. We were scheduled the next week for John to have his monthly checkup. Dr. Shimp arranged for John to come in the next day and to instruct the radiologist to be sure to take a good look at the results of the brain portion of the CAT scan.

Usually the CAT scan didn't take long, but this time I seemed to be sitting in the waiting room longer than usual. I asked the receptionist if she could check on him. A few minutes later, John came out. He sat down beside me and told me that a small tumor was found in his brain. I sat there dumbfounded. Everything had seemed to be going so well. The reason it took longer this time was that John had already spoken with his oncologist in the room where his test had been performed. We were to go immediately to Methodist Hospital for John to start radiation on the brain portion. I broke down.

"Why is this happening to us?" I cried. "We've done everything we're supposed to. We are good people!"

John, who should have been the one more upset, put his arm around me and quietly said, "Don't cry, honey. We have to play the cards we're dealt."

177

We drove over to the hospital, and John had his first radiation treatment. To avoid any aggressive growth, radiation would be given to him every five days for the next six weeks.

John was taking a shower after his third radiation treatment when he noticed clumps of his hair on the shower floor. He had a receding hair line for most of his adult life, but now his head appeared to have missing splotches of hair in random locations. We both laughed as it did look ridiculous. We called a friend who owned a beauty shop in our neighborhood. John wondered if she would come over to the house and shave his head. He felt if he was going to lose his hair, it would be on his terms. Cindy was happy to do this. She came over with her clippers and took before and after pictures. John actually looked quite handsome without the hair. It also gave him the opportunity to wear cool looking hats.

One day when I came home from work, I received a package in the mail. It was a beautiful porcelain doll. There was a note enclosed. It was from John. It read "To the best nurse I have ever had." He told me when he saw the doll, he thought it looked like me when I was a little girl. He continued to surprise me with gifts he ordered. One day I received a Precious Moments plate of a boy and girl in love. I told him he didn't need to give me gifts, but he replied, "You've done so much for me." I always told him, "You would do the same for me. Besides, you're going to get me hooked on QVC."

The cancer illness journey is like a rollercoaster with many ups and downs. The radiation was a success on the brain tumor. For several months, we continued with John's appointments. We developed a routine. Each month we went to the radiology clinic for John's tests and waited for the pictures we hand-carried to the oncology department. After John's appointment, we would have a late breakfast or early lunch at Byerly's in St. Louis Park. We did this as we knew there were going to be days after getting chemotherapy when John would not be able to eat. We also did this because it made us feel human again, getting out in public. When receiving chemotherapy, and especially if your blood count lowers, your immune system is at risk. You can't be around anyone ill or small children. Depending upon how John felt each day, I needed to monitor people who wanted to come and visit.

My cousin, Michele, was a registered nurse specializing in cancer research. We were thrilled when she started doing work with Dr. Shimp. Michele had an incredibly warm and loving bedside manner. She was also a wealth of information for both of us. When you are living each day with cancer, you are opened to a whole new world you never knew existed. There is so much to learn, and I thank Michele for her patience, love, and caretaking.

It had now been more than six months since John's diagnosis. We had already been through some chemotherapy, a blood transfusion, and radiation. Overall, John seemed to be handling things well. Once again, he started taking more Percocet. John was constantly on Prednisone and Percocet. The problem was pain had started again in his back, and the Percocet didn't seem to be doing its magic any longer. His next appointment was not good news. Although the tumor on his back retained its shrunken size, new smaller spots were now starting to appear in his lungs. He needed to start aggressive chemotherapy once again.

Does the treatment do more harm than the disease itself? We constantly wondered about that. Chemotherapy is like injecting a poison into your body with hopes that it will only damage cancer cells and not the good cells. Before John got sick, we knew a few people with cancer. Once they started chemotherapy, their appearance changed drastically. They seemed like a shadow of what they had been. John often said if he was ever diagnosed with cancer, he would take his chances and not subject himself to treatment. Now that he had the illness, he said the reality was you would do anything to live longer and stay around for family. He didn't want to die, so no matter what it took, he would do it.

The chemotherapy treatments were starting to wear John down drastically. He didn't vomit as often, but his weight loss was substantial. His strength was diminishing, and the feeling of mortality weighed on our entire family. He had lost over 50 pounds and now weighed under 200. He needed the help of a cane to walk any distance. The pain was getting worse. He needed several more blood transfusions between chemotherapy treatments. The oncologist prescribed a low dose of morphine by pill in addition to his other pain medication.

Being the stoic person he was, John insisted on still driving. I was fearful of him being on such strong medication while driving, and I told him so. His response to me was, "Please. I'm no longer able to smoke, drink alcohol, or eat what I want. I can't even make love to my wife. Please don't take away my last freedom." As he pleaded with me, I didn't have the heart to deny him this one last pleasure, but I was still not comfortable with it.

We didn't have a large Thanksgiving meal that year. Everything seemed to make John nervous, and he couldn't eat much anyway. I started putting up a small Christmas tree, and John got so anxious, I took it down. He had lost more weight and was starting to look quite frail. The week after Thanksgiving, John wanted to go out Christmas shopping alone. I did not want him to go, but he insisted. John was gone about an hour when it started snowing heavily. I panicked. He was gone too long. I called Steve and Greg, but there wasn't much we could do as we didn't know where John was. I prayed for his safety and for the safety of others.

Finally, after another hour, I heard the garage door open. I helped John into the house. He sat down on the first step going up to the living room. He looked exhausted and scared. After he rested a while, I helped him off with his coat. He sadly looked at me, handed me the car keys, and said, "That was the last time I will ever drive a car. Take these keys and keep them."

"What happened?" I asked.

He wouldn't answer me. He simply repeated that it was the last time he would ever drive. I never found out what happened that day but it was the last time he drove.

Chapter Twenty-Four

The kids and their families came over for Christmas. We had a nice time, and John seemed in good spirits. After the holidays, John requested I buy a spiral notebook. Each day we would go over things that needed to be done with the house and cars throughout the year. I was to write it all in the notebook. This was probably the most difficult thing for me to do. It was obvious John's pain was steadily increasing. He sat up in a chair next to me. He was shaking and sweating profusely. When he told me to write down to remember to shut off the outside water next winter, I burst into tears.

John said, "Don't cry, honey."

I was crying uncontrollably as I told him, "I can't help it. I don't want to live without you!"

"You have to live, Patty. Who would take care of our dogs?"

He was trying to make me laugh. He then said, "That's enough for today. We'll do some more tomorrow."

John's sister, Marilyn, and brother-in-law Dorrell, drove up from Missouri several times. Marilyn wanted so badly to stay and help take care of John. John didn't want that. Marilyn's feelings were hurt, but John didn't want anyone, especially his family, to see what he was going through.

John's mother called from Missouri almost every day. It was so difficult for her, and each phone call ended in tears. We were all trying to be strong for John, but sometimes it just didn't work.

So many friends and co-workers of ours came to visit and offer whatever help they could. Rosalie stopped by almost every day. Rosalie's husband, Don, who worked with John, was also diagnosed with lung cancer a few months after John. We were heart sick about it. John often commented how he didn't want Don to go through what he had. Janet and Leroy stopped by regularly. Leroy would visit with John while Janet and I went to a movie or shopping — anything to get out of the house for a while as I had now taken a leave from work so I could be with John as much as possible.

One afternoon when Rosalie and Don were over, we started talking about mortality. Don had started chemotherapy and was still doing OK. Suddenly John looked at me and asked, "Where are you going to bury me?"

I didn't know what to say. We had never discussed this before. John said he wanted to be buried close to our home in Dawn Valley Cemetery. Rosalie suggested we go look at it. John didn't want to. The only request he had was he didn't want his grave facing the new massive homes just built on one side of the cemetery. He said he didn't want to spend eternity looking at the "rich sons of bitches." That was John, always trying to make us feel better and laugh, even under such dreadful circumstances. Thank God for Rosalie. She was my angel on Earth. We went to the cemetery, and I picked out a lovely spot with two side-by-side graves, without any view of where the "rich bitches" lived.

approaching. Neither Greg nor I slept that night. We just kept looking at John, remembering better times.

John was not really conscious in the morning. It had been fifteen months since he was diagnosed, and he had surprised the entire oncology department that he was still hanging on. I sat by his bedside and tenderly spoke with him. I didn't know if he could hear me or understand me. Maybe I was talking to help myself, but the nurse said it was a good idea. She constantly monitored his heart and breathing. If he made any twitches or moans that would indicate pain, we pressed his morphine button. Steve and Greg were downstairs. They knew their dad would be passing soon and wanted to be close to him. The nurse said it was like John wouldn't let go — like he needed to still hang on for us. While holding his hand, I stood up, and kissed him. I whispered to him, "Honey, it's OK for you to let go. I can't stand to see you suffer anymore. Please remember to save a place for me."

The nurse and I were both shocked as John nodded. Then he died. It was 4:30 in the afternoon on March 5th, twenty-two days short of John's 58th birthday. Fifteen months ago, John weighed 250 pounds. When John's life ended, he weighed not much more than 100 pounds.

Chapter Twenty-Five

The doorbell rang just as John took his last breath. It was Rosalie. She had been planning to be over earlier but had been delayed. Was it coincidental that the doorbell rang just as John took his last breath? Or was it my angel on Earth watching over me?

Even when death is expected, the finality of it strikes your soul. The hospice nurse immediately called the necessary people at our mortuary to pick John up. I did not realize that when a person dies at home, the law states that a police officer must appear at the premises before the body is removed in order to rule out any foul play. In situations of terminal cancer, it is simply a formality.

I sat in the bedroom rocking back and forth, weeping, while I kept asking Rosalie, "What am I going to do now?" Then I begged her not to let anyone put John in a body bag. "Please, please don't let them put him in a body bag!" Rosalie put her arm around me and sat with me, reassuring me. After the police left, John was taken out on a cot with only the sheet covering him.

I don't know what I would ever have done without Rosalie. She was sixteen years older than I was, yet she moved around my house like a white tornado. The nurse gave instructions for Rosalie to flush all John's leftover medicine down the toilet. Rosalie took all the bedding that John had used and disposed of it. She and the nurse took care of cleaning the hospital equipment and arranged for it to be picked up. She did all this for me, and yet her own husband was stricken with the same type of cancer. I prayed if she ever needed me, I would have the strength to be there for her.

Steve and Greg also stayed, and after the inevitable sunk in, all three of us made phone calls notifying loved ones of John's death. I called Marilyn. I wanted her to go over to John's mother's house and tell her in person. John's mom was not well, and she needed someone to be there with her. Poor Marilyn and Dorrell had just gotten home, and now they had to turn around to return for the funeral.

If you could ever describe a funeral as beautiful, it was John's. I was proud so many people came to the visitation and the funeral the next day. The funeral home received so many flower bouquets and plants, during the visitation another room had to be opened just for the flowers. The funeral director said she had never seen so many flowers at one person's funeral. I requested after the visitation the majority of the flowers be sent to hospitals and nursing homes. There were over 200 people at the visitation. The funeral the next morning was held at Pax Christi Catholic Church in Eden Prairie with Father Tim presiding. When planning the funeral, Father Tim asked me approximately how many people I thought would stay for the luncheon after the funeral. I guessed maybe 50. There were at least 150 people at the funeral, and most stayed for the luncheon. I did not have to worry as Father Tim came up to me before the service started and said the funeral staff was on it, and they had plenty of food.

I was surprised when my brother Curt showed up with Veronica at the funeral. The only thing he said to me was that he was "so sorry." He didn't stay for the luncheon, and I was glad for that. I thought maybe Veronica would have contacted LeeAnne, but LeeAnne wasn't present at the visitation or the funeral. The police escorted line of cars going to the cemetery was over two blocks long. Steve, Greg, and I kept looking out the back window of the hearse, amazed at the number of cars and agreeing that John would be proud and happy.

Chapter Twenty-Six

I was thankful for my many friends who made sure I was busy that first year after John's death. People say the first year after a loved one's death is the hardest. I disagree. I believe that first year people are concerned about all the holidays that all of a sudden they will be spending alone. Efforts are made and invitations given. It is the years after that are rough, as people have their own families and feel they should move on. You can't expect to be "babysat" forever. Life goes on.

I did have some unbearable moments that first year shortly after John died. It was on St. Patrick's Day, less than two weeks since John passed. John and I always celebrated holidays and special occasions. We would make corned beef and cabbage. I decided to go to the grocery store to see if I could find a small one-person size corned beef. Before John got sick, he did all the cooking. He loved to cook and did a great job. Now I had to learn not only how to cook but how to cook for just me. I was standing at the meat counter looking at the different cuts of meat, and it suddenly hit me. Why should I even cook? It's just me. Then the thought of past St. Patrick's Days with John tugged at my heart. Tears were rolling down my face when someone tapped me on the shoulder. It was Rosalie. She always seemed to pop up whenever I needed her. My angel on Earth. We hugged, and she invited me to go to a movie and out to eat. I knew Don was getting worse so I told her "no", but I would stop by later.

I decided not to cook. I bought a dozen green carnations for St. Patty's Day. I took six and put them on John's still fresh grave. I would put the remaining six in the house. There wasn't much snow left on the ground, but it was a cold, rainy, and dreary day. I left the cemetery and headed home. As I pulled into the garage, I thought, "This is so difficult. Why should I bother?" I was so sad. John was my life. I didn't know what happiness was until I married John. I didn't know what the love of a family was or how people truly cared for each other. With the car still running, I put my finger on the garage door opener. I thought it would just be so easy to lower the door and die. Just as I was about to press the button on the garage door opener, my three dogs started barking like crazy. I could hear John telling me, "You have to live, honey. Who would take care of our dogs?" With tears running down my cheeks, I started laughing and thanked John and God. Was it fate? Was it a sign? I wasn't sure, but my dogs needed me. I shut off the car and went inside.

I couldn't sleep in the bed we had shared together for so many years. I didn't know if I was scared or what. Since John's funeral, I slept on the living room couch with all three dogs either on the carpet or curled up with me on the couch. Occasionally I woke up swearing I could smell John's cologne, or hear the change jingling in John's pocket. John always jingled change in his pockets and whistled.

My good friend Kathy came over several nights in a row to help me with the funeral thank you cards. She did so much work addressing cards, looking up addresses and zip codes. I will never forget her kindness and friendship.

Six weeks after John passed away, Rosalie's husband, Don, was put in hospice. Like John, Don choose to be at home. The day he was put in hospice, I went over to their house to see if I could help with anything or just to be there to comfort Rosalie as she did for me so many times and still does to this day. The hospice nurse was there and had inserted a similar morphine pump like John had. I was over to see Don the day or two before and was shocked now to see what a difference a few days made. He was in that almost unconscious state. Rosalie had set a plant next to his bed. It was a Christmas cactus Don had given her. He really liked it but was disappointed it hadn't bloomed again since before Christmas. He complained about that a lot. The nurse left her number in case of any emergency, however, she felt Don would sleep comfortably that night and would be in hospice for about 30 days. I told the nurse as she left that Don had changed so much in just a short time, I worried he would pass soon. She told me not to worry, that he still had some time.

Rosalie had a friend staying with her for a few days. I felt reassured that she would have someone with her. Before I left, Rosalie asked me to stay with her too. I would, of course, but first I had to go home to take care of the dogs. I hugged Rosalie and told her I would be back in a little bit, but as I opened the door to leave, this feeling came over me that I needed to be home that night. All the memories of John instantly flooded into my mind. I turned to Rosalie with tears in my eyes and told her I really wanted to stay with her as she did so much for me, but I couldn't do it. Maybe it was too soon. I had been close to illness and death for over a year and couldn't bring myself to stay. Rosalie told me she understood. It was OK as she had someone there. Maybe another time.

As I drove home, all I could think of was what an awful friend I was. I had this feeling I couldn't explain. It was like death was near. I went home, played with my dogs, and fell asleep on the couch.

I had a wonderful dream. I was looking up into Heaven. John was standing behind a wooden fence. There were flowers and greenery all around. John looked so healthy and had a full head of hair. He looked so happy. He was smiling and whistling while he jingled change in his pocket. All of a sudden, Don walked up to John. He too looked happy. John smiled and said, "Hello, Don. I knew you would be here, but I didn't think it would be this soon."

Suddenly I was awakened by the sound of my telephone ringing. I looked at the clock. It was only 5:30 in the morning! Who could be calling me this early? It was Rosalie. She called to tell me Don had just died.

Chapter Twenty-Seven

I got dressed, took care of the dogs, and went over to Rosalie's house. We were both crying and hugging each other. Don's body had just been taken away. I told Rosalie how sorry I was that I didn't spend the night. I told her about my dream. She said it was meant to be that I went home and had that dream. It was proof John was giving me a sign. Then she led me over to the now empty hospital bed saying, "I need to show you something." She pointed at the Christmas cactus, and overnight a bright red flower had blossomed. This may have been her sign.

Together Rosalie and I grew to be close friends. If ever I needed her, she was always there for me. We took adult education classes together in electronics and plumbing, thinking we could learn something as the guys were no longer here to do such tasks. Neither one of us felt very celebratory during the holidays, so we took a night class and made Christmas cookies. There were enough cookies made in the class we did not need to worry about making any more for kids or grandkids. I know that Rosalie was stronger than I was. A few times if I was having a bad day, I would drive to her house. She would open the door, and I would just start crying. She always gave me a big hug and said, "Let's go to the movies."

Rosalie has the strongest faith in God of anyone I know. She always told me that God will take care of us. We just need to believe and honor him. I have never seen her in a bad mood. I remember one day she was a little upset when small neighbor children were at her house and broke a key for her beloved grandfather clock. Her husband, Don, built these clocks as his hobby. Her clock stood tall in her entry way. The children were over and inserted the key into the lock on the door of the clock. They then tried turning the key but they either turned the wrong way or turned too much as the key broke off in the lock. It broke into two pieces with the bottom half stuck inside the lock. Rosalie tried hard to get out the piece trapped inside the lock but couldn't. She placed the broken top half of the key on top of the clock. The next morning when she woke up she decided to take the top half of the key to a locksmith to see if they could replicate the key. She also needed to figure out how to get the other half out of the lock. She reached up and grabbed the top half of the key and was astounded that it was no longer broken! It was complete, one piece, like it never had broken. While shaking, she inserted the key and there was no broken part stuck in the lock. She turned the key, and it worked! A miracle? A sign? I believe it was just like my dream telling me Don had died.

My friend Mary Beth, her husband, and kids had been our next-door neighbor for many years. They now lived in the next town, about a half hour away. Mary Beth and her husband both worked for the then "Northwest Airlines". Mary Beth invited me to go to Hawaii with her. She, of course, flew free. She had won a companion pass. She was willing to give me this free pass to go to Hawaii with her. It had not yet been a year since John's death, but how could I refuse? We

198

both flew "first class" to the Islands. I had not flown first class before, and it was a real treat I will never forget. Once we boarded the plane, Mai-Tai drinks were waiting for us, and we even ordered food off a menu. The best part was how comfortable the seats were and how much more room there was. The closer we got to our destination, memories of my trips to Hawaii with John clouded my mind. There was still the sweetly perfumed scent of the fragrant Hawaiian flowers that filled the air when we disembarked from the plane. The women of Hawaii, called Wahines, were waiting to welcome tourists with their hand-made leis of gardenia, white ginger, and orchids. Hawaii was truly paradise. I had found peace here with John, but John was gone, and I felt the emptiness and pang of loneliness in my heart. Mary Beth was patient and wonderful. She understood. We checked into our hotel, ate dinner, and witnessed a beautiful sunset. Mary Beth just let me cry when I needed to cry, which was often. I told her I had recently read a book stating that sunsets are beautiful, but if you really wanted to feel the presence of God and creation, get up early and experience a sunrise. We set our alarm for 5:30 am, and the next morning grabbed a cup of coffee from the lobby. We headed out onto the white sand beach. As we stumbled in the darkness, we settled on some large rocks once we heard the ocean water lapping up against them. We soon realized other people were there waiting for this same wondrous sight. We waited, and with that first crack of dawn, it's brilliant reddish-yellow beams birthed the separation between sky and ocean. It did feel as if creation had just been born. The significance of beholding such a phenomenon brought tears to our eyes, and yet there was a sense of peace — a knowledge that something else existed beyond our lives. I will never forget that first sunrise. Any doubt I may have had of the existence of God was completely obliterated from my being. I highly recommend this experience for everyone.

I may have thought the trip was too soon after John's death. The fact that it rained steadily for half the time we were there didn't help. But that sunrise did something to me.

My next trip was by myself to Branson, Missouri. I wasn't going to see John's family. I was going at the invitation of friends Doc and Sue. Doc had been a doctor in Branson for many years and had known John while they were in school. They never hung around together, but John's mom re-introduced us to Doc and his new wife, Sue, on one of our trips to Branson. We hit it off and became good friends. When John got sick, they felt sad they lived so far away. Sue would often call asking if there was anything she could get for John. John enjoyed coffee, so once when Sue called, he told her before he died he would like to taste Blue Mountain Coffee. Back then the price of this coffee was about $50 per pound. I think today's price is about $60 per pound for the true Jamaican Blue Mountain Coffee. In a few days, a package came from a coffee shop in Chicago. It was a pound of Jamaican Blue Mountain Coffee. When I spoke with Sue, she told me she had called twelve places before she could find it.

Now, almost a year after John's death, they had invited me to their home to rest and relax. They knew I was still grieving. I had lost weight during John's illness and was determined to lose even more. I struggled with my weight for years and not used to cooking or eating for one, thought this would be a good opportunity. My friend, Bobbi, suggested I try a new drug. She had been using it and lost a lot of weight. It was two pills you take together. The short name for it was Phen-Fen. I made an appointment with the same doctor that helped John discover his cancer. Although the drug was new, most doctors had a good feeling about its benefits. I got a prescription. Not only was I losing weight, I was getting so much done around the house and yard. I hardly slept and had unlimited energy. Everyone commented on my great weight loss. I looked good, but I felt too jumpy. I wasn't happy. It seemed that I was missing John more now than when he passed. I started thinking everything was so difficult and maybe too difficult to continue. I decided to go visit Doc and Sue. I felt a little guilty about not seeing John's family, but I wasn't in a good place to visit with them.

Sue met me at the airport. I was light headed and dizzy when I got off the plane. Sue sensed my instability and asked if I was OK. We sat down and got a bite to eat until I felt better. We then drove to her house. Branson is very hilly. Suddenly I was too hot and had to throw up. Sue pulled over, and she sat with me on a curb while I vomited. Sue was a nurse, and as her husband was an emergency room physician, I knew I was in good hands.

"I am so sorry, Sue. I must be getting the flu or something."

"Nonsense", Sue firmly told me. "You are thinner than I have ever seen you! What are you on?" she demanded.

"Sue, you know me better than that. I wouldn't take any drugs."

"Well, how did you lose all this weight?" she asked.

I told her about the prescribed meds I was on. She took my pulse. She wanted to take me to the ER to be seen by her husband. I told her I just wanted to go to her house and lay down for a while.

At her home, Sue took a stethoscope and listened to my heart. She called her husband at the ER. After his shift, he came to the house with a small portable EKG machine. He checked out the prescription bottles I had brought with me.

He shook his head, looked in my eyes, and said, "Patty, these pills are amphetamines. This Phen-Fen you are taking is not good for you. It could kill you. It is a good thing you didn't come to the ER because in the state of Missouri, amphetamines are illegal."

"These are prescribed by my doctor," I told him.

"I don't care. I don't want you taking them. Why are you so obsessed about losing weight? You are a beautiful person inside and out. Don't do this to yourself."

Meekly I said, "OK."

I still wasn't feeling good. They made me some chicken noodle soup. I was tired and wanted to go to bed early.

Doc said he wanted to give me an EKG. He also gave me some kind of medicine as my heart seemed to be racing.

They put me in the spare bedroom but told me they intended to check on me throughout the night. Doc was going to run the EKG machine during the night if he felt it was needed.

I was tired, but it took me a while to fall asleep. I said a few prayers and then thought about that Hawaiian sunrise. I drifted off to sleep. I had a strange dream. I could see myself in this bed, and I was sweating. I heard a voice calling out to me. It was John's voice. It just kept saying, "Patty, Patty, Patty." Then, a bright round circle with the brilliant colors that were in that Hawaiian sunrise appeared. Within the circle emerged a large figure of a head. I thought it would be John, but it was a man with long hair, a beard, and a moustache. It was Jesus Christ. In my dream, I was in awe and could not speak, but this figure spoke to me. It was the face of Jesus yet the voice sounded like John.

He said, "Patty, we cannot make you live. You have to want to live. It is not your time yet. You have much to do."

In my dream, I found my small voice and said, "But you are God. You can do anything. Can't you make me want to live?"

"I gave you life, and I also gave you free will. You need to find the desire within yourself to live. We want you to love yourself as we have loved you."

This face was so large. I did not see the body but only the head. As quickly as it appeared, it vanished. I woke up sweating. Both Doc and Sue were standing over me looking concerned.

"How are you feeling," Doc asked.

"I'm not sure." I didn't want to tell them about my dream until I processed in my own mind what it meant.

"Well, I think you are over the worst of it," Doc said.

"What do you mean?"

"Patty, we almost lost you five times last night. I flushed the rest of your meds down the toilet. You are not leaving here until I know you are completely healthy. I cannot allow you to fly until your pulse and heart rate remain normal for at least 24 hours." Doc's voice was so firm I knew he wouldn't take no for an answer. I felt my skin being pulled and saw that I still had the markers on me from the EKG machine. "You have been stable for a while now, even though you were talking in your sleep. Grief is handled differently by everyone, but we believe you are going to be OK." I thanked both of them for everything, for taking care of me, for their concern, and most of all their understanding.

That afternoon I was in the garden with Sue. I told her about my dream. She was absolutely sure what I had was a near-death experience. She then asked me, "Do you know what a gift that was? A gift from God and from John. You must treasure that. Not many people receive such a gift."

We went back into the house, and Doc was on the phone. He had called my clinic in Eden Prairie, Minnesota, and with a raised voice, demanded a message be given to all the doctors there to not prescribe the medicine I had. He didn't mention my name but wanted them to know of the near fatal side effects.

A few years later, the Phen-Fen would be banned with multiple law suits for damage to the heart and lungs. I was one of the fortunate ones as I no longer would have those issues.

I came home with a determination to create something to honor John — to not let his memory fade. John loved cooking and everyone loved his cooking, especially his lasagna. I decided to do a compilation of John's favorite recipes. Each recipe would have a story of it's significance in our lives. This compilation soon became a complete cookbook. The cover had a picture of a comical John smoking a stogie and wearing a chef hat. That picture was taken during a rigatoni cook-off with friends of ours from Cargill. Of course, John won. Liz and Karen, who worked with John, helped with the editing. My other friends Kathy, Rosalie, Janet, Mary, as well as my sister Kimberly and John's sister, Marilyn, all contributed help where needed. It took me a year to compile the final product as writing the stories and memories of each recipe tugged at my heart. I took the pages to Kinko's and had them spiral bound. I made 100 copies. I wanted to give a copy to our families and friends who shared in John's life. I was proud of my accomplishment, but more importantly, it was good therapy for me. I gave John's sons copies. They both loved it. Greg said it made John come alive again. Next, I wanted to give John's mother, Wanda, and the rest of his family, their copies in person. John's mother and I had grown so much closer since John's illness. She knew I loved her son, and we now respected each other. Marilyn and Dorrell picked me up at the airport. I had checked all my clothes as I wanted my carry-on to be only the cookbooks. I didn't want to risk anything happening to them. As soon as John's mother saw the cover of the book with John's silly picture on it, she cried. I named the book "The Best of the Best" and there were many notations about his family within the stories. She never stopped thanking me for it. I never mentioned my earlier trip to Doc and Sue's.

John's death took its toll on his mother. She had lost her husband to cancer several years earlier, and now her only son. Marilyn and John were her only children, with John being the younger one. So many people I know find it hard to believe that I have kept in contact over the years with John's family. Why wouldn't I? I had been married to John almost 21 years and never knew the depth of family love until I became a part of his family. I still visit his sister, nieces, and nephews in Missouri. I have also visited his cousin, Bev, in Chicago. You just don't stop being a family when someone passes.

John's mother was ill. Now in the hospital, she told Marilyn she wanted to see the millennium come in and then she would be ready to go. On January 1st, a few hours after she knew she made it to see the millennium, she closed her eyes and took her last breath.

Chapter Twenty-Eight

Rosalie and I often joked around about writing a book of things you should not say to a person in grief. Our husbands dying within six weeks of each other brought us even closer. I remember our first and last grief group we went to at Methodist Hospital. We went around the room telling everyone who we lost and what was the hardest thing to do right then. It was amazing how many women never even balanced a checkbook or knew anything about insurance. I will be the first to admit that John spoiled me by doing so much. I did not know how to pump gas as he always filled up my car for me or insisted I go to the full-service lane. But these women couldn't say they missed anything lovingly about their spouses. Rosalie and I were fortunate as we both had loving relationships with our husbands. There were a few men at the grief group. One older man made us smile by saying he would miss his favorite cookies that his wife made for him. He said there was only one small container left in his freezer, and he didn't know what he would do once they were gone. Then he shocked us by saying, "Oh, well, I'm ready to move on, after all it's been a month. I'm ready to find someone else." We never went to another grief group after that. I don't know how anyone can disassociate themselves so quickly with someone they had shared life with for so many years.

Many people told me that I should date as I was only in my early forties when I lost John. I couldn't think of dating for almost five years. I spent the first few years after John's death trying to hold onto what family was left. After paying off our debt, I used some insurance money and took my grandsons, Greg's boys, Joe and Brad, to Disney World. One long weekend we went to Chicago and stayed with John's cousin, Bev. She took us over to the museums and Navy Pier. We had fun. I had such wonderful memories of my marriage, and I now wanted to keep "creating memories". That became my motto.

Several months after John died, I got a phone call from my sister, LeeAnne. She did not know about John's passing. She was now in contact with our sister Kimberly who told her about John. LeeAnne told me how sorry she was. I was thankful she called me. She was getting a divorce and wanted to reconnect again. She told me how to reach her. It had been ten years since I had heard from her.

Kimberly's son, Shane, always had a weight problem. It was now getting out of control. He weighed 600 pounds. He developed gout and an infection called cellulitis. Like Kimberly, Shane had a strong personality. He didn't care what people thought of him or his size, but he had a good heart. He stood up for what he believed in. He didn't work but was a championship dart player in many tournaments at local bars. When his infection came back full force, he was admitted to Hennepin County Medical Center and died at age 30.

LeeAnne, now divorced, had moved from Chicago to Poplar, Wisconsin. She had the cutest little stone house. It was tiny with only two rooms and a small area for the bathroom, but it was adorable.

Kimberly and I drove up to see her a few times. LeeAnne came for Shane's funeral and was good support for Kimberly. She stayed with Kimberly for a while and came back to take care of her when Kimberly had gall bladder surgery. LeeAnne and Kimberly were now planning to live together. Kimberly and LeeAnne were both now alone. It was a good move.

My sister Veronica had been working with an organization for disabled and underprivileged people. She met and fell in love with a co-worker. Never thinking she would marry again, she called me to say they set a wedding date. She wanted to prepare me as she needed to tell me something about the person she was marrying. I knew it was a guy, so I couldn't imagine what it would be. Then she said, "He's black". I said, "So?" Deep down I was surprised only because of her rape by four black men when she was fourteen. She told me how wonderful a person he was — very caring and understanding. I told her as long as she was happy, it didn't matter what anyone else thought. Less than a year after Veronica and James were married, he got sick. Diagnosed with leukemia, I knew the burden Veronica would have. Like me, she took a leave from work to be by James' side. He was sick all the time, and after less than a year, James had lost a lot of weight but was cancer free. They rejoiced. James' family came up from Kansas City to celebrate the good news. When James' family returned home, James' younger brother stayed. Veronica wasn't happy about that scenario. The younger brother was trouble. He had been arrested several times and had numerous encounters with

209

drugs. Within a few months, James seemed to change. All sorts of company would be at the house when Veronica came home from work, and they wouldn't leave. Veronica realized that James was dealing drugs along with his brother. James explained to Veronica that he had been near death and came back. He now wanted to live life to the fullest and that may be by getting the best high. A few months later, they divorced. James moved to Kansas City. He and his brother were driving down the highway in Kansas City one night and got into a gang shoot out involving drugs. James' brother was killed. Veronica never heard from James again.

A year later, to my surprise, Curt and Veronica purchased a trailer home and lived together. Veronica financed the purchase of the rundown trailer house, and Curt agreed to do all the remodeling in exchange for a place to stay. For a few years, it seemed like it was working out. But of course, anyone knowing my family's track record would know better. Curt was getting high again and doing shoddy work. His now teen-age daughters visited regularly. Veronica told me all of them were into crack.

There was never any mention of his twin daughters by his first wife. His son by his first marriage had been in and out of jail and was classified as a level 3 sex offender.

Suddenly Veronica moved to Colorado. I didn't know about it until after she was there. She called me on the phone and begged me not to give anyone her phone number. Something had happened between her and Curt, and she wouldn't discuss it. She also had a falling out with her daughter, Patsy. Patsy, now divorced, had three children and was in contact with her father, now released from prison. She also was friendly with Curt.

Veronica's son Michael, who lived for most of his teenage years with his father, now lived in Colorado. Michael was living with a girl he met several years earlier. He had been up to see his mother and didn't like the situation Veronica was in. He offered to move her to Colorado. He knew of a small apartment close to shopping centers that Veronica could walk to. Veronica was now legally blind and collecting disability. Michael wanted to help her in any way he could. He was starved for his mother's love that had always been given to Patsy. Michael came up again during a week that Curt was going up north. With Curt away, Veronica and Michael loaded up a U-Haul and left.

My brother Richard remained a strong, positive father for his two sons. Always involved in sports, the three of them were inseparable. He was still not in contact with his girls from his first marriage. His son, Junior, was also from his first marriage. Junior, now an adult, was back in Richard's life. Junior had a tough life growing up with his abusive mother and in and out of foster care. He had gotten into trouble in his teenage and early adult years. He got drunk and in the parking lot at Mystic Lake Casino, he dragged a girl into his car. He attacked and raped her. He was also now classified as a sex offender. After serving time, he was finally getting it together. He had a good job and had purchased a house not far away from his dad. Richard was still employed at the same company since his discharge from the service. He had been promoted to a supervisor with many people under him. He had many opportunities to travel for the company. I saw him just before he left on a business trip to Paris. A dream trip for him. I thought he looked pale. He developed breathing problems in Paris and had to be sent home. When he arrived at the Minneapolis airport, he was so ill he could not get off the plane. An ambulance was called, and Richard was taken to the hospital. Richard was diagnosed with late stage lung cancer. It was inoperable. His children were devastated and helped in every way they could. Rose still lived in the same house, and she too looked out for Richard. She took good care of him while he was ill. Kimberly, LeeAnne, and I visited Richard every day we could. Like John, once a strong, large man, Richard was getting too frail. Somehow, someone contacted Curt. I didn't know who or how, and I didn't want to know. We knew Curt was staying somewhere in northern Minnesota. Richard was expecting his brother to call him, but Curt never did.

I called my sister, Veronica, telling her of the severity of Richard's illness. I knew she wouldn't be able to come up, but I asked her to call Richard. She said to me, "You don't understand. Richard tried stuff on me. I can't forgive that. I won't call him." She would not go into detail as to what that "stuff" was.

A week later, Richard was given the last rites. He was aware of what was happening. Kimberly, LeeAnne, and I stood by his bed as he softly said, "I don't want to die." It was so heartbreaking. Then he asked, "Did anyone call Veronica?"

I told him I would. That night I called Veronica again. Veronica was an atheist. Without any belief in God, she had a tough time with death. I begged her, "I know you said you couldn't forgive him. Maybe you can't forget what happened, but can't you find it in your heart to forgive him? He is dying and you will never have this opportunity to talk to him again."

But I did understand as I knew I didn't have it in my heart to forgive Curt of his transgressions. I often thought, "What difference does it make if I can't forgive him as God is his judge?"

Veronica was crying as she quietly said, "I'll call him." I gave her the number, and she hung up. Rose told me the next day that Veronica called. Rose held the phone for Richard. She didn't know what all was said. It wasn't a long conversation, but she did hear Richard tell Veronica he loved her. When the call was over, Rose said he wept for a long time.

Why does life have to be so difficult? Why do we live most of our lives before realizing we didn't have to follow in the footsteps of our dysfunctional family members?

Richard's suffering came to an end. The night before Richard's funeral was the visitation at the church. I was standing by the casket, when Rose tapped me on the shoulder.

She said, "Patty, there is someone who wants to meet you."

"Who?" I asked.

"Well, there are two girls, and one is in a wheel chair." Rose then whispered to me, "I think they are Curt's twin girls."

Oh my God. I couldn't believe it! How many times I had wondered what happened to them. How many years had I thought about them? I hurried to the front lobby. They were both there, smiling. I would not have recognized them. I yelled for Kimberly and LeeAnne. We went over to a table so we could all be together and talk. I couldn't stop staring at these two grown women. These women, Cathy and Carla, who I had held in my arms when they were only days old and I was just a teenager. A lifetime of questions could not be answered in one evening.

Carla had developed RSD, a dystrophy syndrome that causes swelling and pain in the extremities. It is a rare disorder involving the nervous system which causes chronic, severe pain. I would learn more of that later when we had a chance to meet again and discuss our lives for the last several decades.

It was fate or maybe a miracle when the twins came to Richard's visitation. Cathy had been in the waiting room at her dentist's office reading the newspaper. She glanced at the obituaries and our last name shouted out to her. Not many people would have that same last name. She read the obituary over and sure enough, their father's name, Curt, was listed as a surviving sibling. Cathy contacted Carla. They were hesitant about coming as they did not want to see their father; however, they wanted to meet anyone from their dismantled family to see what we were like.

214

We exchanged phone numbers and email addresses promising to remain in touch. These two women were so strong and had been through so much. Over the next several months I would learn how true that really was.

Richard was a veteran, yet his family did not have him buried at Fort Snelling. He was buried at a very nice cemetery within the city. Uniformed soldiers played taps at the gravesite as well as presented a twenty-one-gun salute. It was hard to believe Richard and Rose were not married as Richard treated her like his wife until the day he died. The American Flag, folded in military style, was handed to Rose. She then rose and spoke to everyone. She relayed how Richard always had her back. He protected her and stood up for her when people had given up on her. She would always cherish that great love.

Chapter Twenty-Nine

In the months to follow, the twins got reacquainted with me, LeeAnne, and Kimberly. Their story is one that should be told only by them. The short version is that they were separated for years and didn't find each other until they were adults. After they were taken away from their parents, they were taken in by foster parents. Not all foster parents are good parents. Some are in it just for the money. The twins went through a few foster parent assignments of which some were very abusive situations. They had already been beaten by their own mother and now the wrath of sadistic foster parents threatened them. Eventually the girls were torn apart and sent to separate homes. Years passed, and Carla finally found a good foster parent. But tragedy didn't end there. One day when she was fourteen, her deviant brother discovered where she was. He broke into the house, beat, and raped Carla. She became pregnant. Carla's foster mother helped her. She sat by Carla's side while an abortion was performed. Then, they filed criminal charges against the brother. He was found guilty and sentenced to many years in prison. The judge told Carla she had been through so much, and if she wanted to change her name, she could do so right then. She could change her name to anything she wanted. And she did. She changed the spelling of her first name and completely changed her last name. She was now in a wheel chair with a disease that doctors were certain was brought on by the constant beatings she endured during her earlier years.

Cathy too finally found a caring home. Unfortunately, one night the family was in a car accident. A drunk truck driver slammed into the car the family was in. The foster mother and two of the children were killed instantly. Cathy was in critical condition. She had major head trauma and almost every bone in her body had been broken. She spent a year in the hospital. By the time Cathy was released from the hospital, she had grown up beyond her years. She had a good head on her shoulders. She decided to go to college and work part-time. Cathy eventually married, so her last name was now different.

Over the years, both of the girls tried to find each other but were never successful. Neither one was aware of the other's name change nor where they resided. One day, while Cathy was at her part-time job at a Burger King Restaurant in Wayzata, Minnesota, a man who was a regular, said to her, "You must love this place. You're here all the time."

"No, I'm not", she said. "I go to college in the evenings, so I'm only here mornings or afternoons. I don't work at night."

This man looked at her closely and said, "Well, girl, I swear you have a twin who comes here almost every night for dinner."

Cathy's heart skipped a beat. Her face went white. She stared at this man not knowing what to say.

"Are you OK?" he inquired.

She said, "You don't understand. I do have a twin, and I have been searching for her for years."

This man told her to come by some evening and she would see for herself. With tears in her eyes, Cathy thanked the man.

That night, Cathy did not go to class. She sat in the restaurant waiting and waiting. When Carla finally entered the restaurant, they both stared at each other in disbelief. Many tears and hugs later, the sisters were inseparable and are still to this day. It amazes me that these two remarkable women have been through so much and yet they now spend their time helping others. Traveling to African villages, donating time and money to help those less fortunate, giving of themselves shows the love and faith they hold dear. It proves that in every darkness we fear, a bright light of hope can shine through. I believe they have found their peace.

Chapter Thirty

Almost five years after John's death, I started dating. It was difficult for me as the men I met were usually my age or younger. I had been used to a husband who was fourteen years older than me. He treated me well and spoiled me.

My first date was set up by a friend. He was a few years younger than I was but very sloppy. He didn't seem to care about his appearance. We had one date.

I had gone back to work at a printing company. I was hired as a transportation manager. I met a lot of men. I was asked out by customers, but I declined those invitations. I had several dates with a younger man who supervised the printing lines. We had a good time but he had too much baggage. He had already been married three times, had kids from each marriage, could barely make ends meet with all his alimony and child support payments. This I did not need. Then there was a driver, older than me, who treated me with such kindness. We had lunch a few times, but before it went any further, he confessed he was married. I didn't need that either.

My boss was a problem. He was older than me and quite often would call me into his office for pointless meetings. One day with the door closed, he wanted to have me look at his computer to help him figure something out. I sat in his chair and while I was studying the problem, he stood behind me and suddenly grasped my breasts! He said that as I was a widow he thought he could help me out, sexually.

I jumped up and yelled at him. He apologized and I left the office. I didn't know what to do. I was going to go to Human Resources to report him, but again I did not need any of this crap! I didn't have to work full time thanks to John's pension. The next week I quit. It was a good decision.

I stayed home for a while. In our neighborhood paper, there was an ad for a part-time position working with artists. It sounded like fun and something so different from what I had ever done. The company was about six blocks from my house. I was hired, and it was a fun atmosphere. I enjoyed the work, and the people were much more professional than anyone I met in the transportation industry. My boss, Michael, was a few years younger than me. We got along great. He talked a lot about his wife, Judy, and their children.

After a few months, I asked Michael, "Don't you have any friends like you that you could introduce me to?"

He said, "You know, I do have one friend who has just gone through a divorce. I think you two would be great together, but I'm not sure he is ready to date. Steve has three teen-age children, and the divorce was kind of messy. He really is a good man and I think you two would enjoy each other."

The four of us met one Saturday night. I felt more comfortable with Mike and Judy there as I am sure Steve did. We had dinner at Kincaid's. My first impression of Steve was that he was very handsome in a reserved sort of way. The four of us went to my house after dinner and got better acquainted. I really enjoyed Judy. She was easy to talk to. Steve gave me a hug goodbye and said I would hear from him. I told him I would like that.

It had been almost a month, and I never heard from Steve. Mike had been out of town for a few weeks. When he came back into the office I asked him, "I guess your friend didn't like me, huh?"

Mike said, "Oh yes he did! Didn't he call you yet?" Mike said he didn't understand but suspected it was because of the recent divorce and probably issues with his kids.

A few days later I received a call from Steve asking me out. I didn't want to go out with him if Mike had to coax him into it, and I told him that. He told me that wasn't the reason, and he would explain if I would see him again. So, we started dating. Steve didn't want his children to know yet that he was seeing someone. The arrangement for custody was that the children would stay one week with their mother and the next week with Steve. Steve and I only saw each other on the weeks the kids were with their mother. I was OK with that.

We dated for about four months, and it was great! I knew I finally had found someone who was caring and respectful. I was really falling for him. One night he called me and wanted to come over. I was surprised as it was a week that he had the children. He said he just wanted to come over and talk. I sensed this wouldn't be good. He came over to tell me he couldn't see me anymore. What had I done? Steve told me his children were still upset over the divorce. They needed him 100 percent, and he felt guilty. He couldn't lie to his kids, but he just didn't tell them about me. I cried. I thought we really had something together. He begged me not to be angry with him.

I said, "Steve, I am so hurt. I really care about you, and I thought you felt the same way. I finally met someone that I truly connect with, but I can't be mad at you because you are doing it for the right reasons. Your children need you now. I understand, but I am sad."

He kissed me goodbye and left. I relayed my sob story to Mike and Judy. They told me Steve needed to start doing things for Steve, but they knew he wouldn't. They said they knew Steve cared for me. Maybe someday it would work out.

I knew I wouldn't be happy with myself waiting for "maybe someday." I kept busy, went out with girlfriends, and spent time with grandkids.

Almost three months after Steve broke up with me, he called. He asked me out. I declined. I was afraid of getting hurt again. A week later he called again. I wasn't home, but he left a message on the answering machine. When I heard his voice on the recorder my heart beat faster. That always happened with Steve. Whenever we spoke on the phone, as soon as I heard his voice, my heart leapt. I remembered how kind he was and pleasant to be around. He also had a great sense of humor. The next day I called him at work. He was surprised to hear from me. I told him we should meet for dinner, just as friends. Hah! Who were we kidding. We had dinner, came back to my place, and well, we've been together ever since. That was 16 years ago.

Starting out with another family has its ups and downs but just like with Stephen and Greg, is well worth it. I sold my house in Bloomington and moved into Steve's townhouse.

I reflect on my life now as "Peaceful." I am fortunate to have five stepchildren: Stephen, Greg, Joshua, Sarah, and Rachel. Their children will always be my grandchildren.

After 65 years, I have come to terms with my life. I have lived through circumstances and moments of hell, but I no longer blame my parents for my life or the screwed-up lives of some of their children. I truly believe my parents did the best they knew how to do. I have no idea what their own childhood was like as I did not have the opportunity of knowing what a grandparent was. I have chosen not to dwell on the sorrowful life of people I have known. I don't know why it had to be like it was. I don't know why some people can cope and others can't. I do know that when I married John, I found happiness, and when he died, I was lost. I know that I was fortunate to find happiness and love again while I share my life with Steve. The spiritual experiences I have had are real. People may not believe that, but that isn't important to me as I have found peace. Peace is inside yourself. My peace is in knowing there is a God. Peace is reflected in the faces of all the people I love and the animals I cherish. During my journey to this point, I came across quotations that I often reflect on. These are a few of them.

What is life about?

The rabbi asks in his book.

"It is not about writing great books, amassing great wealth, achieving great power.

It is about loving and being loved. It is about enjoying food and sitting in the sun rather than rushing through lunch and hurrying back to the office. It is about savoring the beauty of moments that don't last, the sunsets, the leaves turning color, the rare moments of true human communication. It is about savoring them rather than missing out on them because we are so busy."

"They will not hold still until we get around to them."

---unknown---

AFTER A WHILE

By Veronica A. Shoffstall

"After a while, you learn the subtle difference
Between holding a hand and chaining a soul,
And you learn that love doesn't mean leaning
And company doesn't mean security,
And you begin to learn that kisses aren't contracts
And presents aren't promises,
And you begin to accept your defeats
With your head up and your eyes open
With the grace of a woman, not the grief of a child,
And you learn to build all your roads on today
Because tomorrow's ground is too uncertain for plans.
And futures have a way of falling down in midflight.
After a while, you learn that even sunshine burns if you get too much.
So you plant your own garden
And decorate your own soul,
Instead of waiting for someone to bring you flowers.
And you learn that you really can endure…
That you really are strong,
And you really do have worth,
And you learn and learn…
With every goodbye, you learn."
Peace,
Patty Ronchetto

226

Made in the USA
Monee, IL
07 May 2022

96057326R00164